LIGHT'S AWAKENING

MICHELLE MURPHY

BOOK 1: ALACORE'S APOTHECARY

The characters and events portrayed in this book are fictitious. Any similarity to real persons, living or dead, is coincidental and completely a byproduct of the reader's overactive imagination. Why are you reading this excerpt when you should be getting a snack to go with your book?

Alacore's Apothecary, Book 1: Light's Awakening

© Michelle Murphy; D. M. Almond; 2023

All rights reserved.

No part of this book may be reproduced, or stored in a retrieval system, or transmitted in any form or means, electronic, mechanical, photocopying, recording, virtual reality, painting with meaning, emoticons, interpretive dance or otherwise, without express written permission from the author.

1

This is the story of how I found myself locked in a basement with a serial killer. It gets better, though, because there's also a werewolf upstairs trying to break down the door. They're both here to kill me. I'll likely die down here, so I better tell my story quickly.

Six weeks ago, before my life was turned upside down and shaken through a strainer, I was caught up in the mundane task of leaving work. A far simpler thing than pining after werewolf detectives and frequenting fae-exclusive nightclubs, I promise you.

I loved my job in the city. I worked at a florist shop on the corner of 10th and Grande. My boss, Marjorie, had asked me to stay late again so she could get home for her anniversary. It's an enigma to me that two people can be so in love that they still want to be around each other after fifty-five years. I can't even get a guy to stick with me for two months, let alone multiple decades.

I loved the city itself too. I could stare at the towering buildings, and their magnificent architecture for hours. Those buildings were loaded with people from all walks of life. It was fascinating how so many different cultures could exist in the same place in time. It's staggering to think about how many people live in the city. I used to watch them as they went about their daily business and tried to imagine what their lives were like. To think, each of them had a lifetime of memories in their own little bubble of the universe. Anything you like can be found in New York City. Well, except trees, unless you go to Central Park. Not that I did anything with my spare time other than read or feed pigeons at the park. Or tend to my plants. I have a lot of plants in a beautiful rooftop garden I'd been cultivating for a few years. Yeah, there was so much to love about New York City. But, for me, the best part of living in a place with so many people and so much going on all the time was the anonymity. When you are just one face out of thousands, people tend to leave you alone. No one asks too many questions, and you can enjoy your life bottling up all the dark crap deep down where you don't ever have to acknowledge its existence.

Wow, I'm not good at this. Where was I? Okay, so I stayed late once again for Marjorie, and now I was on my way to meet Deedee at a pub. She's my best friend. I personally don't enjoy the experience of going out like she does, but it was a short walk to the pub, and it made Deedee happy. I forget the name of the place. It was one of those Fox and Hound or Drum and Fife British faux flair watering holes. Somewhere above the city's smog, I could feel the moon's luster, and a brisk breeze shook some dried petals out of my hair. Casualties of a long day arranging bouquets.

The pub was dark and unusually packed with patrons for a Wednesday evening. My stomach growled at the mouth-watering aroma of fries and chicken wings. First task would be to shove some food in my face. Deedee stood at the bar, her face lit up in laughter at something one of the men ogling her had said. She always commanded attention in every room she entered, partially because she was 5' 11" and partially because she had the most infectious smile.

"Lanie!" Deedee waved to me and pushed away from them.

That earned me some scowls, as usual. I could read the thoughts behind their eyes. *Who is this frump? Here comes the ugly friend to ruin our fun.*

"I was beginning to think you were going to ditch me again." She giggled, wrapping me in a warm hug. Her hair smelled like jasmine and lavender.

I blushed. "I had to stay late and close the shop."

"'Course you did. When don't you get roped into closing?" Deedee grinned down at me, her fingers twirling a strand of my curly hair. "Did you at least talk to her about that raise?"

My stomach growled again. "I'm too hungry to have this conversation."

Deedee laughed as we found a tall table with two stools. "You know I'm not trying to be a jerk. I just want you to stick up for yourself." She waved over the waiter.

"Ugh, I know, I know." I climbed up on my stool. "It's just that Mrs. Marjorie is such a sweet old lady, and it's not like she's swimming in gold herself, you know. I was thinking, maybe I can scrape by with a few adjustments to my budget."

Deedee furrowed her brow at me. "Changing your budget isn't going to stop your rent from going up. Besides, what is there to cut? You're the most frugal spender I've ever met." She sighed. "The lady owns a successful florist shop in New York City. Trust me, she's loaded."

The waiter handed us menus, but I waved mine away. His eyes lingered on Deedee before roaming over to me. The jerk didn't even try to hide his disappointment. I could practically read his thoughts. *Why is a ten like her hanging out with this three?* Because I'm a fucking joy to be around, you little weasel. "I'll have twenty wings, mild, with a side of bleu cheese and two glasses of Moscato."

"Excellent. I'll be right back with some small plates for the wings."

As if Deedee has ever eaten a chicken wing in her life. "Nope, they're just for me." More silent disapproval as he walked away.

"Seriously, though, I've known you for eight years now," Deedee said, "and in all that time, I don't think you've stuck up for yourself even once."

I met Deedee at Columbia. I was going for botany, and she was studying graphic design. For some reason I still have never been able to understand, we hit it off right away and have been friends ever since. "I don't know…"

"You're living paycheck to paycheck." She clicked her glass of wine against mine. "With the stuff I've seen you do with plants, you should be developing the next watermelon-pluot hybrid or something, not arranging flowers for cheating husbands in deep water."

I bristled. I thoroughly enjoyed arranging flowers. And sure, we got cheating husbands at the shop, but we also got celebrations and love. "Pluots *are* hybrids. Farmers cross plums and apricots to make them."

Deedee snorted. "Whatever, you know what I'm saying. Your time is precious, and there is no shame in asking for what you're worth from Marjorie."

She was right. I was living paycheck to paycheck as it was, and with the recent rent hike, things were going to get financially dangerous soon. "Okay, I'll ask her for a raise tomorrow morning."

Her eyes widened. "You will? Yay, you just made my day."

I wanted to point out that it was actually nighttime, but it was good to let Deedee have this victory. She had probably worked herself up to this exact conversation the whole day. There was something else, though, something off about her demeanor. Why was she looking over my shoulder?

I narrowed my eyes. "Wait, that's not all you wanted to talk about, is it?"

Deedee bit the corner of her lip. "Well..."

I could feel my stomach churning. "No, please don't do this to me again," I groaned.

She was already off her stool. "His name is Ralph. He's Ricky's cousin from Yonkers, a programmer for some tech startup. *And* he's super cute too."

I grabbed her wrist as she tried to pull away from the table. She was waving at someone. "I am going to murder you in your sleep, Dee." I hated that my palms were all clammy.

A short black man wearing a nervous grin walked up to the table. "Hey there, Deedee."

"Ralph, this is my good friend Lanie." I could see his disappointment as he looked from Deedee to me. She waved her free hand to the empty stool. Ralph quickly fixed his reaction and grinned at me. "I wish I could stay and hang out with you two lovebirds, but I have to go feed my cat." She wrapped her arms around me for a hug and whispered in my ear. "He's really cute and he's a nice guy. Try to have some fun for once in your life."

"I'm going to kill you."

Deedee pulled back to look me in the eyes and then gave one of her mischievous laughs. "Call me tomorrow after work!"

Then she was gone, out the door back into the city.

Ralph sat across from me and adjusted his glasses.

"She doesn't even have a cat," I said.

Ralph chuckled. "I wonder why she said that, then?"

Because that was what she called her vagina, and she was undoubtedly meeting Ricky so she could *feed* it. "Who knows, she's an *enigma*." Who I was going to murder. This had to be the fifth time Deedee had tried to hook me up with someone. I didn't do too well with relationships. I'll explain why in a minute.

"So, Ricky tells me you're a botanist?"

"I work at a florist." Damn it, why couldn't I think of anything clever to say? *Why, have you botany plants lately?* No, wait, that's not funny. Just cheesy. Oh god, he *is* cute. Stop looking at me, cute man.

"Oh, a flower shop. Well, that sounds interesting. You must get some interesting requests, huh?"

Say interesting *a couple more times, buddy.* You had to give him credit for trying, though. "It's mostly roses and angel's breath."

The waiter appeared, slapping down a heaping bowl of chicken wings in front of me. "Your friend left, huh?" He added a small plate for bones beside it. "Anything for you, fella?"

Ralph ordered a light beer. What a weenie.

"Anything to eat?"

Ralph eyed my plate of chicken wings and frowned. *Yes, I'm going to eat twenty wings by myself. And why shouldn't I? I worked twelve hours on my feet and skipped lunch today. Screw your judging little perfect hazel eyes.* "I can't eat all these myself," I lamely offered.

The waiter opened his mouth, no doubt to remind me that I had insisted they were all mine only a few minutes ago. "Didn't you say—?"

"That we might need two plates? Yes, we would love that, thank you." *Now go away, you little toad, so I can make a fool of myself in front of this handsome man who has no idea what level of disaster he just stumbled into.*

Once Ralph had a beer in him, he loosened up a bit. He was actually a pretty *interesting* guy. See what I did there? He had moved to New York to make a name for himself in the tech game and was developing an app that would help port VR experiences to user's phones. He seemed like a kind person, and he had the kind of thick lips any girl would like to nibble on. None of that mattered to me. All I wanted to do was get out of there.

Why, might you ask?

To understand that, I have to take you back to teenage me in the dorm of my boarding school. I was going steady with a boy named Kyle for a few weeks and had decided it was time I take it to the next level. So there I was with my panties down to my ankles while Kyle's fingers awkwardly slipped inside me. And then I blacked out. Because that's what happens to your girl Lanie. Whether it is another person or myself, if I get sexually stimulated enough, my stupid good-for-nothing body shuts down, and I black out before it can happen. As if that wasn't bad enough, when I came to that first time, I convinced Kyle to keep going and found out about my second massive problem. No matter who the guy is or how much they try, any man who has ever pressed himself inside of me suddenly finds himself limp and not up to the task.

Doctors tell me it's psychological, and maybe I have not met the right man, and it happens to men all the time. Bullshit. I know there is something fundamentally wrong with me, and no amount of embarrassment from repeated attempts has convinced me otherwise. What man is going to stay with a woman he can never have sex with? How do you spring that on someone? *Oh yeah, I forgot to tell you, guys can't get hard when they're inside me. Bonus points, I black out and have never actually had sex. Oh, and I can't even do normal stuff to you because I'll black out with my mouth on your—* Well, you get the point.

So blind dates. Yay.

That's my sarcasm.

Ralph was great, but after an hour of him talking about himself and six chicken wings, I let him know I was heading home for the night.

"Oh, was it something I said?"

"No, just a long day, and I have to open the flower shop at six AM."

Ralph hopped off his stool. "Well, then let me walk you home."

I snickered. "It's not that kind of night for you, Ralph. I'll see you around, though."

Probably not.

I bolted before he could say another word. Damn Deedee for putting me in another of these situations. After the last time she had promised it would not happen again. The cool night air hit me hard as I stepped out onto the sidewalk. I was surprised to find tears clouding my vision. You would think I'd be used to this by now.

I think that was why I never saw the man who crashed into me. The tears, I mean. We collided hard. I fell sideways onto the sidewalk and narrowly missed hitting my head against the pub.

A man in a knee-length jacket leaned down to help me right myself into a sitting position.

"Oh, I am so sorry, I did not mean to knock you over, Lanie Alacore."

"That's okay. I'm sorry, I must have stepped right out in front of you." Why was I apologizing? Damn it, Lanie, grow a backbone. "Wait, how do you know my name?" I wiped the tears out of my eyes and tried to stand, but the world pulled sideways, and my head spun. "Why am I so dizzy?" I mumbled.

The man pressed something into my hand. It stung me like an angry bee. "Lanie Alacore, I deliver this unto you."

"What?" My vision was cloudy, but it had nothing to do with the tears. *Did Ralph put something in my drink?* I had seen that a million times on *SVU*. Oh no, was this man his accomplice? Were they going to sell my organs on the black market? I looked at my hand where it stung and found a letter. Organ thieves didn't usually deliver letters, did they?

"Lanie! Get the hell away from her!" I heard Ralph shouting from somewhere far away before I was sucked into the abyss.

2

I do not recommend waking up in an unfamiliar place wearing only your bra and underwear. It is an experience I can only compare to having an anxiety attack while also having your bowels hollowed out.

A dreamcatcher hung above the bed, swinging lazily in the breeze from an open window. By the sounds of the traffic outside, it was midday already. Cold sweat broke out all over my body as I flung the white comforter off me and bolted upright. The room swam in my vision like a lazy river as it tilted crookedly. Whatever drug I had been given was still in my system. I was scanning the bed for my clothes when a hand grabbed hold of my arm.

"Get the fuck off me," I shouted and flipped sideways, feet up in the air, off the bed.

Deedee broke down into a hysterical fit of laughter at the sight of me, heels up on the side of the bed with her blanket wrapped around half my body. "What are you doing, wild woman?"

I could feel the heat blooming around my face. "It's not funny, I thought you were going to steal my organs."

Deedee came around the side of the bed, her laughter cut short by a serious frown. "You're safe, Lanie. I'm right here."

We untangled my legs until I could sit upright on the carpet. "I don't know what's wrong with me. I didn't recognize your bedroom." Something about the smog around my brain muddled the recognition of it. "That Ralph is a creep. He must've slipped something in my drink last night."

Deedee shook her head. "Ralph called me to come get you, said some asshole outside the pub assaulted you. He stayed with you until I got there and then helped me get you into a cab."

The man outside the pub. I had completely forgotten. "Oh yeah, that's right, there was someone there. He—" What did he do? It all seemed a blur. "He knew my name…"

Deedee shivered.

"He must be the one who drugged me."

"Ralph said you did have a lot to drink."

"No, it wasn't from that. I was buzzed, at best. But even today, everything looks weird. Like it's too bright or too colorful. There's this weird feeling like everything I look at is over-focused or something."

Deedee rubbed her warm palm on my back. "I'm so sorry, Lanie. I never should have left you there like that. I don't know what I was thinking."

I'd forgotten how furious I was with her until she reminded me. My blood felt like it was boiling, and I shook her hand away. "How could you set me up on another blind date, knowing how messed up I am?"

She pulled a wounded expression. "You are *not* messed up. You're my wonderful amazing friend. I can't stand to see you so lonely. You deserve it all, Lanie. But you're right, I shouldn't have done that to you. It was dumb and pigheaded, and I should trust you to handle things your way."

She sat there like a wounded doe until I caved and pulled her in toward me so she could rest her head on my shoulder. Deedee was someone who always got what she wanted. Her life was filled with success and excess. She could never understand what it was like to live without being able to be touched or loved. I knew she was only trying to help the best way she was able, and I could never stay mad at her, anyhow.

"Do you think that's what happened?" Deedee broke the silence. "Did that man outside hurt you…down there?"

I thought about that for a minute. Nothing felt sore. "No, it was something else. He..." What did he do? I hated not being able to picture it clearly. "I remember running into him and then falling over. The he pressed something into my hand." I was shocked to my core when I looked down to find I was still clutching an envelope in my left hand. "He gave me this."

"Oh, that paper, I tried so hard to get that out of your hand when I put you to bed, but it was like trying to wrestle salmon from a bear. What the heck is it?"

Tingling numbness spread through my fingers as I uncurled them from around the crumpled envelope. It was clearly addressed to me, with a wax seal that looked like a willow tree.

"That's fancy."

I nodded. My palm ached. There was a tiny red scab where the corner of the envelope had pricked my palm. "I better put some ointment on that so it doesn't get infected."

"Really? C'mon, read the letter first. I'm dying of curiosity over here."

The letter was written in what looked like classical calligraphy, with swooping curves and dangling ends to cursive letters. "Looks like it fell right out of a Jane Austen novel," I mumbled. Even the paper was fancy, handmade with dried yellow flowers I didn't recognize pressed into the mesh.

> *Dear Eleanor,*
> *I am sad that this letter does not find you under better circumstances, though I can finally confess that my life has been filled with sorrow since the day you were born, as I have been forbidden from seeing you. If this letter is in your hands, then I am living no longer. I beseech you to go at once to the law offices listed below, where Sir Horrick will affect my last wishes. Present this letter to Sir Horrick, as he will see the truth in the dweomer placed within.*
> *I have always loved you, my dear sweet granddaughter. Not getting to watch you grow and be a part of your life has been the ultimate regret of mine.*
> *Sincerely and always,*
> *Rosalie Iris Alacore*

My mouth felt dry as sandpaper, having read the letter out loud. I scanned it again, gobbling up each confounding word with my eyes. "No one ever calls me Eleanor…"

"I thought you never met your grandmother?" Deedee whispered.

"Looks like I never will either." I tossed the letter onto the bed and rubbed my eyes with the palms of my hands. Why was I crying? I never even knew this Rosalie woman.

Deedee hugged me from the side, rocking me like a child. I felt so stupid sobbing in her arms over someone I had never even met. "Wait, there's something I don't get." She stopped rocking. "If you've never met your grandmother, how did that creep know exactly where to find you?"

Ice trickled down my spine. Had the hooded man been following me? If so, for how long? Goosebumps rose on my forearms. "I don't know, but I'm guessing this Sir Horrick knows something about it. I should probably go speak to him like the letter says."

That was the first mistake I made.

3

I was seven years old when my mother sent me away to boarding school. Her art and antiquities business frequently took her overseas for months at a time. The few times I can recall her being around before that, I was thrust into the arms of whatever nanny she managed to scrounge up that month. Once I was in boarding school, her visits became less and less frequent. I was in essence a nuisance that was discarded so she could run all over the world living her emotionless life without her little brat holding her down. When I was eight years old, the visits only came on holidays, and by the age of ten I was lucky to see her once a year. The boarding school became my home, where I slid into the background as other children came and went. Even the teachers of that dreary institution looked at my loveless life with pity. In all that time, I was led to believe that we only had each other, all her blood relations having passed away, and that my father had died in a tragic accident a few weeks before my birth. My mother's only tie to him, my grandmother, had died of cancer before I was born.

I happily ran off to Columbia when I left boarding school, eager to sink into the obscurity of the Big Apple. I have not seen or heard from my mother in years. Deedee knew all of this, drunkenly confessed over a bottle of Red Cat, albeit without the jacuzzi, our first year as dorm roommates at Columbia.

While we waited for the train, Deedee let me know she had called Marjorie that morning to tell her I had food poisoning and would not be coming in to work.

"What did she say to that?"

"That you didn't have work today anyhow."

"Yeah, I kinda fibbed about that so I wouldn't have to stay out all night with Ralph."

"Got it," Deedee said. "So how do we get to this Figbottom Lane?"

I frowned at the app on my cell phone. "According to this, only the 9 train goes to Figbottom."

The subway was packed with people as usual. The South Ferry platform smelled like a mixture of urine and desperation.

"Never heard of a 9 train." Deedee wrinkled her nose. "Lemme see that. You sure you read it right?"

I showed her the phone, then looked up as a train approached. "Here it comes now."

The train rolled up to the platform in a haze of heat and then hissed to a halt. Only a handful of passengers got off. I shrugged at her and boarded. There were a lot of seats available for that late in the day, but I didn't read too much into it at the time. I was still feeling lightheaded from whatever had happened to me the night before, and even through the sunglasses Deedee let me borrow, the world felt too bright for my eyes.

If I had any sense in me, I would have asked better questions. Like, who ever heard of a 9 train? Why was any train in the city that empty? And why was a businessman at the end of the car wearing an extremely lifelike dog mask?

In my foolish self-indulgent bliss, I did what I have always done so well, and put my head down and receded into the background.

It was a quick ride to our destination. Figbottom was an interesting neighborhood. For one, the street was empty, as if no one knew we lived in NYC, where people crowd every sidewalk. It looked to be very well maintained, as clean as if we were walking through a backlot set at Disney World. I've only been there once, and it was awesome. The buildings around us felt like that, as if they were staged to fool the eye. To that point, I had never seen redstones before. These too were immaculately tended to, each building unblemished and with white steps that starkly contrasted with their redstone edifices.

None of it seemed to surprise Deedee, so I thought perhaps it was simply the effects of the drugs making me paranoid and kept these observations to myself.

Sir Horrick's law offices were thankfully directly across the street from the subway entrance, as proclaimed by a gleaming bronze plaque set into the redstone. Statues of winged lions sat on either side of the steps. I could not help touching one of them as we climbed up to the door. It was so pretty in the bright sunlight and felt as soft as a bar of Dove soap against my fingertips.

The front doors were unlocked. We walked into a lobby that was larger than it seemed would be possible from outside. Clearly this Sir Horrick had procured the buildings to either side of his to create such an impressive complex. A rounded cherrywood kiosk dominated the center of the hallway, with twin elevators behind it, a richly colored mahogany staircase just to our left, and closed doors lining the wall to our right. A tall man worked in the kiosk, his head bald on top while the sides curled in tufts of hair that stood horizontally and level on either side. He looked up at us with red-rimmed, droopy eyes.

"May I help you?" he asked.

"I, um." *Wait, does he have a third arm?*

"My friend and I are looking for a Sir Horrick." Deedee cut in, flashing her patented grin.

One of the man's three arms raised so he could point. "Second door on the left, ladies." The phone rang, and I thought my eyes might tumble out of my head when he indeed reached for it with a third hand.

Deedee briskly ushered me away from the desk. "Geez, Lanie, have some tact."

I gaped back over my shoulder, but the lobby receptionist had already forgotten about us and was marking something down in a ledger while he spoke on the phone. "Did you see that, though?"

Deedee grunted as she opened the door and pushed me inside. "You act like you've never seen anyone with a disability before. The last thing that guy needs is some cute chick gaping at him."

I shook my head to screw my brain on right. What was I doing? I care about people, I really do. When I see a homeless person, I always stop to give them change. When there is a charity event, I am right there ready to help. I believe in equality and equity, all of it. How could I gape at this man's disability? Shame crept into my cheeks as they grew hot.

It was a quick walk down a silent hallway to the only door at the end. We entered a waiting room that might have fallen out of the fifties, with green plush couches and what sounded like elevator music dimly playing from overhead. A lone woman half my height sat behind the desk. We looked to be the only patrons in the lobby. I approached the desk and found one of those ticket dispensers like you would use at

Sam's Deli. The woman did not even lift her eyes to glance at me as I approached. I looked at Deedee, but she just shrugged.

I grabbed a ticket from the dispenser and tore it off.

The woman's eyes shot up to meet mine. "What did you go and do that for?"

"Oh, um, I thought you needed it to tell when it was my turn."

The woman looked past me at the waiting area. "There's no one else in here, love. Did you think I'm a wee bit daft that I wouldn't have noticed ya?"

Deedee looked like she'd swallowed a fly. I was not getting any help there. "I have this letter from my grandmother." I thrust out the letter so she could see.

The woman looked from the letter to me then tightened her eyes. "You're an odd duck, ain'tcha?"

"So I've been told."

The phone on her desk rang so unexpectedly that I nearly jumped right out of my Vans. She answered it, and I noticed she only had three fingers. I quickly looked away. I wanted to say something to Deedee, but after embarrassing myself in the hallway, I thought better of it.

"Yes sir, absolutely." She hung up. "Sir Horrick will see you now, Eleanor."

Deedee and I shared a collective gasp.

"How do you know my name?"

The woman rolled her eyes. "It's written plain as a baboon's arse there on your envelope, isn't it?"

Deedee giggled.

"It's that door there," the woman pointed.

We moved to walk around the desk.

"Fairies only," she commanded.

I did a double take. "Excuse me?"

"She said family only," Deedee replied. "That's okay, sweetie. I'll just wait out here for you, but if you need me, I'll come right in, no matter what this rude lady has to say." With that, she eyeballed the receptionist with her best *nobody puts Baby in a corner* look.

The woman rolled her eyes and waved me on.

Sir Horrick was, for lack of a better expression, a goat.

I do not mean he was old or sheepish or any of those things. He literally had the face and cloven hands of a goat. Combine that with his fantastic three-piece cashmere suit, and you have the perfect recipe for confused as fuck. Which I was. I scarcely remember what his office looked like with all my attention devoted to the impossible figure standing behind a desk patiently waiting for me.

He motioned for me to have a seat at one of the chairs directly in front of his desk, which I did, too stunned to be disobedient. "Good day to you, Ms. Alacore. I believe you have something that requires my attention."

I numbly handed him the letter. His eyes were like hourglasses, and his face covered in soft fur. He plucked the letter from me and sat down to read over it. "Hmm, yes, I see. Oh, this is a rather sad turn of events, isn't it?"

"You're a goat."

I know. It was all I could think to say.

He studied me for a moment in a look that said, *I might have to ram my forehead into you for that statement.* Then his eyes softened. "Not a goat, madame, and that is considered a rather rude thing to say, rather like calling an Italian a dago. A racial slur, if you will."

That shook me out of my stupor. "Oh my, I'm so sorry, I don't know what's wrong with me today. I think—I think I am in shock over everything, and to be honest, I might be having a mental breakdown."

"Nothing of the sort, Eleanor."

"Lanie."

He bowed his head. "Lanie. Your grandmother was a dear customer of mine, and I do know she placed a dweomer on this letter."

"A dwee-homer?"

"Close enough, I suppose. In the best way you can understand, it was a *spell.* More of an enchantment, really, or anti-enchantment, in this case. It seems someone bewitched you and placed a glamour over your mind so that all these years you have not been able to truly see the world around you."

"Then I am having hallucinations?"

"Quite the opposite. You are seeing things that have always been there, which the humans you've lived around aren't privy to."

I shook my head and rubbed my eyes. None of what he was saying made sense. "So you're not a goat?"

"No." His voice had an acid edge to it.

"Then I *am* seeing things."

Sir Horrick took a deep breath and stood. He turned his back to me, flashing a tail that twitched as he paced. His trousers were very neatly sewn with a button above the opening to let his tail wag freely. I fully believed in that moment that I was touched in the head and imagined what life was going to be like in the asylum.

"Please listen to me carefully, Eleanor. I am trying to comprehend how confusing this must be for you. What has been done to you is nothing short of an abomination. You *are* seeing things. Think of it like this. Your life up until the point you touched this letter has been lived under a veil. Someone placed a very powerful spell over you so that you would see the world as any ordinary human does. Now that veil has been lifted, and you are seeing the world as it actually is. I believe that is a supreme shock to your mind. I am *not* a goat." He curled his lip at the word. "I am a gwyllion, my receptionist is an ornery brownie, and Gustav, who works the lobby of our building, indeed has three arms."

He paused to study me. It took me a moment to realize he wanted my confirmation that I understood. "The man in the lobby has three arms, but my friend Deedee doesn't see that?"

"Correct. A human would see Gustav as a man with one arm. Their brains cannot process the incredible, and so they fill in the blanks with the probable."

"So to a human, your receptionist would be a nice old lady?"

"No, she's always a little bitch. That wouldn't change."

Fantastic, I'm talking to a not-goat goat. I felt that the best thing to do was just go along with this merry charade and get the hell out of there. "Well, this has certainly been enlightening." I rose from my chair and evened out my skirt. "I do appreciate your time, Sir Horrick."

A sound that only a goat could make came out of his throat in what I could only believe was exasperation as he reached out a halting cloven hoof. "Wait, you can't leave yet. We still need to go over your inheritance."

That stopped me in my tracks. "She left me something?"

"Rosalie left you everything, child." Sir Horrick went over to a filing cabinet behind the desk and rifled through it until he found the correct file. "Yes, here it is, the Alacore estate. Please, Eleanor, sit down so we can discuss the details."

I would rather stand, but I was still feeling dizzy. "My name is Lanie. No one calls me Eleanor."

"Yes, erm, I apologize. I drew these papers up with your grandmother quite some time ago, possibly twenty years."

"When I was just a little baby?"

"Your grandmother always lamented she could not see you," he stated with a high level of seriousness. "Here it is. Yes, your paternal grandmother Rosalie Alacore, of sound mind and body, bequeathed the entirety of her estate to one Eleanor Alacore as sole heir. That is you. This includes her antique shop, her apartments, and all that lies within or is connected throughout. It also includes her title as Warden to the province. Everything she had to her name, she ordered to be legally bound to your name upon her death. And if that letter came into your possession, it means she must be of this mortal realm no longer."

That sounded like a lot. Also, he was very well-spoken for a goat. "You mentioned she was a Warden. What is that?"

"A role of the utmost importance to the community of Willow's Edge," Sir Horrick replied dubiously.

"Which means?"

"As Warden you would provide assistance members of the community rely on in hard times. It is not an easy title to explain and not my purview. As your lawyer in this inheritance, I am more qualified to speak to the holdings and estate than of provincial titles."

"But why would someone who never even had the time to speak to me leave me everything they owned?"

"I don't believe you are listening to me, Lanie. Rosalie long lamented that she could not speak with you. Forgive my saying so, but she and your mother were ever at odds, and it was your mother who tricked Rosalie into that wretched vow that ensured she could never contact you as long as she lived. This letter, which found its way to you, was enchanted to be delivered in the event of her passing. It carried the anti-enchantment to lift the veil clouding your reality. This was something she was barred from doing in life but that she vowed she would see to in the afterlife."

The scab on my palm tingled as if in response to his revelation. "Are you saying the envelope cut me on purpose?"

"The cost of blood to release the enchantment is a common catalyst."

Fire burned behind my eyelids. This was all too much for me. I stood abruptly and snatched my grandmother's letter from the desk. "I do not want any of it."

"Be that as it may, it is her death right to bequeath it as she saw fit. Please, Elean—*Lanie*, your grandmother was a good woman. I know all of this is terribly confusing to you right now, but at least go to her shop and look over her things. Perhaps you can find some common bond to understand Rosalie better, as it should have been all these years. Your mother robbed you of your grandmother in life. Do not let her also do so in death."

The damned goat's words hit home in my heart. I was not about to forgive my grandmother for some ill-placed promise to my mother never to speak to me, but the least I could do was go check out this shop. It might even be worth something. And my rent was going up soon. I decided I would make quick work of selling my grandmother's estate and then move on with my life as promptly as possible. That, and quickly get an anti-psychotic prescribed to me.

"Fine, I'll go to the shop. Give me the address, please."

This was, of course, my second major mistake.

4

Willows Edge was not what I expected. Goat men were speaking to me, and my world was beginning to unravel. Despite this, I was determined to move forward. How could I not be curious about a grandmother I never met?

We hopped on an early train out of the city for a short three-hour ride to her last living residence. I'd shared Sir Horrick's outlandish claims with Deedee on the train and we both had a good chuckle over it. Of course, I left out the part where I was seeing goat faces and three-armed receptionists. No sense in letting her know I was losing it. The town of Willow's Edge was nestled amongst swooping valleys, nearby gorges, and wide forests. There was not much that could be seen of the town from the train ride in, but what I did glimpse was sheer beauty. Autumn was in full bloom. The forests were blanketed in wide swaths of coppery orange, golden yellow, and scarlet leaves. Willow's Edge looked quaint as we eased into the station, though the platform was absolutely bustling with "people."

I might have marveled over the array of creatures swarming to get on the train if I hadn't thought I was in serious need of psychiatric assistance. Amid human-ish people were mushroom-capped gnomes, brownies half my height, shimmering beings I glimpsed only in my peripheral vision, and even a man who appeared to be a shirtless minotaur. *I guess it might be a challenge to pull a t-shirt over horns that large. Though they could just wear a button-up.* I snickered at the idea of the muscle clad behemoth wearing a dress shirt and tie.

"All this time, your grandmother lived so close." Deedee took a deep breath and smiled. "Ah, clean country air." A tiny woman sporting a business suit and gossamer wings flew past her head. What did she see? A hummingbird?

"Three hours isn't exactly next door."

Deedee frowned at me. A seven-foot man with leaves growing out of his arms cut between us on his way down the platform. "Why do you always do that?"

I gawked at the man as he shambled past. Were his leaves always that golden hue or were they changing for the fall weather? It was impossible not to stare. Besides, once the doctors diagnosed my insanity and pumped me full of prescriptions, it would all become a smear on my brain. I figured it was better to enjoy the spectacle while I had the guilt-free pleasure of doing so.

"This is better than that time we did 'shrooms," I mumbled.

"What?"

"I said why do I always do what?"

Deedee hailed a taxi driver waiting at the roundabout. "You have this uncanny ability to make excuses for people who slight you."

We met the driver at the rear of the car and waited patiently as he placed Deedee's suitcase and my duffel bag into the trunk. At least he was human. I thought. I forked over the address, and we scooted into the backseat.

It was a short drive to my grandmother's property, swooping down steep hills lined with colorful houses and ancient-looking trees. I hadn't seen so much green since our weekend trip to Vermont. We drove past an elementary school where little girls played hopscotch during recess. One of them had a face like a faun. As we dipped deeper into the valley, we came to Willow Avenue. It was lined with quaint shops that hailed memories of a simpler time. A tailor, an ice cream shop with one of those long bars you sat at to get your malt shake, a five and dime, and even a cobbler.

"That café looks tasty," Deedee giggled.

She was right. The cafe could have sprung from an ad for Parisian vacations, with little black tables and chairs set up on the sidewalk, where townsfolk dined and chatted away. The waitstaff was even wearing black and white as you'd expect. I didn't know what they were serving, but the whole ambience sucked me in as we drove past. "We should definitely go there before we leave."

A few blocks later, the taxi pulled to the side of the road. "Here we are, ladies." The driver hopped out to retrieve our luggage.

Alacore's Apothecary

Alacore's Antiquities was a stark contrast to the colorful wonderment that made up Willow's Edge. The picture glass storefront windows that faced the street were in bad need of a cleaning. The painted words on the glass were cracked and peeling, and what could only be described as junkyard scrap blotted out the few parts of the windows not obscured by dust. An old dented and unpolished French horn, a typewriter missing a dozen keys, and stacks of newspapers were the items grandmother had chosen to display. The whole storefront had a ramshackle air to it. I honestly could not tell you what I was expecting, but I knew with one look that this was not it.

"Oh," Deedee said.

"That's overstating it," I added before comparing the address I had written down with the one near the door on the side of the building. "Looks like it's the right place, though."

The driver waved as he pulled away, his eyes lingering on Deedee's ass. I emptied the bronze key from the tiny envelope Sir Horrick had given me. It was grandma's spare. A quick turn, and the front door opened with a jingle from a tiny bell propped above the doorway. It was dark inside, with the little light coming in through the front windows showcasing dancing dust particles.

Deedee sneezed. "Well, the storefront has to be worth something at least."

We stalked into the shop. It was small and cramped. Wooden shelves lined the floor, making up two aisles. They were all clotted with garbage that I supposed would have been antiques to the right flea market shopper trying to flip something vintage. An old tricycle with rickety wheels built for an adult hung from one wall. A small music box with a crooked hinge. A bin of ornate metal frames.

"The property itself is bound to sell for a good price," Deedee assured me.

"I hope so, because the rest of this is complete trash."

"There's those charmin' city manners they talk so much of," someone said from behind the checkout counter.

I did not blame Deedee for screaming or for jumping back to grab hold of my arm. I almost peed my pants on the spot, or I would have, if I were wearing any. So I guess I almost peed my skirt. Could be a new saying, it's kind of catchy.

Behind the counter, a small creature with red-hot skin, razor-sharp fangs, and tiny leathery wings sat smoking the stub of a fat cigar. He was reading an aging newspaper from 1912. Deedee simply saw a small person, though I can't imagine how anyone could hide leathery wings like that. He wore a black buttoned-down shirt with suspenders and grey slacks and a hat that could have marked him as a member of the Peaky Blinders.

"What the hell are you supposed to be?" I blurted as Deedee tucked herself behind me.

He looked up from the paper to regard me with shrewd eyes. "Somethin' wrong wiv your sight then, love? I'm an imp, ain't I?" He blew out a ring of smoke, then another that chased through the first.

"Well, I suppose you are. But what are you doing in my grandmother's shop?"

"You're Rosalie's kin? Thought you smelled familiar. Guess stupid runs in the family, then. No surprise there, huh? What's it look like? I'm workin', aren't I?"

I felt Deedee stiffen behind me, her momentary fear replaced by indignation at the little imp's attitude. I put a hand up for her to hold that thought. "*You* work here?"

Someone's gotta keep an eye on the place when Rosalie's out and about." The imp had returned to his perusal of the newspaper, his cigar hanging from one side of his mouth like a cartoonish nightmare.

I felt a pit open in my stomach. "Then you haven't heard the news?"

"Tryin' to catch up on it as we speak, love." He waggled the paper, then resumed his reading. "Almost finished 1912 too before you trollops came strollin' in disparaging the merchandise."

Deedee shot me a harrowing frown. I'd never had to be the person who delivered the news that someone had died. I thought the best thing to do was just get it all out. "I'm sorry to have to tell you this, but my grandmother, I mean Rosalie, well, she's passed away."

Finally, the imp's eyes met my own. He searched there for a moment, as if trying to gauge if I was being sincere. The smirk dissolved from the corner of his mouth. Deedee pulled tissues from her handbag to hand the imp. "Rosalie went up and croaked, yer sayin'?"

"I'm afraid so."

Alacore's Apothecary

Flames spit out of his little mouth as it opened in a roar. The imp tore the vintage newspaper to shreds, even biting some pieces of it off as his body shot upward in flight. He whirled around the room, throwing antiques and swearing. "That good for nothing hack of a bitch! How dare she leave me here like this!"

"The little old guy's really upset," Deedee whispered. "I bet they were close."

"Please, mister, calm down before you hurt yourself," I said.

The imp landed on the floor nearby and punched a hole in a shoe box, scattering loafers onto the floor. He was panting as he rounded on me with a crazed look in his eyes. A three-and-a-half-foot-tall man does not sound very menacing until you see flames spurting out of his mouth.

"Calm myself?" he growled.

I nodded with upraised palms. "The death of a loved one can be very painful, but you must not let it tear you apart."

The fire fizzled out in a puff of smoke followed by the imp's tears. He hunched over, sobbing uncontrollably.

Wait. No, not crying.

"Are you laughing?"

He slapped his knee and wiped a tear from his eye as he tried to stifle his laughter. "Imagine that. Me, Sacha, cryin' over Rosalie the trickster." He mocked crying and then fell on the floor, rolling side to side and slapping his round belly.

"Okay, you're being a little disrespectful, don't you think?" Deedee snapped with her hands on her hips. This was her disapproving stance, perfected through years of lording over alpha males who would grovel at her feet for a chance to spend one more night together.

Sacha gave her the finger. "Here's your respect. This little trollop's grandmummy has had me chained to her service for sixteen years now. Can you imagine the nerve? Summoned like a dog to this pathetic realm of human under-indulgence. I would have killed her with my own two hands if it were possible. So sorry, no tears to shed here over Rosalie."

At that moment, the front bell clinked as the door swept open. I probably should have locked the door behind us. "Sorry, we're closed," I tried to say, but when my eyes landed on the man who slid inside, the words twisted around my tongue.

He was six foot two, with muscles that bulged beneath his grey suit jacket. His jaw looked hammered from marble but was covered in a thick blanket of close-cropped facial hair, bordering between five o'clock shadow and *I'm growing this shit in*. I felt warm all over the instant I saw him, but it was his eyes that made my knees go a little wobbly. They were a sharp golden color, and he swept the room with them like a predator looking for something to sink his teeth into.

"Did my ears pick up a confession there, Sacha?" His low rumbling voice reminded me of a snarling hound.

The brash little imp immediately stared at the floor and scrambled back toward the security of the counter. "C'mon now, Lobo, you know that was just shop talk."

The man slowly strolled past me and Deedee, his nose raised as if he were smelling us, but those bloodthirsty eyes remained locked on Sacha. The imp climbed back up on his stool, trying very carefully to maintain an air of aloofness, but I could see this newcomer had shaken him up a bit.

"So, you're Rosalie's kin, eh?" the man said to me.

I rubbed my forearm to hide the goosebumps that sprang to life. "That's what I've been told."

Sacha reached down to retrieve another newspaper from the counter stack. Lobo slapped a hand down over the top of the newspapers and eyeballed the imp hard until he squirmed in his seat. "Oh, leave off, you fiend. I haven't done nothin' wrong."

There was something primitive about Lobo's mannerisms that I could not place at the time. I mean, had I known then what sort of fae I was speaking to, I would have likely run out of the shop screaming and headed back to the city, where I belonged. As they say, forewarned is forearmed. Or was that foreheaded? Pig-headed? Oh, I don't know. Whatever the saying was, it would have been smarter to leave.

He snapped his gaze to my own, and I felt suddenly that my heart was racing. And I thought to myself, *He can hear it. He can hear the blood pumping in my veins and throbbing behind my eardrums*. "Tell me, when was the last time you saw your grandmother?" he asked.

"Half past a quarter of never." I snorted a bit too loudly.

Lobo flared his nostrils in disgust, as if he had smelled rotten cheese on my breath. "You claim you never met Rosalie, yet you are here to take over her estate?"

Who was this asshole, to come waltzing into my life and calling me a liar, bold as brass? Heat bloomed in my neck. "That is correct."

"And who the hell are you, strolling in here like you own the place?" Deedee cut in.

His eyes never left my own. I could feel him reading me. "Detective Lobo, at your service."

That shook me. Of course he was a cop. That explained why his presence set me on edge. He was probably trained to throw people off during interrogations. "I don't understand. Why would a detective be interested in my grandmother?"

Detective Lobo studied me for a moment more, then finally released me from his scrutiny. He turned back to Sacha and raised a hand. The imp winced, but then Lobo's hand swiftly plucked a pencil and notepad from his breast pocket. "My interest is simple. I am investigating the unknown whereabouts and possible abduction of Rosalie Alacore."

5

Someone approaches you after years of living alone and says, *Hey, guess what. Remember that family that didn't want you? Well, one of them actually did, and all these years you could have been hamming it up together, happy as pigs in mud, but now she's gone.* That's my rotten luck summed up.

I already had those thoughts niggling away in the back of my head when Detective Lobo, sat on my face with his headline: "I'm investigating the possible abduction of Rosalie Alacore."

I was almost too astonished to speak, but I saw Deedee's lips moving and needed sorely to beat her to the punch for once. "Are you saying that my grandmother is still alive?" My stupid voice cracked as I spoke, like some sob story damsel in distress. I bunched my hands into fists to steady myself.

Lobo noticed my clenched fists. "Did anyone show you a body?"

A body? What was this common-sense sorcery he spoke of? "No. They just called me to the lawyer's office out of nowhere to tell me she'd passed away."

Lobo arched a brow, and I felt ten inches tall under his judgment. "In my experience, when someone dies, there's a body left behind."

"He's got a point," Deedee agreed, much to my aggravation. Why was she siding with this police thug who just threw a hand grenade in my plans to be in and out of this estate nonsense? "It *was* kind of strange how they dropped that news on you."

"I just assumed she was sick or something," I said lamely. Isn't that what happens to all of us eventually? We get old, we get sick, we die. Ugh, that's morbid.

"I just visited Rosalie a few weeks ago, and she was doing fine," Lobo said.

Oh, he knew my grandmother. This was not just some random police check on a missing person. There was some sort of personal connection between the handsome detective and my grandmother.

"Then out of the blue she disappeared, along with her assistant, and no one has heard from either of them since."

"That's not entirely true," Sacha interjected. "Ya did find Jalk's hand."

"You found somebody's hand?" Deedee yelled.

"Where was the rest of their body?" I asked in exasperation.

Lobo screwed up his face into a snarl at the imp. Sacha shrank back from his feral gaze, puffing on his cigar.

"Detective, if it's dangerous to be here, you need to tell us," Deedee demanded.

"I don't *need* to tell you anything," Lobo growled. He thought over something for a minute then trained his eyes on me as he spoke. "Rosalie's assistant went missing the same night she did. A week ago we found his severed hand in upstate New York, indicating foul play. No news of Rosalie has cropped up in any of the provinces so you can imagine I was surprised to suddenly hear you were coming to push this family claim on her estate."

What was he insinuating? "I didn't *push* anything. I've never even met her before."

Deedee nudged me in the ribs. I guessed that kind of statement did not help my cause, but for some reason, her nudge just irritated me. "What's your deal, Detective?" she cut in. "If you have something to say, out with it."

"I hope you're not thinking I had something to do with my grandmother's death," I spurted out. "'Cause that's insane. And what's your big theory, I did it to steal an inheritance I didn't even know about until yesterday?" I waved my hands at the dusty shelves littered with junk around me. "'Cause this pile of garbage is my big payday, right?"

"Hey," Sacha scowled.

Detective Lobo looked around the room. He searched my face again and then moved on to Deedee, and a light went on somewhere in his canine brain. "Ah, a human," he mumbled. "Yes, of course, it seems I have caught you at a bad time. I can see you're feeling…*emotional* at the moment. How about I swing back around tomorrow morning, and we can discuss this matter further?" He paused to look back at me and emphasized, "*In private.*"

"What the fuck did he just call me?" Deedee asked.

He did not want to talk around Deedee, or more aptly, he did not think I wanted to talk around her. I should have told him to go fuck himself with his condescending *emotional* remark. "I would like to hear what you think happened to my grandmother," I agreed instead. If there was any chance Rosalie was alive, I wanted to seize it.

"If you think of anything in the meantime, give me a ring." Lobo dropped his card on the counter before strolling out of the shop. The door rattled shut behind him.

"What an asshole." Deedee huffed.

"Is he always like that?" I asked Sacha.

The imp slid off the stool and slunk toward an office behind the checkout counter. "I'm going to bed." He slammed the office door behind him without so much as a backward glance.

"He's a bowl of sunshine," Deedee grumbled. "You think he lives back there?"

I scanned the store. It was such a disappointment. Every boarding schoolgirl's dream is to find out they have some secret rich relative who will sweep them away one day with a grand inheritance that turns their whole life around. I should have known when that day came, I would have the misfortune to end up in a place like this. It fit me, really. The store was unremarkable and irritating. A dusty, trash-littered shithole that I would have to sort through to find something of value. As much as it sucked, I couldn't deny that I needed that money.

I sighed. "I just want to go home."

Deedee rubbed my back. "Oh. I'm sorry, sweetie. I know this isn't what you were expecting."

"It's fine. I'm tired too, though. Let's go upstairs and crash for the evening. I'll sort all this out tomorrow." Rosalie owned the whole building, including two apartments upstairs, one of which was hers. I couldn't care less what her apartment looked like, as long as there was a place to sleep.

As we locked up the shop, I noticed something odd. There were no streetlamps outside. That's something you sorta take for granted until they're gone. Streetlamps cast wide circles of electric light. The sidewalk was lit, but it was a natural light. The warm kind you get from the glow of a candle.

"Where?" I thought out loud, then followed the source of the light up. Cast-iron lanterns hung from tree branches overhead. There were dozens of them hanging up and down the street. They cast flickering orange light on the sidewalk and road. The only thing missing was a horse and buggy passing by to make me believe we had somehow fallen out of time.

"That's weird," Deedee said. "Must be some sort of green initiative, huh?"

"I didn't notice those earlier," I said, suspecting the reason for that was that they were not there when we arrived. How did that work? Did the lanterns appear when the sun set? Was it magic, or did someone have the job of setting out all the lanterns each night?

"Whoa," Deedee gasped.

I followed her wide eyes. An owl the size of a small dog was perched almost directly overhead. Its round eyes watched us with an alarming degree of intelligence, which was scary for two reasons. First, I had always read that owls aren't as intelligent as some other avian species. So why was this one looking at me as if it were about to ask my name? Secondly, the owl was not alone. As I gazed across the trees, I found three more of them. At least the others were looking at different things around the neighborhood. If they were all staring at me, I would have probably headed back to the train station on the spot.

"You see those owls too?" I asked.

Deedee snorted. "You crack me up sometimes. Come on, let's go get some rest."

I led her to the side door of the building, never taking my eyes off the owl watching us. It should have creeped me out, but there was something serene about the owls. They fit in with the world, they belonged. I'm not sure if that makes sense, and it didn't to me at the time either. Not logically. All I can say is I could feel their rightness in my bones.

As we made our way up a particularly old-looking inside stairwell, Deedee calculated the surprising amount of money that could be made selling old antiques online. "You should take a week off and catalog the storefront. Let me handle getting a realtor for you."

I tried to pay attention to what she was saying, but my mind kept wandering back to Detective Lobo's penetrating eyes. What if he was right? Could my grandmother really still be out there somewhere?

6

I slept unusually well that evening. My grandmother's apartment was a cozy one-bedroom affair. We shared her bed. It smelled like one of those 'clean cotton' candles you buy at the grocery store.

Deedee was getting ready in the bathroom as I made the bed in the morning, tucking the heavy down comforter back in place. I was setting the pillows when I saw the light catch on something hanging from the right side of the headboard.

The light came from in between a bunch of pretty silk scarves hanging from the bedpost. It was a crystal pendant wrapped in braided leather. I carefully lifted it off the corner of the headboard. Light from the bedroom window hit it just right, reflecting dancing blue lights all across the wall and ceiling.

"That's really pretty," Deedee said.

I jumped. I hadn't heard her get out of the shower, let alone come into the room. Embarrassed that I had been so transfixed, I let the pendant drop onto my palm. Without the light hitting it, I could see the crystal better. "I think it's azurite," I said, showing her the blue crystal.

"It kind of looks like a horn."

"Huh, I hadn't noticed that before. It sure does. Whoever polished this must've really known what they were doing."

"You should wear it," Deedee said.

"It's probably just some junk she picked up at one of those little holistic shops or something. It would look silly on me."

Deedee saw right through my bullshit. "Either way, if it was your grandmother's, you should wear it."

The crystal was smooth to the touch. It had been polished and shaped with precision so that it had a tapered spiral effect, like one of those long seashells you could find on the beach. With Deedee's nudge, I decided I would keep it.

"Do you think that detective is right?" I asked softly. "Could my grandmother still be alive?"

Deedee frowned. "That guy doesn't know his ass from his nose. He was grasping at straws last night."

"But what about her assistant? Who would cut someone's hand off like that?"

"Lanie, some of these crackheads in the city would slit someone's throat for twenty bucks so they could scrounge up their next hit. It's sad to say but that's how things are. If she was traveling with her assistant and they found his hand... It doesn't sound like she's a *missing person* to me."

I clutched Rosalie's crystal for comfort. "Yeah, I think you're right."

There was no Uber or Lyft in town, which we both found strange, so Deedee called the local cab company, and one met us in front of the store.

"You sure you're going to be okay here on your own for a week?" Deedee asked as the driver put her suitcase in the trunk.

"I'll be fine."

"Even with all the...," she giggled and flapped her hands behind her back like wings. We both felt it was cooky that the people in this community called themselves fae. Of course, Deedee hadn't seen what Sacha looked like as I did, but even so, the idea of it all was preposterous and we both shared a good laugh.

"You have meetings all week, and I'm a big girl," I reassured her. "Besides, we have a good plan. I'll catalog the inventory while you choose a reliable realtor."

Deedee frowned at the storefront. "They're going to have to be a really good realtor." We shared a laugh as the driver got in and leaned over to wave her on. Deedee opened the backdoor, then paused. "What about what that detective was saying, though?"

As if I had not been replaying Lobo's words in my head the whole morning. I rolled my eyes. "He's paid to be paranoid. I'll hear him out when he comes by today, but there's no point in stalling things. The worst that happens is my grandma turns up after all and I get stuck with her."

Deedee shook her head with a knowing grin. She wasn't falling for my false bravado. The truth was I would have given anything to have a grandmother in my life. There were so many questions about my childhood I wanted answered, and if there was any chance Detective Lobo could find Rosalie, I would take it. However, he had not wanted to speak in front of Deedee for some reason. I wished she could stay. The idea of facing all of this on my own left me queasy. Unfortunately, I was more worried that, if she didn't leave soon, he might pull up and change his mind.

Deedee gave me a warm hug. "Okay, you're right. As usual. But take care and call me. I want to know what that jerk says."

"And please stop by the apartment to check on my garden," I reminded.

Deedee chuckled. "You know I will."

Then she was off. And I was alone. I unlocked the store and half expected to find the imp waiting for me on his little stool behind the counter, but the store was empty. The office door was still shut. I decided to let him rest. Who knew how much sleep a flying daemon needed? I rolled up my sleeves and took the place in again.

Dusty shelves? Check.

Rubbish for sale? Check.

A loser in aisle two? Checkmate.

Unfortunately, nothing had changed in the overnight hours.

I decided to tackle the counter first. That way I could stack things on the checkout area and take photos and make notes. A quick scan behind the counter revealed shelves underneath and a worn notepad I could fit in my pocket. The top sheet had a handwritten address circled. I tore off the sheet and tossed it in the bin, then found a pencil to write with.

I felt very pleased with myself to already have a plan. Detective Lobo would be by soon, and I wanted to make some progress before he came. I quickly cleared the newspapers off the checkout counter as well as a tin overflowing with ashes and cigar butts. All of this I stacked neatly outside the office door so Sacha Cranky Pants would have no trouble finding it when he finally woke up.

The hanging shelves behind the counter were interesting. I had not noticed them the previous evening. Their contents were some of the only things in the shop that were not dusty. Small glass vials and amber jars littered them. None of it was labeled, which was truly odd. Some of the vials contained what I assumed were essential oils. They smelled wonderful. Lavender as fresh as a summer evening. Frankincense and peppermint that tickled my nose. It was a splendid array of aromas.

"Rosalie made those herself." Sacha nearly made me jump out of my skin when he spoke. I dropped a vial. He fluttered forth fast as a bee and caught it before it touched the bare wooden floor. Then he grumbled and eyed me sideways as he slapped it on the counter and walked over to his ash tin.

"Thank you, Sacha," I said.

He grunted and fished around in the ashes until he found a cigar butt that met his approval.

"I see she has some herbs here too." I waved a jar of sage at him. "Does my grandmother have a garden around here somewhere?"

Sacha shrugged. "She helps out at a communal garden on the weekend, but she doesn't have her own. Rosalie doesn't have that kind of time on her hands." He took the cigar butt in both hands and pulled it like putty until suddenly there was a full cigar again. "Or had, I guess."

My eyes felt like they were going to fall out of my head. "That was a neat trick! How did you make it grow like that?"

Sacha did something shocking. He smiled. It was the grin of a cat that had just dropped a dead mouse at your feet and was receiving praise. "Just a little trans-dimensional acceleration to start the day, love."

"Shit." I sat down on the stool. The room was moving in a circle around me as reality finally slapped me full in the face. "You really are an imp, aren't you?"

Sacha's grin was gone, replaced with the cross pout of a bulldog once more. "No, I'm a flippin' kangaroo is what."

"Oh, please don't be upset. I just—it's all just...so weird."

"Being an imp is weird?" Smoke came out of his nostrils.

I raised my palms in surrender. "Hear me out. Until two days ago, I had never seen another creature other than a human. I grew up reading fairy tales about fairies and demons and whatever else. I had no idea any of you actually existed."

Sacha scrunched up his face. "You're pulling my leg?"

I pointed to my exposed palm. "The letter my grandmother sent me did this. Sir Horrick said it dispelled some sort of enchantment someone put on me to make it so I never saw what was really around me."

Sacha snapped his fingers, creating a small flame that he used to light his cigar. He took a couple of puffs to get it started, then let the cigar dangle from the corner of his mouth. "Pretty nasty trick to pull. Sounds like my type of prank."

I scowled. "It wasn't a prank. Jesus Christ, it was my life."

Sacha hopped back a step, then snarled. "Whoa, there. No need to be throwing out insults."

That gave me pause. I replayed my words in my head. "You mean Jesus?"

Another hop backward. Sacha looked around the shop. "You better quit it with that talk. Don't know how those halfwits in the city handle that kind of shit, but around here you're likely to be lynched for it."

That was interesting. Apparently the fae folk didn't like mention of Christian orthodox martyrs. I filed that one away. What did this mean for my world? "If all of you creatures are real, how can I see you?"

Sacha took a deep drag. I noticed something odd. Cigars normally made me want to gag with their odor, but Sacha's didn't smell like anything at all. "With your eyes," he replied.

"I know you think you're being funny, but I'm trying to be serious. Sir Horrick said humans can't typically see fae folk. So why can I?"

Sacha narrowed his gaze and let out a double circle stack of smoke. "Wait, do think you're a human? Oh, that's rich. Is that why you was hanging out with Miss Sex Pants last night?"

I stared at him.

His eyes popped open, and he swallowed the cigar whole, then just as quickly spat it out onto his hand with a voracious round of knee-slapping laughter. "You do! Wow, whoever pulled that spell on you did you up rotten, kid! I love it."

"You're being stupid. If I'm not a human, then what am I?"

Sacha wiped a tear from his eye and waved a hand at me. "How should I know? You all look the same to me."

I crossed my hands over my chest and frowned at him. "All of us who, women?"

36

"No, spell casters, you daft trollop. You know, speaking with you is worse than poker with a sphynx."

"Spells? I'm not a magician, you little weirdo." I started moving the oil vials and glass jars as if to organize them. It was the type of irrational busy work I usually did when annoyed. Organizing is my calm place. "Don't you have some work to do?"

"You tell me. You're the boss," Sacha replied with all the warmth of an icicle.

I was the boss. Imagine that. I had never been the boss of anyone before. If anything, I was used to people largely ignoring what I had to say. There was something equally empowering and terrifying about that title. Also, there was a larger problem. "I can't pay you."

Sacha stared blankly at me.

"I'm sorry, it's just that I don't have two dimes to rub together, let alone enough cash to support an employee."

"I ain't yer employee," Sacha snarled. "I'm an imp."

"Well, what's the going rate for imps these days?" I threw my hands up in exasperation. "Because it will still be far more than I have in my checking account."

His shrewd little eyes narrowed again. Sacha studied me for a few moments, then chuckled. "It's all trolls under the bridge, love. I'll stick around, since I'm a bleedin' heart and all. I'll help you out with my usual duties while you get things sorted."

I could feel my eyes light up at the prospect.

"Under one condition."

"Name it."

"Rosalie and me, we had an agreement on duties around here. There were things she did to take care of me that I'll need assurances will still be completed."

"Like what?"

"For starters, the office is mine. That's where I have my privacy."

"That's fine." I was not about to kick a flaming daemon out of his bedroom anyhow.

"And Rosalie, she took care of food around here."

"Room and board. I can manage that, I think." He was a small fellow, and Grandma had ample food in the cabinets upstairs. How much could he possibly eat?

"And she got me new cigars whenever she went out. I like the Maduros, rolled tight and aged."

I frowned and shook my head. "I don't have money for that."

He snarled.

"Maybe after we sell off all the crap in here, I can give you a cut of the profit? Then you can buy whatever cigars you want."

Sacha's eyes flickered with firelight. "You'd do that for me?"

"In exchange for you telling me more about my grandmother. I want to know what kind of woman she was. Her life, her story, you know?"

Sacha chewed on his cigar. "Fine. But I want fifty percent."

"You'll get five percent. Take it or leave it."

Smoke came out of his ears. He took off his cap and wrung it in his hands, then smoothed out the strip of hair in the center of his skull. He had two tiny horns I hadn't noticed before. "You drive a hard bargain, and I'll meet you there under one condition."

He had already asked for several conditions at that point. I did not like the way he threw that *one condition* nonsense around.

"Rosalie has something of mine, and I want it back. It's a family heirloom and not yours to sell. It's a small pendant about the size of my palm with my family crest on it."

"Why does my grandmother have it? Or why did she?"

"Doesn't matter why. I want it back. It's mine." He folded his arms and let smoke trail from his nose and ears as he glowered at me.

I shrugged. "Sure, no problem. Do you know where she kept it?"

Sacha grinned. "Not a clue. But I'll expect you to hand it over as soon as you find it."

"Deal."

Sacha snickered and shook his head at me. "A day in, and you're already making deals with daemons." He turned his back to me and waltzed back toward the office.

"Where are you going? I thought we had a deal. You have to help me with the store."

"I agreed to do what I normally do around here," he said without turning around. "And it's time for my nap. After that I'll tend counter and haggle with customers."

I frowned and looked around the shop. "What customers would ever come in here? And who in their right mind would haggle over the trash we have for sale?"

"I'm very good at haggling, trust me," Sacha said. He slammed the office door behind him and left me standing there, wondering what had just happened.

I am ashamed to admit that I spent the next three hours zoning out. I had gone in that morning determined to have a productive day cataloging all the merchandise. Instead, I spent my time meticulously organizing and rearranging my grandmother's glass vials and jars. What you need to understand about me is that I am a sucker for herbs. My favorite thing to do in the whole world is tend to my rooftop garden in the city. I know it sounds silly, since I spend my days surrounded by plants and flower arrangements. But before I settle down to binge-watch television or read a book from my massive TBR stack, I spend my evenings tending the soil, weeding, and caring for my garden. Plants are miraculous little creatures who want nothing more than your love. They do not tell you how frumpy your hair looks, they do not ask you why you have not had a boyfriend in nine years, and they do not expect you to say witty things. And the things plants can do! It's astounding what nature can provide.

It started when I popped open another of the amber jars on a whim. I took a deep sniff, hoping to catch the scent of jasmine or more peppermint. Instead, a sweet woodsy aroma hit me. It was minute, barely discernable to most people. Not to me, though. I instantly recognized that this was root of wolfsbane. I slapped the jar down and took a step back, quickly trying to remember if I had touched any of the root when I opened the jar. What the hell was my grandmother playing at? Wolfsbane was highly toxic. Why in the world would she have some randomly lying in a jar on her store shelf?

I quickly grabbed a roll of masking tape I had seen under the register and tore off a piece. I slapped it on the jar and wrote "Wolfsbane – Do Not Touch" on my makeshift label. Once the jar was sealed back up, I surveyed the shelf. There were dozens of jars and twice that number of vials. What if there were other horrid specimens among these? *I can't just leave them lying around if they're dangerous.*

That was the start of a three-hour rabbit hole I happily fell down. I carefully inspected each jar both visually and aromatically. Once I knew what was inside, I labeled them. I found so many different varieties of herbs, oils, and minerals. It was like dipping my toes into heaven.

The first jar was jasmine, always a pleasant smell and very good for relaxation. I found the pungent earthy aroma of pine, citrus, and spice, sharp on the senses. *Ah, frankincense.* I marveled at the clarity of the resin chunks my grandmother had procured. There were so many uses for this resin, everything from perfumes to clearing skin imperfections. Many believe burning it during meditation could provide clarity and independence. Even more thrilling was to find a jar of myrrh resin just beside it. This was frankincense's unpopular stepsister, even though they had almost the same uses. Egyptians even used it in their embalming agents. Fascinating stuff.

Anyhow, you get the point. I was infatuated. So when the storefront door jingled, I nearly jumped out of my skin in surprise. My roll of masking tape was down to a thin ring by then, and almost the entire shelf was labeled. I sighed to leave that work, but that irritating Detective Lobo was finally here. What a jerk, making me wait all day for him like that. I had thought about grabbing something to eat a couple of times but didn't want to leave and miss his visit. Purely because of the information he would have about my grandmother, of course.

I turned around to greet the rude man.

"Oh, hello. You're new."

It was not the gruff, scruffy-necked, chisel-jawed detective. This was a woman, a deeply beautiful dark-skinned woman with curves in all the right places and full lips that were smiling at me beneath cobalt-colored contact lenses. She wore a fantastically hip-hugging dress that cut off just above her knees. I wasn't sure if it was because I was embarrassed to have mistaken her for Lobo, or just the fact that she was absolutely breathtaking, but my body temperature spiked. This woman looked like she could easily grace the cover of *Vogue* and was wildly out of place in my grandmother's dusty storefront.

"You're not the detective," I said.

She giggled. "Not that I know of. I'm Taewyn. I live upstairs. Is Rosalie around?"

"Upstairs?" Well, that couldn't be. My grandmother's apartment was upstairs. My brain was not working properly. "Oh, wait. You're the other tenant. The second apartment." *And you don't know my grandmother's dead,* I thought. I'm not sure why I had assumed everyone would know Rosalie had passed away. I hadn't even placed an obituary yet. Was I supposed to do that, or had Sir Horrick already take care of it? "Rosalie's…not here right now." Why was I lying? I realized I was exhausted by all this death business and wasn't in the mood to answer another litany of questions about my relationship with my deceased grandmother. "Is there something I can do for you, though? I'm Rosalie's granddaughter, Lanie."

She frowned. It was as if a Victoria Secret's model was in my store, frowning. Even this looked alluring. "Rosalie always knows how to help. Do you know when she'll be back?"

In her next life? "Let's just say she'll be gone for a while. Is it something I can help with, though?" *Ugh, Lanie, what are you doing? Just get this gorgeous creature out of the store and go hide in a corner where you belong.*

Taewyn shrugged. "I've been having awfully bad stomach pains lately. The human doctor said it was acid reflux, but that chemical crap she gave me isn't doing anything. It's like someone is giving me cramps at the same time that they're stabbing me in the intestines."

"Hmm, that sounds horrible." I winced. "Wait, I know just the thing." I held up a finger and spun around to my freshly labeled stash of remedies. "I just saw—let's see, yes, here it is. Slippery elm." I waggled the jar at her with a triumphant grin.

Taewyn leaned on the counter, giving me an ample view down the front of her dress of her breasts pressed together. How the hell did they look so perfect? I felt my face flush and quickly snapped back around to pour some of the bark into my palm. What was I doing? Something about Taewyn set me on edge. I was not even into girls…at least, I didn't think I was. I certainly experimented a little, but it never clicked that way.

I found a stone mortar and pestle amongst Rosalie's herbs and oils. "Let me just grind this up into a powder, and you can use it to make a tea. It should settle your stomach in no time." I made quick work of the dried bark but then realized I had nothing to put it in. All the jars were full, and there were no plastic baggies lying around. "Here, just take the mortar and bring it back when you're done."

"You're a delightful little woman, aren't you?" Taewyn took the stone bowl in both hands with a slight bow of her head. "How much would you like for it?"

"It's on the house."

"Oh no, I simply couldn't."

I held up a hand to stop her protests. "Consider it a gift. We are neighbors, after all."

"Oh?"

Yes, and Rosalie is dead. Tell her, you idiot. "The store and apartments are under my care for right now. I'll be staying across from you for a while."

"That's wonderful! It will be fun to have someone young and hip to shake things up around here."

No one had ever accused me of being hip. It made me blush even deeper.

Taewyn looked around the shop. "Is Sacha here, or is he with Rosalie?"

"It's the imp's nap time."

"Nap time?" Taewyn snickered. "Rosalie would have his hide if she found out he's lazing about at this time of day. Be careful with that one, you know how these daemons can be."

"Yeah, of course." *Shit. Did that little rat trick me?*

The office door popped open, and Sacha came twirling out on flapping wings. He plopped in place on the stool and reached for his ash can. "Afternoon there, love." He tipped his cap to our customer. "Was just catchin' a wee bit of shut-eye to make up for a long night."

Taewyn trilled a laugh that tickled my ears. I could listen to her laugh all day. "Right, you better keep an eye on this one, Lanie. Anyhow, it was lovely to meet you, and I hope we can hang out soon. I'm going to run upstairs and try this stuff out on my aching guts."

And she was off.

"She was really nice," I said to no one in particular.

"And she made off with your grandmum's bowl."

"She'll bring it back."

Sacha snorted as he lit a cigar. "Can't never trust no succubus, love. You're not careful, you'll end up signing the deed to the shop over to her if she bats her pretty little eyes at ya."

"Succubus? I've heard that term before. That's like a sex demon or something, right?"

"And then some. Better watch your knickers around that one."

"She wasn't even flirting with me."

Sacha puffed a ring of smoke. "And yet she made off without paying ya and with the mortar. More folk hear about that, and we'll have boggarts and brownies popping out of the ceiling looking for handouts."

Sacha's words made me angry. Not because he was being annoying, but because I could see he was right. I was in way over my head with this fae stuff. Who was I to say that Taewyn did not glamour me or some such thing? She seemed nice enough, but who knew what kind of powers these fairies and daemons possessed over humans? Plus, this was a business, and I needed every penny I could scrape together. I suddenly missed the tranquility of my rooftop garden and curling up on my sofa without a care in the world.

I wanted to scream at Sacha. *Well, I would not have been duped if you'd been out here helping me run the shop instead of taking advantage of my good nature.* I chickened out, though, as usual. My stomach rumbled. I had been at it half the day or so without eating. "I'm hungry. You want some lunch?"

The imp's eyes flashed with enthusiasm, and he nodded his head like a puppy dog.

"I'm going upstairs to rustle something together. When that detective shows up, come and grab me."

I eyed the front door as if expecting Lobo to come strolling through on command. I could picture his cocky swagger and know-it-all stare. Why did I feel so disappointed? The guy was a creep. I decided then and there I was not going to let that jerk push me around when he came in. People had been taking advantage of me all day, and the least I could get out of it all was some answers. I wanted to know who my grandmother was and what the heck happened to her. That detective thought he could walk into my life and intimidate me? Absolutely not. When Lobo came by, I was going to rip him a new one.

7

Detective Lobo never did come by. I cooked some boxed macaroni and cheese Rosalie had in her pantry. She did not have milk, so I had to use water and butter, but it still came out tasty with the salt and paprika I added. The butter was stored in a wooden bowl and looked to be locally sourced. If someone had asked me what I thought supernatural folk ate for lunch, I would have never landed on mac and cheese. Her cabinet was full of processed garbage like that, from canned chicken noodle soup to instant Rice-a-Roni. I did not mind, and Sacha practically inhaled his bowl of pasta. Deedee would murder me if she heard me call mac and cheese pasta. I could never tell the difference between noodles, macaroni, or pasta. It all tasted good. Don't judge me.

I decided to indulge myself after lunch and went back to working on my little labeling project. It was good to sink my teeth into something that helped the time pass. All the while I waited and waited for Lobo to make his appearance, but before I knew it the whole day was gone and it was eight o'clock at night.

"I don't think that detective's coming by, is he?" I said.

Sacha was reading a newspaper from March 1913. "Good riddance. Who needs cops around?"

I heard my sigh before I registered it was happening. Sacha rolled his eyes at me. Great, now even an imp was feeling sorry for my pathetic ass. At least I had finished getting all the jars and vials done. The glass looked much better now that I had dusted each container. I arranged them by genus, with plants, minerals, and oils grouped together. The shelves looked very pretty, like some hip apothecary in Brooklyn. It made me feel all warm and fuzzy inside.

The idea of owning an apothecary in the city suddenly revved up my engines. Could I do something like that? If I could muster up enough cash flow from Rosalie's estate sale to pay my rent for a year and open a new storefront in the city, that might be enough to kickstart the business.

The store mocked me with the miserable contents of its dusty shelves. Who was I fooling? I would be lucky if I didn't have to rent a dumpster to clear out all of Rosalie's "inventory" so we could at least get the store presentable enough to sell the building. I was looking at days of hard work, up to my elbows in rubbish. *Why did I just waste my whole day playing with herbs and oils?*

My head sank low, and I felt shaky with exhaustion at how stupid I had been. The truth was ugly, and I hated myself for it. I did not want to be there, and the only reason I had even mustered up the energy to come downstairs was because I had thought that jerk Lobo was coming by.

"You're so pathetic, Lanie," I muttered.

Sacha raised his head to look at me. He did not say a word.

"I'm done for today," I said, unable to make eye contact, lest I break down and start one of my famous *Lanie is sobbing all over the place like a hot mess* specials.

"You want me to lock up for the night?"

"Yeah, whatever." I felt like a puddle of mud on the floor. I just wanted to get upstairs and crawl into bed.

I let the door rattle shut behind me and ignored the oversized owl staring at me from the tree in front of my building. The lanterns were back, swinging from trees up and down the road. *This place is so weird*, I thought. I frowned and entered the stairwell to the apartment.

Taewyn ambushed me halfway up the steps. "Hey there, sweetie."

"Oh. Hey, Taewyn."

"You can call me Tae if you want, all my friends do. That slippery elm was a dream come true, thank you. My tummy feels so much better!" She handed me Rosalie's stone bowl.

"You're giving this back?"

Tae grinned down at me. Her teeth were perfect and so white they almost glowed. "I was just coming down to the store to return it. What's wrong, sweetie? You look a little upset."

My faith in the goodness of others was temporarily restored. Taewyn had not only returned the bowl, but she also seemed genuinely concerned for my emotional wellbeing. I waved a hand in the air. "It's nothing. Just a tough first day here, is all."

"Aw, you poor thing. Feeling a little homesick? You know what, why don't you let me take you out for some drinks tonight, and we can give you a proper welcome to Willow's Edge?"

I felt myself caught up in her infectious smile. To be honest, I was probably grinning back at her like some dazed mooncalf. Wait, was this another of her tricks? I studied her warily. "I don't have any money for that kind of thing."

"Nonsense, it's on me tonight. That's the least I can do after you healed my stomach."

"I couldn't let you do that."

"You wouldn't let me pay for the slippery elm. You're not getting out of me paying for drinks. C'mon, you look like a lightweight, anyway. It'll probably only set me back one drink. The fellas will be paying for our cocktails by then, anyhow, especially when they see a cute thing like you come strolling in."

It seemed Taewyn hadn't gotten the memo that Lanie Alacore is a stick in the mud. The last thing I wanted to do at the end of a long day was have guys hitting on me. And I was not known for being the most fun person to bring to a bar. I was more of a go-straight-to-pajamas-after-work kind of gal. Luckily for me, Taewyn did not know that.

"Alright, I would love to go out with you tonight."

Fae bars—in this case, a fae nightclub—were exactly as amazing as you would imagine. The little glimpse of Willow's Edge I had gotten on my taxi ride in led me to believe it was a quaint country town, perhaps with a taste of Parisian flair. So you can understand why I pictured Tae buying me drinks at some local watering hole. And it looked like one, nondescript on the outside, next door to a park on one side and a bookstore on the other.

There was not even a sign posted, and for a moment I panicked, thinking I had misunderstood and that we were going to a house party. I have never done well at house parties. They're too intimate, and I have a history of bad luck at them. The idea of some random guy closing in on me and asking all sorts of questions about my life scared me worse than a root canal.

The second we stepped inside, I saw how wrong I was. The main area was at least four times the size of the outside. My brain said that was impossible, but I felt it in my bones. I was witnessing magic. The bar area looked like some sort of Dungeons and Dragons adventure, with a proper inn-like atmosphere. There was a massive bar to one side of the space and round wooden tables at intervals all around it. The tables were all different sizes, some small enough for a couple's night out and others built for a party of twelve. They were different heights but uniformly dark walnut in color.

The chandeliers above us were downright mystical, large silver circles with spokes like a wheel. Above them in dizzying patterns floated a myriad of glass globes. The glass was so delicately blown that they could just as easily have been bubbles you could pop with the tap of a finger. Candles melted inside each globe, and there had to be hundreds of them amongst the four chandeliers. I should have marveled over the floating globes. Instead, I kept wondering whose job it was to light that many candles every day. Did they blow them all out at close or just let the wicks burn down to nothing?

As if those amazing chandeliers were not enough, I then noticed sunlight filtering through the branches of a giant weeping willow in the farthest corner of the room. *What is a tree doing growing inside a nightclub? Wait, it's dark outside. Where is that sunlight coming from?* The canopy swayed as if in a breeze as motes of light danced all around the boughs and upper branches. I instantly felt a tingling sensation in my chest that I knew was an affinity for the place.

"Welcome to Free House." Tae spread her arms wide, gesturing to the marvelous room before us. A man with antlers waved at her as he walked past with his friends. She gave him a wiggly finger wave back that almost made me groan.

"This place is amazing," I said.

"Best spot to grab a drink in the entire province," Tae agreed, grabbing me by the hand and pulling me toward the bar. The place was so large that it was hard to define it. This was not a pub or a club. I knew that intuitively. Free House was something else entirely.

"Is it always this busy?" I asked.

Tae giggled, waving at three women sitting at the bar. "Will a brownie shine your heels for a bowl of cream?"

I did not follow, but she said it so matter-of-factly that I went along with a giggle of my own.

"Hey, Tae-Tae!" One of the women threw her arms around Tae. "Getting a late start to it, eh?"

Late? It was only nine-thirty.

Tae kissed her friend on the cheek and stepped aside. "This is my new friend, Lanie Alacore."

It struck me that these women were not human at all. At first glance they appeared to be. However, a closer inspection revealed eyes a little too large, necks slightly longer, and their skin, whether ebony or ivory, held a slight shimmer when they moved.

"Ooh, are you related to the Warden, then?"

"The Warden? Um, I don't think so."

Tae laughed and elbowed me. "Stop teasing my friends. Yes, in fact, Lanie is Rosalie's granddaughter."

The women shared a tittering laugh that sounded like plucked harp strings and should not come from anyone's throat. That sounds strange, but it was actually lovely to hear. The one who hugged Tae tackled me in her arms next. "Well, it is fantastic to meet any friend of Tae's." She pressed me in a hug. Her hair smelled just like vanilla ice cream, and her sweet breath tickled my ear lobe.

"Nice to meet you too," I said, politely trying to push her away.

The women tittered again and told us to take their seats at the bar. "It's past time we hit the dance floor."

We watched them go, rounding the bar to the nearby room. A wide set of doors revealed scores of people in a two-tiered dance hall with flashing lights of all colors. A DJ with three arms was on an enclosed stage floating above the crowd. The music was something from an EDM concert, with heavy bass, and the women immediately began dancing to the beat as the doors closed behind them.

"Your friends are gorgeous. How do they shimmer like that?"

"That was Cleo, Seo, and Mao," Tae said. "They're all muses."

"What did I tell you about bringing strays in here, Taewyn Śaṅkhinī?" The barmaid was stoic, like a warrior you would read about in a Norwegian fairy tale. She was tall and sturdy, with eyes that lit up with mirth and a smirk that left you feeling at ease. Her hair was white as the bark of a birch tree, pulled back into a thick braid like a Disney princess. She stood there with her muscular arms crossed, eyeing both of us.

Tae flashed her a wide grin. "Lanie, this is Drys, the proprietor of this fine establishment and heart of Willow's Edge."

"It's nice to meet you," I said. Drys's eyes were piercing. That was the way with many of the fae, but I still was unused to it. I nervously glanced around the tavern until my eyes landed on the corner of the room. "I love your tree. It's one of the most beautiful things I've ever seen."

Drys let out a boisterous laugh, like rumbling logs rolling down a hillside, and her cheeks turned rosy. "I like this girl."

"Drys, meet my new friend, Lanie Alacore. She's Rosalie's kin, holding down the fort for her grandma right now, so to speak."

Drys sobered up all at once, her grin replaced by lines of sorrow etched around her eyes. "Oh, my little dearie. I'm so sorry." Apparently, news of my grandmother's death had reached this enigmatic woman. She studied me with that penetrating gaze. "You look so much like her, you know. When she was younger. I wish we had met under happier times, child. But you're here now, and if you prove to be half as kind as Rosalie, you shall always be welcome to Free House and Willow's Edge."

Tae listened to our conversation, puzzled. "Kind of heavy for a first-time customer, Drys."

The barmaid's smile was back, and the air around us brightened. She chuckled at Tae and slapped her bar towel over her shoulder. "'Spect it would be for little Lanie here, growing up with humans. What a wild introduction to our world this must be."

I was taken aback by Drys's intimate knowledge of my life. "You know where I'm from?"

"Oh yes, and 'tis a shame Rosalie could not be here to guide you, lass. But chin up and feet back, because you are in truly good company all the same."

"Aw, that's so sweet of you, Drys." If you ever saw a succubus blush, you would know how delicious it looks. I swooned under Tae's succubus powers, whether she meant me to or not.

"Tell you what, Lanie, how about old Drys fixes you up with a nice big mug of mead, seeing as it's your first day under my boughs?" the bartender offered.

Mead? Isn't that something old Nordic gods drank? It sounded weird, but I was not about to be rude to a woman who looked as if she could bench press me without breaking a sweat. "That would be great, thank you."

Drys was off in a flash, down the long bar, past the other barmaids—two dwarves and a doe-headed woman.

"What was that she was talking about?" Tae asked. "You lived with humans?"

I suddenly felt a guilty lump in my throat. I don't know why I felt I owed her an explanation, as if omitting details of my personal life to this stranger was somehow a violation simply because she had offered to buy me a drink. "My mother sent me to a boarding school when I was a little girl. It was all humans."

Tae's eyes were wide saucers. "No fae at all? What was that like?"

"Let's just say I had a sheltered upbringing."

"Here we are, ladies." Drys plopped two wooden mugs in front of us, some of the foam sloshing out onto the bar. She stood back with arms crossed over her chest and watched us.

"Thank you." I grabbed the mug, which was so wide I needed two hands, and took a small sip. I was expecting beer, which I hate, but was not going to be rude about it. Something about the hops in beer always turns my palate. It's like rusty water. Instead, I was greeted with a thick liquid that warmed my mouth and throat. It was honey-sweet with spicy notes that lit up my palate. "This is delicious!" I marveled.

Drys nodded confidently. "I knew you'd love it. That one is on me, lass, for having such a sweet way with words."

I hid my blush with another quick sip of the mead. "Can you tell me about my grandmother?"

A breeze blew through the packed tavern, tickling the willow branches into dancing fronds. "I will, to be sure. Though tonight is not the best time. You come by anytime this week before four, and we can sit and talk for a spell."

"I would love that, thank you."

Drys gave another of those belting laughs and smiled approvingly at Tae. "Such a polite little lass. You ladies have fun now." And she was off again to tend to her business. Free House was overflowing with patrons. I didn't think there was an empty seat in the house.

"Well, you made a good impression on her," Tae said, downing some of her mead. "But what's all this talk about Rosalie? Is she okay?"

There it was. The question to ruin the evening. I took a deep breath to steady myself. "Can we talk about that tomorrow? It's…a lot to share. I would like to just enjoy our evening, if we can."

Tae hesitated. She frowned as she searched my eyes. I saw her clear intelligence shining through. The woman was nobody's fool. I had an uneasy feeling she wasn't going to let it go. I prepared myself to come clean with her about Rosalie, but then she nodded as if she'd made up her mind about something and lifted her mug in salute. "To a laidback night with my new pal, Lanie."

We clinked wood, and I cannot tell you how relieved I felt in that moment though I did feel a trace of guilt lurking in the background of my mind. Tae was so nice to me from the second I met her, and here I was in town on a mission to sell the place where she lived. How was I going to tell her that she'd be homeless soon? I felt like a horrible person.

I quickly looked around to find something else to occupy my thoughts. Golden eyes were locked on me from the other end of the crowded bar. They were feral, and I had a fleeting image of being stalked in the woods by a predator. I let out a small gasp.

"What is it?" Tae followed my gaze. She rolled her eyes. "Oh, Detective Lobo."

"You know him?" I asked, more eagerly than I would have liked. Lobo was listening as a black man spoke earnestly to him. The other man was dressed similarly, and I assumed he was another cop. Lobo's eyes wandered back to the man as he replied. They were too far away and the bar was too loud for me to hear what they were speaking about.

Tae snorted. "He likes to lurk around Rosalie's shop sometimes. The two of them are strange when they're together. He's a prick though. There's always something about him that grates against my nerves."

"Was he stalking my grandmother?" I asked, my gaze flicking back to him. He was fully engaged in his conversation now.

"No, nothing like that. I think he helps Rosalie with some of her wards occasionally. They're friends, far as I can tell. But you know how it is with werewolves, always lurking about and throwing their weight around."

I sprayed some of my mead in a sputtering gasp. Tae was instantly there, wiping my chin and chest with a napkin. "Oh no, are you okay?"

I snatched the napkin and dabbed at my blouse. "Wait, he's actually a werewolf, then? Like barks at the moon and runs around on all fours werewolf?"

Tae quickly looked around us, as if checking if anyone had heard. "Yes, but lower your voice, silly. There's probably more of the mutts around, and they can get kinda salty."

"Sorry." I shrank in on myself. "Like I told you, sheltered."

"You seem really surprised to see werewolves, and then you talk about them like a human. And that's because you grew up with them." Tae tapped her lower lip in contemplation. She was talking more to herself than to me.

"There's a lot I don't know about our world," I admitted.

Tae's eyes brightened. "Wow. That's so interesting. I can tell you everything I know, if that helps."

This was like striking gold. I had not realized how little I knew about fae and supernatural creatures until the last few days. I had so many questions that they were practically spilling from my head. "What's that creature over there? Why is there a tree in the middle of the bar? Who is that grumpy guy in the corner? Why is—"

"Whoa, whoa, slow it down." Tae laughed, emptying her mead, and pushing the mug forward for another. The dwarven barmaid was just making her way down to us. "One question at a time. Let's see."

She gestured covertly at the short man wearing a mushroom cap on his head. "That's a gnome. He probably just got off a stint tending the Gardens of Eriliah, by the looks of his boots. They're cute little fellas, and most of 'em are kind as a dandelion."

"Why does he wear that mushroom cap? Is it like camouflage or something?" I quickly finished my mead and pushed my mug next to Tae's just as the barmaid reached for them.

Tae wrinkled her nose. "Uh, it's not a cap, that's his head. All gnomes have mushroom-looking heads. You know, I never thought about it, but blending into the forest probably has something to do with why they evolved like that."

"So, you fairies believe in evolution?"

"Yes, *our kind* understand that creatures great and small must adapt to nature in order to survive. Now, you asked about Drys."

"No, I didn't. I wanted to know about that grumpy guy over—"

"Yes, but before that, you asked about her willow." Tae directed my attention to the glorious tree, with its swaying branches and lines of sunlight filtering through the canopy despite it being nighttime. "That tree *is* Drys. They are one and the same. She's a dryad, and that is her other half."

My mouth hung open. I peered down the bar at Drys, a stoic Norwegian woman, and then back at the tree. And heaven help me, it made sense. There was something similar about them both, something that resonated and made it easy to believe that the hearty woman and her larger-than-life laugh were one and the same as the tree and its great boughs. "That's amazing."

"Why else would she give you a free drink? Drys isn't exactly charitable. It was your compliments on the willow that I think warmed her up to you. But you know, Drys is thick as thieves with Rosalie too." She paused to pull our freshly poured mead back toward us. "Put it on my tab, Bob."

The dwarven barmaid winked at her and moved back down the line of eager patrons. I thought Bob was a weird name for a dwarf, but who was I to judge?

"Ugh, it looks like Bigby is grilling you again." Tae curled her lip. She was right. Lobo was staring at me from across the bar once more. When he saw me look, he casually turned back to his partner.

"What's his deal? He's so weird. The big jerk was supposed to come see me today at the shop, and he never even showed."

Tae looked sideways at me, then giggled into her mug.

"What?"

"So that's why you were all down in the dumps earlier. You got a thing for wolf boy, don't you?"

"Ew, no," I lied. I could not deny to myself that as much as Lobo pissed me off, I felt a strange attraction to him. Which was ridiculous, because we had hardly spoken two words to each other when we met.

Tae giggled again and shook her head. "They're nothing but trouble, trust me. The sex *is* ridiculously good, but they're twice the pain in the ass with all their doom and gloom."

I felt my cheeks blooming red hot. Other than Deedee, no one knew I was a virgin or about all my catastrophic failures. "I said I'm not into him, so please drop it. But what was that you called him just now? Bigboy?"

Tae bit her lower lip. She could see she'd rattled me. "No, Bigby. It's what your human friends would call a derogatory term. Means big bad wolf."

I almost snorted the mead out through my nose. "I could see how that would piss them off." Lobo had diverted his attention again, and I wanted to move the conversation away from my sex life as soon as possible. The willow tree caught my eye, and I smiled at it.

"You know Drys is the protector of Willow's Edge, right?" Tae said.

"What do you mean? Is she a cop too?"

Tae shook her head. "How can I explain it? Humans, if they wanted to protect themselves, they would do something like build a wall or a moat around a castle, right?"

It seemed Tae had a very outdated view of what humans were like. "Sure, to keep people out."

"Well, that's what Drys does. Willow's Edge is her dominion, and she keeps it protected by the magic of her boughs."

"That's fascinating. Is that what those little sparkles of light are that float around the branches?"

"What? No, silly, those are sprites," Tae giggled.

"Oh. My. God," I gasped, watching the motes of light dance around the tree with a whole new understanding. Those were tiny winged people who were partying. "Like Tinker Bell."

A couple seated next to us abruptly stopped speaking and both hit me with looks of disgust. They promptly got up and left the bar, one of them scowling at me over his shoulder.

I leaned close to Tae and whispered, "Was it something I said?" In truth, she looked almost as uncomfortable as they had.

"Most fae don't like the big G guy or his son being mentioned. Lot of bad blood between fae and human religious zealots. Then you threw that nasty little Tinker barb on top of it."

"Fae don't like Tinker Bell?" It was the saddest thing I'd ever heard.

Tae winced. "One of them hears you say that, you're liable to end up with a toothpick in your eyeball."

I clamped my mouth shut and mimed locking it and throwing away the key.

Tae resumed her light-hearted air with a giggle. "No harm done, Lanie. Just watch the names you're calling folk around here."

"What about calling Lobo Bigby?"

Tae shrugged. "Nobody cares if a wolf gets upset. They're not fae."

"What are they, then?"

"Don't know the full of it, but they're bred to do our bidding."

Well, that sounds fucked up, I thought. We sat there for a few minutes in silence, drinking our mead and watching the crowds of people swarming the bar area. Occasionally the double doors would open, filtering in heavy electronica dance music from the other room.

I broke the silence. "There's so much to learn. I feel like my whole life has been a lie, and now…I just don't understand anything."

Tae patted my back, and I suddenly missed Deedee. How much of this would she believe? Somehow, I could see her fitting right in with these folk.

"Don't be so hard on yourself. It must be strange, living with humans all your life." Tae paused to think. "Lanie, I like you. Most of the people I meet would have tried to shove their tongue down my throat by now, but your first instinct was to make sure I was okay. You even showed me trust. I never get that from fae folk. They always think that because I'm a succubus, I must be up to something."

I figured it was bad timing to mention Sacha had me believing the same thing only an hour before. Or that the only reason I had not jumped on her was my condition. "I'm not really into girls," I admitted. I had tried it a few times, thinking my sexual problems were maybe because men were the wrong fit for me. Unfortunately, it always ended in the same disaster, with me passing out. The women would come down with horrible stomach cramps as well, so not much room there for repeat trials.

Tae snorted. "As if that ever mattered. You're so funny, Lanie." She slapped her manicured hand down on the bar. "You know what? I've made up my mind. From here on out, I'm your girl. Anything you need to know about fae, you just come to me, and I promise to give it straight."

I felt my eyes getting damp. *Oh no, not the blubbering Lanie express.* Tae had no way of knowing what a monumental offer that was. To date, the only other person who wanted to be my friend was Deedee. I could not believe my good fortune, but I knew I had to speak before I turned into a hot mess and made her change her mind. "I appreciate that more than you'll ever know. I do have a question. Why do some of the people here look like, well, just people?"

"That's a good question actually."

I am not going to explain it the way Tae did because it took a lot of back-and-forth questions before I understood. It boils down to this. There is a hell of a class system in the world of the fae. And not a capitalist system of poor, middle class, upper middle class, blah blah, but a real class system. At the top of the food chain are pureblood faeries. They look quite human at first glance. A closer inspection reveals the truth—unblemished skin, high cheekbones, larger eyes than a human's, with big round irises. Their fingers were long and perfectly uniform, and their skin has a slight shimmer to it. We have seen some of them before on the covers of fashion magazines. They are beautiful, exotic-looking, tempting. Over time, it appears the fae bloodline has been diluted. A pureblood fairy will have wings, full-sized gossamer wings that shimmer with an opal hue when the light hits them. Most of them keep their wings hidden beneath their clothes. There was only one group of fae in Free House that had wings exposed, bandied like a status symbol for all to see.

The pureblood fae were the rulers of our world—well, of their realms on our world, at least. That part was difficult to wrap my head around. I made a mental note to ask Sacha more about it later. The important part was that the lesser creatures of fae all, for one reason or another, worked for the purebloods. Talk about classism.

"Even the werewolves?" I asked.

Tae was on her third mug of mead while I was still nursing my second serving. "Were-folk are not fae," she said adamantly. "They're either cursed or bred to serve. They are not natural. I don't know the whole story. I'm sure it has something to do with the Court of Shadows though, since that's where they come from."

"The Court of Shadows? That sounds foreboding."

"Because they are," Tae stated simply.

She covertly directed my attention across the tavern. In one corner, on the far side of Drys's willow, was a roped-off area where the winged fae lounged. The wings that could be seen lay flat against their backs. It was just about the only place in Free House where true fae gathered in groups. There were around twenty of them, rambunctiously partying around black leather sofas and cherrywood coffee tables. One of them stood out from the pack, not because of his chiseled jawline or eyes that were so silver they looked like they hailed from the edge of the moon. He was distinct, with an air of *fuck everyone* that he put out to the world. While those around him laughed, and some quite obnoxiously, he sat with forearms on his hips staring out at nothing in boredom. Every once in a while, a slender fairy with fiery red hair would grab his arm or nudge him with a joke. His response was cold as ice, if ice was an indifferent asshole who thought he was better than everyone else in the world.

"That's the grump you were asking about earlier, right?" Tae said covertly.

"Yeah, the guy with the white hair," I said. "Or is it blue?"

"That is Lucien. He is the Prince of the Court of Shadows."

Now, I love my English dramas, so I knew a little about titles. "So he's next in line to be king?"

Tae shrugged. "It's more complicated than that. There are four great houses that really run things, but they're kept in check by the royal family. You're looking at the heir to the Court of Shadows, which is one of the great houses. His daddy is the one who runs their family and their family is the most powerful in their court."

"He looks like a world-class asshole."

Tae snorted and almost choked on her drink. She quickly recovered, dabbing her thick lower lip and chin with a napkin. "He is, Lanie. From what I've heard, he and his entourage over there can be pretty nasty to us 'lesser' fae. So, you do not want the prince or any of his cronies to hear you saying that."

Whatever. I had met my share of pompous elitists in New York City. "And who is the royal family?"

Tae wrinkled her nose and tapped a finger on her lower lip. "That's a weird one for an outsider to grasp, I think. Not that you're an outsider, more of a newbie. Queen Titania and King Oberon have ruled over the fae for aeons. These days they're more figureheads than actual rulers. That's a long story, though, and a bit too dark for casual drinking."

A bell chimed in Tae's pants, jarring me. Not because her pants were chiming but because it was the all-too-familiar sound of a cell phone ringing. After the last few days in this strange and fascinating world of fae, it was disarming to hear and see such an ordinary thing.

Tae smiled sheepishly at me. "Sorry, I have to get this. I'm going to step out front so I can hear. Be right back."

No! My worst fear when going out with Deedee is that she will leave me there alone. The idea of being left at the bar for men to hit on is one of the things that keeps me from going out in the first place. But what could I do, throw a tantrum? Beg her to stay? I smiled like an idiot and watched Tae walk out of Free House talking on her phone. I suddenly felt completely exposed, as if everyone in the bar was watching me. Why was I sitting so slouched? No matter which way I repositioned, I felt awkward. I pulled out my own cellphone. I hadn't been able to get a signal since arriving in Willow's Edge. Maybe I could call Deedee and find out how her search for a realtor had gone. Shit, no signal. Why did Tae's phone work then? Was there a local service exclusive to fae? That feeling of being watched still nagged at me. I peered quickly around to tell myself it was all in my head. *People have better things to do than watch you, Lanie.* Lobo was just turning his head, and we locked eyes. *Oh crap, does he think I was staring at him?* Goosebumps tickled my forearms when our eyes met. He wasn't looking away. *What a dick. Why bail on me earlier today just to stare from across the bar?*

I deliberately turned sideways so he wasn't in my direct line of sight. A group of fairly human-looking patrons sat at the table right beside the bar, playing cards. The cards they used were oversized and brilliantly embossed with silverleaf that reflected the light of the chandeliers. Six of them played the game, with small ivory figures of animals that they tossed into the center of the table, each in turn.

One of them caught me looking and smiled. "Do you like to play Skrop?"

I gulped down my drink.

"You can drop in next game if you want," he offered.

I am sure I looked like a frightened deer shaking its head, because his eyes went wide with concern. "I'm sorry, I wasn't eavesdropping," I said.

"Your link is severed, Sam," one of the others declared, exposing two small tusks with his triumphant grin.

The man who had spoken to me turned back to his friends and threw up his arms in mock surrender. He laughed and tossed his cards into the middle of the pile, and they were quickly divvied up between the remaining players. He was already on his feet, standing before me with a hand outstretched before I could turn away. "Sam Usou, pleasure to meet you."

His hand was warm and calloused, with a clammy grip I took to mean he was nervous. Sam certainly didn't look like the type to have a lot of practice hitting on women. Despite that he was handsome. I shook his hand quickly and pulled away. "Lanie. Sorry. I guess I made you lose your poker game."

Sam narrowed his eyes. "What's poker?" Then he laughed. "Ah, so you've never played Skrop."

"Never heard of it. What were those little animals for?" I hid my face behind my mug of mead, taking a big swallow.

"The children of the forest rally behind the prismatic ones in the ring of the world."

I almost groaned. The only thing worse than being stuck alone in a bar with a guy hitting on me was a man trying to explain a board game. I checked over his shoulder for the front door.

Sam followed my gaze. "Are you expecting someone?"

"I'm here with my friend. She's a succubus." *Shit. Why did I say that?*

Sam laughed again. He had a nice laugh. It danced behind his kind eyes. I don't even know what that means. "I'm surprised. Normally succubi are on the dance floor by this time of night. Wait…are you sure you weren't spying for Derrick?" he said with a light-hearted air, thumbing over his shoulder at one of his friends playing cards.

It was interesting to learn that even the fae had nerds. Sam was nice enough, and I felt myself quickly at ease around him. I snorted. "I don't know Derrick, promise. I was just curious when I saw those cards." I took a heavy gulp of my mead, the honey lingering pleasantly in my mouth.

"I haven't seen you around Willow's Edge before. Is this your first visit?"

"I'm from the city. Willow's Edge is such a nice place. Drys is amazing, and her mead is tasty."

Sam thought that was funny. "It is at that."

"It's my first fae drink," I said.

"Well, if you like the mead, you should try one of her cocktails."

"I wouldn't know what to ask for," I giggled.

"I can help you." Sam waved for Bob. I must have been riding a nice buzz to feel so comfortable flirting. "How about a prickly pink?" he asked the bartender, then turned to me. "You ever try one before?"

"That sounds dangerous," I teased.

"Nothing pink has ever hurt anyone, trust me," Sam laughed.

The dwarf put up two of the cocktails. They were in long fluted glasses. The liquid inside swirled like a tie-dye pink and purple explosion.

Sam waggled his eyebrows at me and lifted his glass. "To new friends."

We clinked glasses, and he downed his drink in one long fluid motion. I brought the drink up to my lips and was pleased to smell peppermint. I couldn't guzzle the whole thing as Sam had, but I did my best to take a heavy gulp. It was like bubblegum and mint, with warm cherries, but thin like a wine. I preferred the mead, but no one could deny this was also a tasty beverage. I wondered why I'd been so scared of being left alone. This was nice. Sam was nice. The room felt fuzzy and warm.

Then Lobo attacked us.

8

"What do you think you're playing at, Sam?" Detective Lobo shoved himself between us. Before I could blink, his hand was wrapped around Sam's throat. Lobo hurled him into the bar as he simultaneously flung the stool aside. Sam flapped left and right, like a trapped rag doll, as Lobo repeated the question.

"Nothing, honest," Sam squeaked.

Things happened so quickly it was hard to keep track. Sam's friends pushed back their chairs and raced over. Lobo snarled at them over his shoulder, flashing razor-sharp canines. His growl was electric, like a whip cracking across the tavern. It stopped the five of them in their tracks.

"What are you doing?" I yelled. "Get off him."

Lobo snarled at me, his face a rictus of canine fury, then slapped the drink out of my hand. "Don't ingest any of that, you idiot." The glass amazingly did not shatter when it hit the floor. It sounded like a dropped plastic plate and spilled out the cocktail in a spattering puddle.

Lobo snapped his head back to Sam, whose face was rapidly turning various shades of purple. "What did I tell you about coming around here and playing your little games? I should rip your throat out right here."

Sam gurgled out something unintelligible.

A hand stretched across the bar and rested gently on Lobo's forearm. It was Drys. "There will be no killing in Free House, Detective." She said it calmly and kindly, but with the authority of an empress.

The veins receded from Lobo's face, and his shoulders loosened as he let go of Sam. It wasn't fear I saw play out on his face but respect.

Drys directed her attention to Sam's friends. "Get this lowlife out of my house. Don't ever come to Free House again Sam. And if any of you ever comes back with him, you'll be banned for life."

Sam's friends helped him to his feet and made a quick retreat from the tavern. I realized that Free house had gone eerily quiet and many eyes were turned our way.

Drys lifted her hands to the crowd and laughed. "Next rounds half off, ya sorry sacks!"

That was met with a round of applause and stomping feet as everyone rushed the bar.

The room was brighter. Had someone turned the candles up? "Geez, it's hot in here," I mumbled. I undid the top button of my blouse and fanned myself. "I don't understand what just happened. We were just talking. Sam didn't do anything to me."

Lobo curled his lip in disgust. "Go back to the city, Lanie. You don't belong here."

I pushed myself off the stool and shoved my face upward to meet his gaze. "How about you go fuck yourself?" *Whoa! What the hell was that?* I covered my mouth in horror.

"What are you bothering my girl for?" Tae was suddenly there, pulling me slightly back by the arm. "Don't you have parking tickets to write or a mail truck to chase or something?"

"While you were out setting up your next hump session, I was stopping a creep from giving her a prickly pink," Lobo deadpanned.

Tae raised a finger to tell him off, then processed what he had said and turned to me. "Oh no. You didn't drink any, did you?"

Why was I suddenly the one in trouble? "The bartender gave it to us," I said sheepishly. My body was already starting to tingle, and the sounds of the room were muddling together.

Tae bit her lower lip in the most seductive look of dismay I had ever seen.

Bob dropped off two mugs of beer to Lobo. ""It's on the house. Drys says no more shenanigans tonight, though, or you're outta here too."

Lobo took it without comment. "Guy's a creep," he said to me. I took a deep gulp of my beer. "He likes to look for nubiles and gets them to 'drink a pink,' then brings 'em back to his haunt so he and his brood can take turns. Usually goes for a lot younger than Lanie, but all the same."

"Wait, have I been drugged?" I was starting to feel awfully odd. "But why would they serve roofies at the bar?"

"It's not a drug," Tae answered, rubbing my back. Her hands sent warm ripples down my spine. "Think of it as more of an aphrodisiac lovers take to experience an evening of pleasure together. Kind of like humans and ecstasy."

Lobo snorted.

I am usually so quiet. I have let some horrible things be said about me or even be done to me in the past without a peep. There was something about Lobo, though, that just twisted in my side. I mean the man really irritated me. I slapped my hand down on the bar, then snapped my fingers and pointed at him. "This is all your fault, you big jerk."

Lobo frowned and knitted his thick eyebrows together. "I'm the one who stopped you from drinking it."

I knew what I'd said did not make any sense, but my face felt like it was on fire, and my brain was fuzzy around the edges. I didn't know it at the time, but the prickly pink was working its magic. "You stood me up today."

Lobo's frown turned to puzzlement.

"You said you were coming by to talk to me about my grandmother," I persisted.

Lobo shrugged. "Yeah, well, there was no need. I ran your info last night at the station. You were telling the truth. There's nothing special about you. You're just some outcast living like a human in the Big Apple."

"Don't act like you know anything about my life," I snapped.

"You live alone, pay your taxes like a good little human, have no friends or known affiliates of any importance, and have worked in the same flower shop for the last four years."

"I have a friend." I crossed my arms close to my chest. Maybe even two of them now, but the way Tae was eyeing me left me unsure. *Oh shit, she probably realizes what a loser I am.* She'd drop me by the end of the night.

Laughter and music spilled into the tavern as a pair of punk rock girls came spilling out of the dance room. The music was electric. It demanded my attention like a moth to flame. Why was this succubus hanging out with me when she could be in the other room dancing to all that exciting music? The idea of all those bodies moving in rhythm made me feel warm inside.

"Uh-oh," Tae said, "we're losing her. Looks like she got some in her after all."

Calloused fingers grazed my cheek as Lobo turned my head with all the compassion of a doctor shining a penlight into your eyes. "Stay focused, Lanie." He studied my eyes, searching them for signs of intoxication.

What surprised me more than this stranger putting his hands on me was the soft look in the werewolf's eyes. They were a harsh gold but ringed with genuine concern.

I smirked. "You like me, don't you?" The real Lanie, the one floating above my body as I spoke, would have died of embarrassment if she heard me. The prickly-whatever-drunk Lanie licked her lips deliberately, just to watch the wolf's eyes trace her tongue's movement. His pupils dilated just a little bit, and I could feel his shock as he grew rigid.

I shoved him away from me while an uncontrollable laugh spilled from my throat. It bent me over, with hands on my belly, and backed me into Tae. She saved me from falling backward.

"Oh shit, he definitely got some of that into you," she giggled.

I looked to her with a devilish smirk I could not shake. "I'm fine. I just had a sip of that stuff."

Yeah, a sip was all it was going to take. Turns out the drink called prickly pink was a derivative of an Eastern medicine, epimedii herba, used to cure impotency. The fae liked to mix it with an aphrodisiac they concocted from fae herbs and drink it at the fall equinox during orgies and weeklong festivities. Who wouldn't need a pick me up after a couple days of solid uninterrupted sexual activity, am I right? A glass of this stuff would have you rubbing yourself up against a signpost like a cat in heat. As it was, I had only had the one gulp. The air around me was hot, but in a delicious way, and my skin felt tingly. I was alive to a world around me that came in waves of pleasure. Each wave that hit me left me giddy.

Then I noticed the fae in the corner, the prince of whatever, the fella who had been wearing his boredom like a neon sign. His frosty silver eyes were locked onto me, studying me like a lizard that sees something wiggly to eat. His gaze cut across the room with a commanding presence that could only come from someone who believed everything he saw was his property. He made me feel uncomfortable, like I was naked in the middle of the room but only he knew. I sidestepped so that Lobo was between us, blocking his view. Lobo frowned at me, and I could not help another bout of trilling laughter.

Tae was grinning ear to ear. "We better get you home." She grabbed my hand and pulled me toward the exit.

I stopped and pulled her back to me instead, laughing. "No, not yet, not yet. I'm okay, really."

Another wave of giddiness washed over me, right on the heels of the thumping bass from the dance room next door. Without thinking, I snatched hold of Tae and tugged her toward the doors. "Let's go dance."

Tae let herself be pulled and joined in on my laughter. It was not too much of a surprise to me. This was more her world, after all. Delightful creatures like Tae weren't built to sit around a bar and chat over a drink. She was alive. She was free. And I wanted to feel that, if even for a few minutes.

We spilled into the dance room, and the music hit me in the chest. It was deep electronica with rhythmic bass that engulfed me in euphoria. I was suddenly amidst a crush of bodies all around, each moving in their own perfect way to the music. My whole life I had been scared to go out onto a dance floor. The few times I did were fueled by way too much liquor and one time a hefty helping of marijuana. Those instances were different than this. They were things I only distantly remembered, waking the next day with a hangover but somehow knowing I had the best night. Liquor dulled my senses, calmed my overly rational mind, so that I could muster the bravery to dance.

Prickly pink did no such thing. Nothing was dulled. I was in a state of complete awareness, alive to the universe, with cascading beats running through my soul. Everything I experienced was hyperreal. The smell of Tae's skin, like honey and lavender, as she danced beside me.

The wave of warmth and pure bliss that washed over the dancers. I never knew this was what dancing was, why people loved it so. We were all alive together. It did not matter what you looked like, just that you were one with the music. The DJ booth slowly circled overhead. Flickering lights patterned the floor to his beats.

Lobo stood on the periphery of the crowd. He looked like such a grump. His arms were folded as he watched us. It's cliché, but he seemed in that moment very much like a guard dog. He looked so rigid, so apprehensive, and it struck me hard that he reminded me of myself. Always on the outside looking in. I beckoned for him to join us.

Tae laughed. "You really got a thing for that pup, huh?"

I laughed and shrugged as innocently as I could fake.

Tae grinned and slid between two women, "Looks like someone else has his eye on you."

I almost sobered up on the spot, following her gaze to find the prince staring at me still. Somehow (I know, *magic*) his entire cadre and seating area had moved to the edge of the dance floor. It was still roped off and no one partying behind it had batted an eye as it transferred rooms, but the prince sat there, cold as frozen steel, unabashedly watching me as I danced.

"You shouldn't be here," Lobo growled. I never even saw him move closer, but he was standing just beside me, close enough that I could feel the heat radiating off his body.

"Oh, you came to join me." I bit my lower lip in a grin. Bodies closed the gap around us, blocking the prince's view.

"Lanie, this is no place for you," Lobo said. "These people are dangerous."

I laughed at the idea of a werewolf telling me other people were dangerous. The music washed over me in another wave of ecstasy. I spun into it, as if caught up in a soft whirlwind, and threw my arms into the air. Lobo was close behind me, his body rocking slightly to the beat. I pressed against him, feeling how hard his muscled chest and belly were. Lobo's arms wrapped around me from behind and his face buried into my hair. We moved together as one with the music, words no longer necessary.

The crowd parted. The prince was still staring at me. His silver eyes could cut across an entire arena and probably still have the intensity of a ray gun. I realized he was enjoying watching me, and it thrilled me to my core.

I spun around and threw my hands around Lobo's neck. He was sneering at the prince, his body rigid and tense. If not for the prickly pink, I would have been shocked to see his canine teeth bared so. I gently shifted his neck as I continued to dance, tilting his head down to look at me. His shoulders softened, and he began to sway with me once more. I could not help myself. I wanted to be in that moment with him, dancing as one, our bodies alive and electric. However, I was just as thrilled knowing the prince was watching me, and I felt my hips swaying enticingly to him as well. If the werewolf noticed, he did not care. His golden eyes remained locked on mine as we danced. He craned down, pressing his face into my hair again. His breath was hot on my throat, and I felt something tighten deliciously in my belly.

As much as I was enjoying myself, I just had to see if the prince was watching me still. I turned, pressing my back against Lobo and grabbing his neck from behind. The crowd parted. The prince was gone.

That was when I saw him.

He was cutting through the crowd in a black hooded robe. I recognized him instantly, the way he stood, the way he moved. It was the same man who had knocked me over that first night in Manhattan. The man who had pressed my grandmother's letter into my hand. He must have felt me looking, because suddenly he stood still and snapped his head around. I could not make out his face beneath the hood, but I could damn sure feel his shock.

The hooded man shifted his attention to the werewolf behind me. His glimmering eyes opened wide in shock as we gazed at each other across the dance floor.

Before I knew what I was doing, my finger was up pointing at him. "You!"

He looked wildly around, preparing to run.

"Stop!" I screamed, throwing myself forward with an outstretched hand. I spun toward Lobo, who was thoroughly confused. "It's him!" I shouted but I couldn't find the right words to explain myself. "My grandmother!"

The man took off in a dash.

"Lobo, grab him! That's the guy!"

I could not possibly tell you what made me crazy enough to chase him. Well, we both know that's not true; it was the prickly pink still messing with my new brand of self-confidence. Before I knew what was happening, I barreled into a couple grinding on the dance floor. I have probably never moved so fast in my life, and I'm known to be a pretty quick runner. I ducked under the arm of a minotaur, slid around a group of three fae, and leapt over a breakdancing dwarf. I caught a glimpse of the man's robe flapping around the corner of one of the backdrops skirting the dance area.

Lobo snarled for people to get out of his way behind me. I rounded the framed backdrop and almost ran face first into the crotch of a hairy man who at first glance I thought was on stilts. Nope, those were his legs. A quick dodge around him, and I was in a long corridor behind the main stage. Squeaking footfalls raced away from me somewhere ahead. I dashed down the hall until it split off to the right.

The hooded man was running as fast as a cheetah down it, toward an exit.

"Wait, I need to talk to you," I hollered. Well, I meant to holler. What actually came out was more of a pathetic pout. Damn you, prickly pink!

Without a backward glance, the mysterious man slammed into the panic bar and out the exit doors. I groaned. More running, and I was losing steam thanks to the damned drink. Lobo zipped past me. He hurled himself into the exit doors with a snarl that stopped me in my tracks. It was the sound of something feral in the wild that was about to leap upon its prey.

A ghastly image of the werewolf crouched over the bloodied body of the hooded man came to me, Lobo's teeth sunk deep into the man's throat as taloned hands tore apart his chest. The imagery of it was so powerful that I almost faltered as I finally made it to the exit doors. Prickly pink or not, I was out of breath and suddenly scared.

The night air hit me in the throat and swirled around my shoulders. The dark, dank alley was a stark contrast to the warm and colorful atmosphere of Free House. What I noticed first was Lobo. He stood at the edge of the alley. He was alone, his head flicking back and forth as if sniffing the air, which he likely was. I skirted an overflowing dumpster, peering into its shadows. It was so dark outside, and my eyes were not adjusted yet. Anyone—or *anything*—could be lurking in those shadows.

"He's gone."

I gave out a little shriek and stumbled back. "When did you move so close?"

Lobo stood just in front of me. He still sniffed the air and swept the area with his eyes. They gleamed in the moonlight. A cold chill ran down my spine. Had I just been crazy enough to follow a werewolf into an unlit alley?

"Who was he?" I asked, pulling my arms tight around my chest to keep warm.

Lobo's eyes locked on mine. Something hot inside me unlatched at that look. "How should I know?" he growled. Then he chuckled. "I just heard you calling for help and pointing at him and took off. I don't even know why we're chasing the guy."

For some reason, the idea of us both suddenly chasing a man through Free House seemed utterly ridiculous. I smirked, and then Lobo broke out in a barking laugh. I could not contain myself. Before I knew it, we were both laughing hard. "Are you sure you didn't have some of that prickly pink too?" I giggled and slapped his chest. It was like slapping marble.

That made Lobo howl with laughter. I mean literally howl. Okay, not *literally*, but it was something to behold.

Until it wasn't. He stopped abruptly and narrowed his eyes at me. Lobo slowly turned his head until his eyes locked on something by the dumpster. I followed him over, still giggling. He snatched a clear vial from the pavement and gave it a sniff. He laughed hard.

"What is it?" I asked, wondering why a glass vial was so funny.

The exit doors popped open, and out came Tae. She quickly took in the scene and shivered. "It is colder than a witch's titties out here." That might have been the single funniest thing I had ever heard, and Lobo seemed to agree, based on how loud his barking laughter grew.

Tae frowned at both of us in turn. She spotted the vial in Lobo's hand. "What the heck are you doing with a stitcher?"

Lobo slammed the vial into the pavement, shattering it and throwing the contents wide.

"What's a stitcher?" I asked, my giggle dying down.

Lobo sneered at the broken glass by his feet. "It's an enchantment. Distracts you by making you giddy."

"That's clever," I said.

"Back there you said something about your grandmother." Lobo turned to me, all seriousness back. "Why were you chasing that guy?"

I shivered under his intense gaze, reminded once more that I was in a cold dark alley with a werewolf. "I...uh—"

Tae wrapped an arm around me and pulled me back out of reach. "Would you knock it off, you big lug? Can't you see you're scaring her?"

Lobo softened up, even looked a little wounded by the allegation. "I wasn't trying—"

"Kumbaya for you," Tae said. "If you want to talk to Lanie, you can come by her shop tomorrow. I think you've had enough for one night, don't you?" She looked at me.

I nodded. I wanted nothing more than to go home and curl up under a warm blanket until my head stopped spinning.

We left Lobo in the alley, feral eyes lingering on me every step of the way.

9

I slipped away from a delicate dream of laughter. In it someone that looked like me danced in a nightclub and frolicked in dank alleyways with a werewolf. My head felt heavier than usual, the muscles in my neck stiff. I worked hard to sit upright, extending my arms and legs in a delicious stretch. I was on a couch in an unfamiliar room. A wide bowl of exotic flowers sat on the coffee table by my knees.

I instantly knew I was in Tae's apartment. Something about the overabundance of comfort surrounding me told me that. I was on a thick cushioned sofa with a matching loveseat across from it. Most of her apartment was hiding in the shadows of night, but I could see hanging silken scarves, lush plants throughout, a gilded altar with some small statue surrounded by dimly burning tea lights. It all confirmed my hunch. I felt for my grandmother's pendant underneath my shirt. The warmth of it against my skin gave me comfort.

Tae had taken care of me, kept me safe while I was under the prickly pink's spell. I smiled and curled the blanket around my shoulders. It smelled like a thick musk. No, wait, that was the air, I realized, wincing as I tried to see clearly. The air was permeated with a dense smoke. Alarmed, I hopped to my feet with the blanket still curled around my shoulders like protective armor.

I was in Tae's living room, which had an open kitchen connected to it, a very similar layout to my grandma's place. The smoke was coming from a hall that shot off toward the bedroom. The floor was covered with a lively shag rug that almost swallowed my feet to the ankles in fluffy tendrils of fabric. I hurried down the hall, then pulled up short when I saw Tae's bedroom door was half open, light spilling out into the hall.

Drums beat inside her room, static with the whirring of an old record player. The smoke was a pungent woody aroma. I thought I could almost taste neroli too, like a bitter orange paired with jasmine. I peered into her room, not knowing what to expect after the strange evening I'd had.

Tae did not fail to make my night even weirder. She sat naked with her back to me, cross-legged on the floor. Candles were lit all around the room and in three points around a circle she had drawn onto the floor in front of her. Each candle was surrounded by a smaller circle that joined the points of a triangle. Other items were scattered about the summoning circle; a dish with crushed leaves, a goblet of red wine. But no incense, as I had expected the smoke to be coming from. Instead, the smoke was radiating from Tae's naked flesh as she chanted in a soft golden voice and swayed sensuously side to side.

I felt shame burning as deep as my awe to be peeping in on her. However, I'd never seen smoke rising from a person's body and I was thoroughly intrigued. Still, there was something clearly sacred about what was happening, something incredibly personal and spiritual, and I had no business spying on Tae's private moment. My face felt hot with embarrassment, and I moved to head back to the living room.

Then it happened.

I had seen many strange things since I received my grandmother's letter, but this took the cake. The air at the center of the summoning circle altered all at once. Like the ripple on a pond, the air bent in concentric circles that spiraled outward leaving a black rift in their wake. Before I could even gasp, a hoofed foot stepped out of the portal. I quickly dodged to the side of the doorway.

Was Tae summoning the devil himself to her bedchamber? I had certainly read stories about witches summoning beastmen to fornicate with under a full moon. Icy dread ran through my veins. Tae's chanting grew louder, as did the record's drumbeats. I dared to peek around the corner. The beast was fully outside the portal now. He was a man, with a barrel chest and powerful corded arms. Thick hair matted his body in segments, and his lower half was distinctly goatlike, which made sense, as he had horns on his head as well.

Tae's chanting was pointed at him.

He replied in a guttural language that might have been German or Norwegian. I understood none of it, but Tae gave a throaty laugh and opened her arms wide. He spilled onto her, their bodies a tumble on the floor, lips roaming over each other passionately. The portal closed.

The beastman pulled back from her, and she produced a bottle of clear liquid. Tae took a bit in her palm and rubbed it over his muscled chest and arms. She worked her way lower and lower until she reached the area below his belly button, where smooth skin gave way to fine, soft tufts of fur. As she did so, he took the bottle and drizzled a small line of oil across her shoulder blades and the base of her neck. He smoothed the oil into her skin and slid his hands down to cup her breasts. I could see him gently twist her nipples between his thumb and forefinger.

"Ohhhh, do the other one," she said.

The beastman happily complied. The two of them glistened, each sensual curve and chiseled muscle accentuated by the candlelight. I was entranced by their courtship. I had never seen or heard of anything like it. Somewhere between the sight of the lovers, the steady beat of drums, and the pungent aroma, I forgot my embarrassment. I lost myself in the moment.

Tae's hands slid lower out of sight as she massaged somewhere that made the beastman moan. She quickly pressed two fingers to his thick lips. "Shhh, my friend's sleeping."

Without taking his eyes from her, the beastman pulled her hand up and nibbled her fingertips. Tae giggled and then traced a line down her breast, past her navel, toward her opened thighs. By the lusty gaze in the beastman's eyes and the sharp breath he drew, I knew she slid them into her parted lips. Now it was Tae's turn to moan. I saw proof of the beastman's excitement when he shifted to the side, revealing his thick rigid cock. I almost gasped. I had seen pictures of naked men before, but the beastman's swollen member was far thicker. I quickly slid to the side of the doorframe again, worried he would see me.

I pressed my back against the wall. What was I doing, peeping on my new friend like some pervert? Why was I not running back to my apartment with embarrassment? Even speaking of sex would usually have me on my heels with dread. Instead, my entire body felt tingly and warm. There was an aching in my core, and my most intimate parts were throbbing and slick. It must have been the prickly pink still coursing through my system, overstimulating my senses in the most precarious and delicious way.

A throaty moan escaped Tae's lips. I quickly peeked inside the room. She was leaning back on the floor with the beastman's face buried between her thighs. One of his hands was caressing her tender thigh while the other pinched and teased the delicate nipples of her heaving breasts. He alternated between kissing and nibbling on her inner thigh then running his tongue over her clit. As I watched, he moved his hand from her breast down her smooth skin and then between her legs where he entered her with first one and then two thick fingers. He slid his fingers slowly in and out while his mouth kept teasing her clit.

 Desire raged inside my core. My own body ached to be touched that way. I shifted my position and pressed my thighs together as rippling waves of heat radiated inside me.

 My eyes shifted to the beastman's rigid cock. What would it feel like to have something like that inside me? Stretching me out and filling me up with hot sweaty pleasure? I longed to see him take Tae, to thrust himself inside her beautiful body. She moaned in ecstasy as he sucked on her clit while moving his fingers in and out of her to the rhythm of the drums. Tae suddenly pulled away from him.

 She flipped over on hands and knees, and lifted her ass up high. "Fuck me, now," she ordered.

 The beastman rubbed up and down her pussy lips as he pumped his cock with his other hand. He pressed the head to her. It was so large I didn't think it could possibly fit inside her tiny opening. He teased her with the head, rubbing it up and down her opening, without entering her. Tae rocked her ass back onto him. The beastman threw his head back as he groaned. He was slick with her wetness. He grabbed her hips and thrust himself further inside of her. I felt dizzy watching them. Tae buried her face into the blanket on the floor, muffling her moaning as he slammed harder and harder inside of her.

 I felt my fingers on my pants, grazing my own sweet spot. I wanted nothing more than to rub the aching passion out of myself. Perhaps the prickly pink made it possible? I had never been so aroused in my life. Was this what sex felt like? I was free. The spell on the envelope must have cured my horrible medical affliction too.

 The beastman grabbed hold of Tae's hair and pulled her head back. Her whole body quivered as she reached the height of her pleasure and screamed. The beastman continued to pump himself inside her, relentlessly thrusting his cock in and out of her cumming pussy.

I could not contain myself any longer. And why should I? My fingers teased up and down where the moist heat was growing, bringing me closer to a climax. Euphoria washed across my body.

And then the world went black.

Shit.

A deep voice broke the nothingness. "She's got a nasty bump on her head."

"I can see that, Billy." Tae scowled. "Go get me some ice like I asked."

I opened my eyes to see the beastman, Billy, stalking off to the kitchen wearing sweatpants. I was lying on the couch in the living room. Tae hovered over me, frowning.

Her eyes lit up as mine focused on her. "There she is. Are you okay, hon? You took a nasty spill in the hallway."

"Fuck me," I groaned, covering my face as I felt it heat up with thirteen shades of scarlet. What could be worse than spying on your new friend while she was having sex? Getting caught red-handed. I was mortified. "I'm so sorry, Tae."

"Sorry for what?" She gently moved my hands away from my face. She was smiling down at me.

Billy returned with a handful of ice. He presented it to Tae.

"Good goddess, Billy. Go get a damn paper towel for it."

Billy jumped to action with a clumsy grin. "Oh, right."

"I was spying on you," I admitted, already thinking, *Wait, that's dumb, what if she just thought you tripped on the rug or something.* "I'm so embarrassed."

Tae giggled. "Lanie, if I had a problem with you watching, don't you think I would have said something?"

"I never should have—wait, what? You knew I was there?"

Tae shrugged. "I figured you would either join us or take care of yourself." She took the wrapped ice from Billy, then pressed it gently to my forehead. "Plus, I saw how that drink affected you, so I didn't want to be pushy."

"You thought I would join in?" I repeated, still dumbfounded by the idea.

Billy's eyes lit up as he quickly looked between us with a dopey grin. Tae caught his look and rolled her eyes. "At the time, in the heat of it, yeah, sure, why not?"

I remembered how large Billy's cock was. I was certain my face was red as a ripe tomato at this point. Tae was so beautiful. I couldn't fathom a world where she would have been happy to have me join in. "I can't believe you knew I was peeping the whole time," I groaned.

"It's not that odd," Tae said. "Plenty of folk like to watch. Nothing wrong with it, and it excites me too. The blacking out was odd, though. Has anything like that ever happened to you before?"

I shook my head. It felt heavy and fuzzy still. "I'm a virgin." *Oh my goodness. What the hell is wrong with me? Why did I just blurt that out?*

"No, I meant when you—." Tae's eyes suddenly bulged. "Hang on. Did you just say you're a virgin?"

I nodded meekly. Billy was studying me like a was an animal in a zoo. You would think after years and years of those looks, I would be used to them, but it still filled me with humiliation.

Tae caught on to my discomfort. "Billy, go wait in the bedroom, will ya?"

He grinned sheepishly. "It was nice to meet ya, Lanie," he said, already heading down the hallway. "I hope your head feels better."

Tae patiently waited for the bedroom door to close, then focused back on me.

"Is he okay in there alone?" I asked. "I mean, don't you have to teleport him back to hell or something?"

Tae's brow furrowed. Her mouth opened with an unspoken question. Then light entered her eyes. "Oh my goddess, you thought…" She giggled. "Billy is not a demon, dear. He's a satyr."

"But you summoned him through that portal thingie," I said. I pushed her gently away and sat up, holding the ice to the lump on my forehead. It was numbing it nicely at that point, but I had a sharp pain upon lifting my head. "I'm not so uneducated that I don't know what a summoning circle is. I have cable television."

Tae shook her head, still giggling. "It's just a bit of roleplay we like to do sometimes. It actually gets Billy off more than me, but I like it just the same."

"Oh, so he's not a spawn of Satan."

"Lanie, you are a hoot. No, he's just a bloke I fool around with from time to time. Don't you remember meeting him at the tavern?"

I had a flash of Billy walking by us when we first entered Free House, waving to Tae. They had waved at each other. "I remember now. How silly of me." The rest of the night was a bit of a blur. I remembered how foolish I had been afterward, on the dance floor. I groaned.

"Billy helped carry you home. You were pretty out of it after we went back inside, so I knew I had to get you out of there. Especially with the way you were all over that creep Lobo."

I covered my eyes with my free hand as it all came rushing back to me. "Oh no. I'm such a nitwit."

Tae giggled again. "Don't be so hard on yourself. We've all had nights of questionable experience. Anyhow, what's this nonsense about you being a virgin? You do know what I am, right, Lanie?"

I dropped my hand to look at her. "You're a...succubus?"

"Do you know what that means?"

"Not really. I think...a succubus is a fae that makes other people attracted to each other or something, right?"

"Well, close. Those are cupix. We succubi are born with the *gift* of fertility. Magic, as humans would say. We are indeed very sexual creatures, but also born with the gift of sight as it pertains to sexuality. Other fae come to us for help in their love life or with fertility issues, things like that. I myself work as a couple's therapist."

I felt guilty. The whole night we hung out, I had never asked Tae what she did for a living. It was remarkable to me that this amazing fae held such a professional job. Then again, Sir Horrick was a lawyer. *I wonder how many other regular jobs fae have.*

"I tell you this so you understand that, well, when you say you're a virgin, I can see Lanie that this is not true. I can spot a virgin a mile away. With my *sight*, that is."

I thought it was endearing how careful Tae was being to tell me she thought I was lying to her. I grinned meekly at her. "I've been penetrated before. But never anything further. I have a...well, a disorder, I guess."

And suddenly I opened up to Tae. The only person I had ever told any of this was Deedee, yet here I was, twenty-four hours into meeting Tae and already spilling my darkest secret. I explained how the first time I tried to have sex, I blacked out. The few times I tried after that would be similar, with me blacking out, but with the boys I was with also being affected. "You see, they can't maintain an erection once they're inside me. One of them tried his hardest. He thought I passed out drunk and was going to help himself regardless. Which apparently was something he'd done in the past, the little pig. But no man can keep maintain an erection once they've entered me."

Tae threw her arms around me. "Oh, you poor dear sweet thing." She cradled me back and forth.

I patted her back, as if she was the one who needed comfort. "It's okay," I lied. "I've made my peace with it. The doctors I've seen say there is something wrong with me emotionally. That I cause this to happen mentally, psyching myself out because of the trauma from the first time."

Tae crossed her arms over her chest. "That sounds like some horrendous human horseshit."

I shook my head. "No, it's got to be right. I've tried everything. I even thought maybe I was into women and didn't realize it, but the same thing happens. I pass out as soon as I get excited, only instead of going limp, they get horrible stomach cramps."

"Your eyes rolled back in your head," Tae said, but she spoke as if she was talking to herself, working out some puzzle. "So even when you try to pleasure yourself, you pass out?"

I nodded meekly.

Her eyes lit up, and she snapped her fingers. "Lanie, we must have met for a reason. This is exactly my territory of expertise, after all."

I put the wet remains of the paper towel and ice down on the coffee table. "You want to be my therapist?"

"Even better. Lie down and let me look at your aura."

"My aura?"

"Just trust me," Tae pointed at herself. "Succubus, remember?"

I nodded. "Fertility magic."

I had nothing to lose, and I was intrigued. I lay down on the couch and held still as Tae worked her hands over me, inches from my body. It was a strange sensation, as if a subtle energy was radiating from her fingertips. I had seen reiki massages on a documentary of Eastern medicine before and wondered if the two were related.

After some time, Tae abruptly stopped. She turned her back to me and went into the kitchen. I heard the water running and wondered if I should sit back up. Were we finished?

Tae came back into the room and handed me a glass of water. She took her own glass and plopped onto the loveseat across from me. Her face looked as if it had aged ten years. She noticed my gaze and explained, "It took a great deal of energy to delve inside your aura. It's a thick tangled mess. This is what I look like when my glamour is worn out."

"Just as beautiful," I said.

She smiled weakly. "You're too kind, Lanie. Which makes what has been done to you one of the cruelest crimes I can imagine."

The water felt great sliding down my dry throat. I could feel it sloshing in my empty belly, ice cold. "I think that stupid prickly pink is finally wearing off," I said. "What do you mean, *'done to me'*?"

Tae frowned, her face wrinkling. A tear trickled out of her left eye. "As I thought, there is nothing wrong with you mentally. I don't know what I imagined I was going to find, but it certainly wasn't this."

"Wasn't what?"

"Lanie…someone has put a curse on you."

10

A curse?

All my life I had believed there was something wrong with me. Like at the core of who I was, I was a failure. I was incapable of one of the most fundamental things in life. I know many other people have struggled with their sexuality and some had probably had far harder times of it than me. But I wasn't them. I was me. It was my life, and for years I felt like a rotten piece of fruit someone left in the bottom of the grocery bag. I stayed out of everyone's way and hid my shame in the corner, resigned to live a life of loneliness.

Now I had a succubus telling me it was a curse that made me like this.

"But, what…? Why would anyone do that to me? I'm a nice person, I think."

Tae her tears away. "I don't know, but I'm so sorry."

I looked around the room, suddenly sober. What the hell was I doing here? This couldn't be real. "Well, can't you just magic it away or something?"

Tae shook her head. "It doesn't work that way, Lanie. Someone put a powerful hex on you. This thing is buried deep at the core of your being. I wouldn't even know where to start."

My throat was dry as sandpaper. I took another gulp of the water. I could hear Billy laughing at something in the other room. "Let me try and understand this. There's nothing wrong with me mentally?"

"Nothing."

"But I have some, what, fae curse on me to make sure I can never be intimate with anyone?" I could hear my voice cracking as a lump grew in my throat. I was going to cry.

Tae pursed her lips and nodded, her own eyes wet.

What did I say to that? In the course of one evening, my entire life had been flipped upside down once more. I could only sit there like a lump, staring at empty space with my mouth hanging open.

"I'm so sorry, Lanie." The way Tae looked at me made me feel small. I was a pathetic creature to her. This was a fae for whom sex and fertility were everything. I was a living personal affront to her. Pity rimmed her eyes. I had seen that look on so many girls in college. *There goes Lanie, the pathetic little sophomore who can't find a man.*

Tae opened her mouth to speak.

I leapt to my feet and fled her apartment. I don't remember if I said goodbye or anything else. I just needed to get out of there before she could say one more thing to me. Otherwise I might scream until my head popped off. I do not remember getting my purse or calling a cab or even buying the train ticket. By the time I could think about anything, I was doing what I should have done several days before. I was going home.

I slept for most of the train ride.

It was late afternoon when I arrived back in the city. I pulled out my phone to check the exact time, except my phone wasn't in my pocket. *Nice, another screwup, Lanie. Great job.* I'd left the phone at my grandmother's apartment. *I'll just have to buy a new one. There's no way in hell I'm ever going back to that horrible place. Let the realtor sell it for whatever they want, as-is. That's not my world. It's a world full of curses and empty promises.* Just more of the same evil I had already lived with my entire life.

We rely too much on technology. I did not even know Deedee's number without my phone. As I thought of her, I realized I didn't want to see Deedee anyway. I could not face her at that moment. She was just another person to pity poor little Lanie.

It was a quick cab ride back to my apartment. Had New York always smelled like the bottom of an exhaust pipe? Had I been desensitized to that, living here all these years? At least most of the people I saw were normal, just plain old humans going about their business. It was a welcome reprieve from Willow's Edge.

A homeless man scurried into the alleyway on the side of my building. He had crow feathers in his hair and mumbled incoherently to himself. I made a mental note to tell the superintendent. The last time vagrants set up shop in our alley, one of them overdosed. It felt good to be back inside my apartment building. It had only been two days but felt like years.

I skipped my apartment and went directly up to the rooftop. *What I need right now is to sit among my plants and zone out to the sounds of the city.* I realized I had missed my garden more than anything. *If I spend a little time taking care of them, everything else will be alright. I can get through this. I'll just put my head down and fall back into my routine, and before I know it, I'll never even think about faeries and curses.*

I felt something was off the moment I stepped out onto the rooftop. Tattered leaves from my crab apple tree littered the exit to the roof. My heart caught in my throat, and I ran around the corner. The breath was taken out of me as surely as if I'd been punched in the stomach. For four years I had worked cultivating row upon row of raised garden beds. I tended everything from a miniature Japanese maple to overflowing wisteria. Hibiscus that would generally die in the colder weather of a rooftop garden thrived amongst lamb's ears and hydrangeas. They were my precious little babies.

And they were all gone.

Someone had destroyed my garden beds. The plants were torn to shreds, some of them ripped out by the roots and maliciously tossed onto the rooftop. White dust dotted the rich soil. I grabbed a handful and let it pour out into the air. Someone had salted my garden beds!

What kind of monster would be capable of doing something so heinous? It was the act of a madman. They had not only ravaged my garden but ensured I could never again plant anything in the soil I had carefully poured my heart and soul into.

I ran down to my apartment. I was numb inside, hollowed out as truly as if someone close to me had just died. That garden was everything to me, and now it was gone forever.

My door was slightly ajar. I burst into the apartment seething with anger. The vandal had better pray they were not still inside, because I wanted nothing more than to choke them to death.

My apartment was completely ransacked. Shelves were toppled over, books torn apart, and my television was shattered. The stereo was on, blasting my Phantogram album from the living room. Something fell in my bedroom. I ran toward the noise, hoping to catch the intruder.

My dresser was toppled over, all the contents strewn across the room. I owned a stack of records. That was what had fallen over, and most of them were shattered to pieces. Then I saw my bed, and my heart went cold. Deep gouges were torn into the mattress, like a wild beast had clawed it over and over again in a frenzy. Someone had used my black sharpie to scrawl a message across the wall over my headboard. It read: *You're Next.*

I finally came to my senses. What was I doing, running toward danger like that? Someone had broken into my apartment and gone absolutely nuts. Then they destroyed my garden beds beyond belief. That message wasn't random. This was personal. Whoever had been here was looking for me. But why?

I eyed the shredded mattress. *What could make cuts like that? Not a knife, right? What if I had been here when they broke in?* I pictured my mutilated body left to rot on the rooftop.

I shuddered. The song playing over the living room stereo started over. Sarah Barthel's voice was calmly telling me to *hide the sun* as the song kicked off. The thing that surprised me the most in that moment was my anger. *Fuck hiding.* I was not going to keep running from room to room looking for the intruder, but I still felt fierce. I should have broken down in tears and called the police or run to the superintendent's apartment for help. Instead, I harbored a scorching fire in my belly that was making its way to my chest.

The intruder had made one fatal mistake. If I had come home to find the apartment broken into and the mattress shredded, I likely would have slipped into that old feeble Lanie who could not look out for herself and wanted to hide in the corner. But this bastard fucked with my garden.

Well, guess what? They'd messed with the wrong person.

I staggered into the living room, still in a state of shock. I locked the door to my apartment, then turned off the blaring stereo. A quick search around the floor led me to my landline. I didn't know Deedee's number, and I was wondering who to call when my hand felt thick paper in the pocket of my skirt. It was Detective Lobo's card. Perfect. I punched the number into my old phone. It rang a few times before I hung up.

My desktop computer monitor was knocked over but otherwise fine. The computer was tucked behind the desk, in the corner of my living room. The desk itself was tossed apart, but the intruder had not made it to the PC underneath. I set the monitor upright and powered the system on.

While it booted up, I dialed Lobo once more. It rang.

I entered my password and opened my DVR folder.

Someone picked up. He was breathing heavily into the line. "Detective Lobo, whaddaya need?"

"Lobo? It's Lanie."

A pause. "Oh, Miss Alacore. Sorry. I was working out. Didn't hear the ringer."

I could tell he was lying. He had ignored my first call. It didn't matter. I scanned the files in the DVR folder until I found the most recent. It was dated two days ago.

"Hey, about last night," he began.

"This isn't a social call, Detective. Someone broke into my apartment."

"Above Rosalie's shop? I'll be right over."

I double-clicked the video clip and set it to 10x speed. "No, I'm back in the city. Someone ransacked my place. Everything I own is pretty much destroyed. The fucker even salted my garden beds."

Lobo went silent for a few moments. I could almost hear the gears in his head turning. "Lanie, that's awfully far away. You shouldn't have left Willow's Edge. I'll hop on a train right away. You better call the police there, though. It's way out of my jurisdiction."

"Got you, motherfucker," I said under my breath. I clicked play. "I got him on my home camera system. Figured a fae might not know to look for that." In the video, my apartment door was open. I rewound until it was closed again and let it play.

"We have security systems too," Lobo said, sounding annoyed. "Do you have a good angle on them?"

My heart froze. A hooded man entered the apartment. I instantly recognized him. "It's the same guy," I mumbled. The man looked sideways, then closed the door behind himself. He turned directly toward the camera. If I didn't know any better, I would swear he was looking directly at me, as if he knew I was watching him across the span of time.

"Shit, you're right," I said. "He saw the camera."

"Lanie, this is serious. You shouldn't be monkeying around by yourself. Just call the police and get out of there."

The hooded man crossed the living room in a dash, his cloak a flowing shadow. I let out a yelp when his face suddenly appeared inches away from the camera. The video turned to static. I looked up at the corner of the room. The tiny camera wires were hanging from the ceiling.

"What is it? Are you okay?" Lobo was breathing hard again.

I rewound the video until just before the static kicked in. There, I had it. A clear picture of his face.

"Shit. Lanie, are you there? Are you okay?"

"I'm fine," I said with a steely resolve I had never felt before. "I got a clear shot of his face."

"Oh, that's good," Lobo said, clearly relieved. "Bring it to the local precinct, and I'll meet you there later tonight."

"I'm not doing that."

"Lanie—"

"*Because* this is the same creep we saw last night at the club. The cops here aren't going to be able to do diddly squat with this, but if I'm right, he's still in Willow's Edge. I'm coming back, and you're going to catch this bastard."

Lobo was silent again. He chuckled. "I was wrong about you, Lanie. You're a very strange person."

"I'm headed back on the first train. Meet me at the shop. And *don't* stand me up this time." I hung up on him.

The face was still staring back at me from the computer screen. He was a soft-looking little bitch, and he was going to regret the day he messed with me. He really should not have touched my garden.

11

Lobo was sitting in an old Chrysler sedan, waiting for me as my cab pulled up to the antique shop. He was not alone. The man he'd been talking with at Free House the previous night was sitting in the passenger seat. *Was that really only last night?* It seemed to me, as I entered the shop, that it had been weeks since my prickly pink mishap. The door rattled shut as I swept inside, waving for Lobo to follow.

Sacha peeked above his newspaper, a cloud of smoke circling his little imp form. "Finally decided to drag yourself into work," he grumbled.

"I know you lied to me about the conditions of your employment here," I said, tossing my purse and jacket onto the counter. "And I don't work here yet."

Sacha swallowed his cigar and almost stumbled sideways off his stool. Then, just as quickly, he spit it out again. He caught it with his lips, still lit. "Hmm, must've been Tae with her big mouth. Can never trust a succubus."

The door chimed as Lobo and his partner walked inside. They came around the shelves, Lobo sweeping the storefront with his penetrating gaze, as if someone might be lurking behind a shelf. "Lanie." He nodded.

Now that we were face to face, I felt a little queasy. A three-hour train ride will do that to you, giving you the proper amount of time to appreciate that someone could be out to kill you. Couple that with my completely out-of-character dance with Lobo, and I was feeling like the old Lanie. "Thanks for coming," I said meekly.

"This is my partner, Doule."

Doule swept off his hat and produced a half-bow for me, accompanied by a mischievous grin.

"Geez, you got a whole pack of 'em in here now," Sacha grumbled. So Doule was a werewolf too? Interesting.

"Nice to meet you," I said. "I'm assuming Sir Smiles over here filled you in already?"

"Did you bring the picture?" Lobo, all business, prodded as Doule hid his smirk behind a fake cough.

"Got it right here." I waved the USB drive in the air.

"You have a computer? In *this* shop?" Lobo growled.

"Of course we do. This is a business, isn't it?" I did not know why he was so annoyed. I looked around the counter, but there was only an old-fashioned register with big metal keys. "Sacha, where is the computer?"

Sacha eyed the USB drive as if I was presenting him with a handful of poo. "Gross. What would we have one of those for?"

"This is a business," I repeated. "How the heck do you print invoices and stuff?"

Sacha had a good chortle at that one. "What, am I having déjà vu? You sent me and the shop back to the sixth circle of hell, and I'm swimming in invoices?"

"I don't have the faintest idea what you're talking about," I said.

Lobo groaned. "Just give it to Doule. He'll run it over to the station and print some pictures out for us."

"Thank you, Doule," I said sheepishly, handing him the USB drive.

"My pleasure entirely, Miss Alacore." Doule grinned. "I'll be back in a flash, *Sir Smiles*."

Lobo growled as Doule took off on his errand. We both watched until his car pealed away. Then we were left standing there in awkward silence.

"Do you mind if I look around the shop?" Lobo asked.

It felt strange for him to be acting so polite toward me. "Search the shop?"

Lobo cleared his throat. "I've been thinking that whatever is going on must be related to Rosalie's disappearance. If we can find some clue to where she went, then it might help us figure out why this guy's stalking you."

"Makes sense," I said. "But didn't you already do that when she first went missing?"

"I did a minor search, found some newspaper clippings and Rosalie's day planner. Unfortunately, that's as far as I got before the chief caught wind and pulled me off the case."

"Because you didn't have a warrant?" I asked, leaning into my extensive *Law & Order SVU* expertise.

"Something like that. There's a lot you don't understand about our world. Rosalie was an important figure in our province. The chief didn't want to risk a scandal by letting me loose on her shop. To be honest, they acted like I was overreacting when she went missing. But I know Rosalie. She never would have missed our plans without calling or leaving a letter. Chief didn't want to hear it. Too much pressure from above. Then by the time folks realized it was serious, it was too late. Rosalie has been gone long enough now that the council has declared her dead. They're usually right about this stuff, but now the case is closed, and we didn't even vet it completely. Nothing new there. They're all too happy to turn their noses away from the stink of reality."

"Are you saying my grandmother is the victim of some political tail wagging?"

"That's one way of putting it."

"That...that pisses me off," I said, feeling the heat rush to my forehead. I could not believe that even here, in the world of the fae, politics reigned supreme. Why was my grandmother's fate left in the hands of bureaucracy? "Well, it's all legally my property now, so go ahead and root away."

I had Sacha lock up for the night so no customers would disturb us. Not that I had seen any since I came to Willow's Edge, other than Tae. If she even counted. I thought about how poorly I'd behaved the previous night. First spying on her, then storming out of her apartment like a child having a tantrum. I owed her an apology.

"I'm going to start by looking through the basement," Lobo said.

"I have a basement?"

Sacha snickered from behind his newspaper.

"Are you just going to sit there giggling all night, reading those stupid papers?" I asked him.

He folded over half of it to peer at me, his cigar hanging from his red lips. "What else is there to do in this wretched fairyland?"

"You could help us search for clues to where she went, for starters."

"Don't waste your breath," Lobo said, unfastening the side of a wall shelf between the counter and the door to the office. "He's not gonna help you. Sacha's just a worthless imp." The shelf opened on a hinge, revealing the basement door behind it.

Tiny flames above Sacha's head ignited as he glowered at Lobo resentfully.

"Nobody here is worthless," I scolded Lobo. Sacha might be a jerk, but nobody deserved to be called that.

Lobo shrugged.

"What's down there?" I asked.

"Rosalie did most of her serious work in the basement, as far as I know." Lobo headed down the creaking wooden steps. "I'll holler if I find something."

"Racist," Sacha muttered under his breath.

Was the imp really bothered by Lobo's words? I had not thought anything could faze the troublesome little daemon. "Well, prove him wrong, then. Help us search for what happened to Rosalie instead of sitting there without a care in the world. I would think you owe her that much."

Sacha growled and tore up his newspaper, the tiny flames floating above his head growing brighter. He scattered the pieces around him on the floor.

"What are you doing?" I asked calmly.

He slapped his face and growled again, then crossed his tiny arms over his hairy chest and settled into a pout. "I could fit what you know about daemons into the heart of a marble, and there'd still be room to spare."

His little display had my heart hammering. It was easy to forget that Sacha was some otherworldly creature, and a very dangerous one at that. At least to me. It was the feeling I got when a dog I was petting started to growl. Like, *oh yeah, the only thing between you being cuddly and tearing my face apart might be the promise of a Milkbone.* Except Sacha did not seem angry as much as offended.

But why? What had I said that bothered him that much? I had a suspicion I knew the answer. "You can't help us even if you want to, can you?"

Sacha was surprised I'd pieced it together so quickly. His tiny flames dissipated as fast as they had come. He gathered up his dropped cigar and fluttered in a circle above the counter. It was his version of pacing. "Rules of Hell forbid it. Only reason I'm here is because that good-for-nothing witch Rosalie trapped me." He landed on his stool and grabbed a fresh newspaper from the stack, then tugged it open with a scowl. "Not like I'd help you if I could, anyhow," he muttered.

He was lying. I could see it plain as day. Whatever strange relationship Rosalie had with this daemon was bigger than he was admitting. I felt like a fool that it had been right in front of my face this whole time. No matter how much he tried to deflect the truth, Sacha cared about Rosalie. And he was trapped here. "Can you even leave this store?"

"Leave me alone," Sacha grunted.

I felt a pit in my stomach. All I had thought about this past week was myself. However, it was clear Rosalie had left a larger legacy behind than just me. People cared about her. Drys, Tae, Lobo, and even Sacha. She had touched the lives of those around her.

My stomach growled, and I realized I had not eaten anything since before I hopped on the train back to Willow's Edge. Something else dawned on me. Sacha had tricked me into cooking for him. But where else was he going to get food if the little imp could not leave the shop? I felt horrible, trying to recall when the last time I had cooked for him had been. If I was hungry, he must have been ravenous.

"Would ya stop staring at me?" he grumbled from behind his newspaper, cigar smoke billowing around him.

"Tell Lobo I'll be right back if he comes up."

I raced upstairs to my grandmother's apartment. I preferred my mac and cheese cooked on a stovetop, but when you have an imp to feed who has not eaten in at least a day, you used the microwave. It still seems funny to me that fairies exist and that they use such mundane things as a microwave. It made sense. I mean, it's not like someone was going to set up a cauldron in an upstairs apartment.

In no time at all, I had some mac and cheese whipped up. I grabbed a box of crackers and a slab of muenster Rosalie had in the fridge, then zipped back down to the shop.

"Dinner time," I trilled, coming around the aisle to the counter.

Sacha slapped down his paper with wide eyes as I placed the bounty on the counter before him.

"C'mon, dig in." I handed him a spoon and nudged the larger bowl of cheesy goodness in front of him.

Sacha sat there eyeing the food and practically salivating, but he did not budge.

"Well, go ahead. Eat up, silly." I nudged his bowl a little closer.

Sacha looked between me and the bowl and whined exactly like a distressed puppy. "I can't."

"That's ridiculous. You had no problem eating it before. It's obvious you're hungry, and I made all this…" Something in his pleading eyes unhinged my brain so the pieces fell in place. "Ah, but before you tricked me into making that food, huh?"

He nodded emphatically.

"I see, so you can take something from me if you've tricked me into it." I tapped my finger to my lips, trying to remember what I had read about fairies and demons in the past. I loved to read, but it was mostly fiction. How much of that might apply to the real world? "There was one story I read where the trickster demon would only help the prince if he made a deal with him. But this is different. I want to help you, not the other way around. So if we were doing things that way, then you would have to pay me something in exchange for the food."

Sacha grinned, and a fire lit behind his eyes. His tiny leathery tail flicked back and forth excitedly. I was definitely on the right track.

I shrugged. "Okay, tell me something about this dumb antique shop, and I'll give you the food."

Sacha let out a gleeful squeal. "We don't sell antiques here." He pulled his suspenders and let them snap back in place, then snatched up his bowl of mac and cheese. He quickly shoveled the food in his mouth.

That was a weird thing to say. "What do you mean? All we have here are antiques." I turned and scanned the shelves. What was I missing? "Then what do we sell?"

Sacha ignored me and kept scarfing down his macaroni.

I picked up a piece of the muenster and wagged it in the air. "I'll give you some cheese if you tell me what we sell here," I said playfully.

Sacha snatched the cheese from my hand without even looking up. "Y'already said I could have the food."

Damn. So, it was going to be like that, huh? I would have been annoyed, but Sacha looked so happy chowing down. My curiosity was piqued, though.

I walked into one of the aisles and grabbed a dented French horn from a shelf to inspect. "Wait, are you saying these aren't antiques?" The implications of that hung over me like a dark cloud. I had hinged my hope for a future on the potential income from selling all these pieces of junk. If they were worthless, if they were just the garbage they seemed to be…then I was royally screwed. I spun around as panic descended and shook the horn at Sacha. "Are you saying this is worthless?" I yelled.

Sacha dropped his bowl on the counter and flew across the store to snatch the horn from my hands. His eyes were wide with fright. "Are you mad? You want to kill both of us?"

I frowned. "With a French horn?"

Sacha rolled his eyes. "It's magical, isn't it? Half the stuff in here is, in one way or another."

Magical? I mouthed the word. Old leather boots, a broken typewriter, a torn gift box. Some of these things were magical? "Well, what do they do?"

"Don't know all of 'em. That was Rosalie's department," Sacha said, carefully placing the French horn back where I found it. "But this one'll open a portal to the Antarctic, freeze us to death before we can blink."

"Fuck me." What else was there to say?

Sacha gave me a tiny nudge on my shoulder as he flew back to the counter. "Why don't you sit down and just leave this stuff alone until the wolf is done downstairs?"

I felt numb as I made my way around the counter to sit on the second stool by the register. My own bowl of mac and cheese waited, but I suddenly had no appetite. In my ignorance, I had almost killed us. How many other items like that were there lying around the store? It seemed danger lurked for me everywhere I went these days.

"Wait," I thought out loud, "why did you warn me? We didn't trade anything that time."

"It's called self-preservation, love." Sacha grabbed a handful of the crackers.

I was starting to understand. Dealing with an imp was going to be tricky. He would try to scam me constantly, as was his nature. If I wanted something, I would either need to make a deal with him or let him think he tricked me into it. But if Sacha's life was on the line, he could act regardless.

"Then why didn't you just tell me about making a deal so you could eat? Isn't it self-preservation not to starve to death?"

Sacha chuckled. "An imp can go a good month without Earthly food before it gets to all that. Doesn't make me any less hungry. Which isn't a pleasant feeling, I'll tell you. But I won't get weak or die for a good bit without."

"Wow, there's so many rules," I said, shaking my head. "Between learning about all the different fae and then this…I think I need to start writing everything down to keep track."

I reached under the register for the notepad I had used the previous day. It was where I left it, on top of a stack of other pads. One of them caught my interest. I pulled it out. It was a small spiral bound notepad, stamped 'Planner' on the front. *That's strange,* I thought.

"Lobo," I called toward the open basement door, "didn't you say you already took Rosalie's planner?"

12

The basement was, to quote Tae, *colder than a witch's titty*. It feels like something a drunk biker would probably say, but in that moment, it was the first thing to pop into my mind. What does that even mean? Do witches have colder titties than other women? If so, why? Either way the basement was frigid. I can attest to this as both of my nipples promptly stood at attention upon descending the creaking steps. I wrapped my arms around my chest to keep warm and tried to get a feel for the area.

The usual hum of hot water heaters and furnaces could be heard from somewhere in the dank basement. Dim light filtered across the gray walls from somewhere deeper. Directly ahead was an area that reminded me very much of the library I worked at in college. It was part of my work study program and one of my favorite places to be. It was called the stacks, basically the backroom area where large wooden shelves from floor to ceiling housed all the backup tomes. It was my job to keep them organized and to retrieve books for students. It was quiet work, and I was surrounded by amazing literature to read. I absolutely loved it. I might have stayed there forever if there was a plant to be seen. Unfortunately, the most you could hope to grow in those dark rooms was fungus, and the moisture required for that was not good for the books. Whatever Grandma Rosalie had set up in her basement looked eerily similar. Except instead of books, it was more antiques. A dusty drum kit on the floor between shelves, worn boxes, an old pair of boots. It looked like the standard rubbish that unqualified buyers at a flea market would label antiques.

Or not antiques, according to Sacha. Some of the items cluttered on those shelves could be mystical relics that could open portals to a freezing tundra. Maybe those drums could conjure up a tornado? What a *fancy* life I had slipped into. As much as I wanted to explore the stacks and accidentally set off some weapon of mass destruction, I needed to find Lobo.

"Lobo," I called for a second time. "Did you hear me?"

There was some shuffling of papers. "I'm back here."

I went to the end of the first row of shelves and turned right, toward the light. Once I passed the rows of stacks, there was a hallway. I passed a couple of rooms with chicken wire doors on springed hinges. One room was piled with stacks of cardboard boxes. The other looked like the place you keep your tools. Was I someone who needed a place for tools now that I was a building owner? How provincial of me. More cardboard boxes littered the hallway, forcing me to snake around them to continue.

"Where is *here*?" I called, mostly to hear my voice. The basement was creepy. I was trying to keep from thinking that someone could be hiding behind one of those box stacks waiting to jump out at me. "This place is like a labyrinth."

"Just follow the hall."

Said the wolf to the girl in the dark basement. Fuck me. What was I doing?

The hall split off to the right, down an even darker corridor that you could not pay me to enter. I quickly moved past it. I had to fight the urge to turn around and make sure I wasn't being followed. *Mental note, never go into the basement alone again. Except I'm not alone. There's a man down here that changes into a wolf and eats people.*

I'm a master at comforting myself.

The hall finally opened into a wide room, the width and depth of the apartment building. Wooden columns were interspersed throughout the large space, supporting the floor above.

"I see my grandmother's a packrat," I said. The area looked like something out of *Hoarders*, with stacks of magazines as tall as me, piles of black trash bags, a mound of brass fittings; there was so much random stuff down there it was dizzying. A narrow walkway worked around the stacks, forming islands like some junkyard bazaar.

"It's not that bad," Lobo said gruffly without turning around. He was standing with his back to me in the lit area before a long wooden table pressed up against the farthest basement wall.

"This hill of dolls from the village of the damned would beg to differ," I said, skirting a creepy pile of dolls that would put the American

Girl collection to shame. Each had the potential to be the star of their own horror flick. I never did like dolls. They look like they come to life when everyone went to sleep, except in more of a *Where's the knife to slit your throat* way than a *Toy Story* kind of party. "I mean, it's just piles of stuff down here. Super creepy."

I quickly wound through and around the piles of neatly stacked rubbish. *Wait, is any of this magical too?* I did not dare touch any of it and almost groaned. Scratch the idea of having movers come in and toss all of it out so I could sell the building. I was going to have to clean all of this myself! It looked like Sacha was going to earn his next meal with hard labor.

The tables Lobo stood before were piled with various scrolls, parchments, books, and interesting-looking trinkets. "Is that lab equipment?" I asked, pointing to the empty alembic and beakers.

Lobo shrugged. "Rosalie was great at making potions. There's not much here pointing me in the right direction. She always had her hands in so many different things. I can't make heads or tails what she was doing most recently, though," he grumbled. "Have you ever seen anything like this?"

Lobo showed me a torn sheet of paper. It looked like the edge of a book. The writing on it was ornately embossed with goldleaf. But the words were in some cuneiform language I had never seen. It was all wedges and tiny symbols. "I'm not much of a linguist."

He nodded and put the paper in his pocket. "It *does* look like someone messed with her stuff."

I wrinkled my nose. "How can you tell? It's pretty sloppy-looking to me."

Lobo gestured to a long corkboard fixed to the wall above the table, as if the answer were obvious. All I saw were different-colored strings hanging from tacks around the board, and a bundle of herbs tacked to the bottom of the frame. "What? It's just some sweetgrass."

"It's not what's there. It's what is missing. I've never seen Rosalie's board clear like this. Whatever she was working on, someone didn't want us to see it." He sniffed the air. "I can smell them in here. It's an odd odor, masked with chaotic magic."

The basement just smelled like dust and old newspapers to me, but I saw what he meant. Some of the tacks had bits of torn paper still underneath them, as if someone had ripped off the contents in a hurry. I met Lobo's gaze and felt an involuntary shudder. His golden eyes glowed in the darkness of the basement, a trick of the light's reflection. I had only seen anything like that in *National Geographic* pictorials of night shoots with forest creatures. We both understood in our silent language what this meant. Someone had deliberately destroyed Rosalie's work. And that someone had recently been in this basement.

"You guys having a private moment?"

I nearly jumped out of my skin, that is how hard I shook when Doule came around the corner. Especially as I twirled around to find his eyes reflecting the basement light the same as Lobo's as he strode out of the shadows. He chuckled when he saw my reaction.

"That's right." Doule smiled. "I forgot Lobo said you're new to all this. Didn't meant to scare you."

Lobo chuckled. I felt my face turning red with embarrassment.

"You shouldn't be sneaking up on people like that," I snapped. I was getting tired of constantly being spooked lately. I quickly broke away from them. "Lobo, I found something. Come upstairs, I can't stand this basement."

I raced around the piles but could not remember which wall led to the hallway. Lobo came up behind me. "Just follow me. Doule wasn't trying to scare you."

"I'm *not* scared." I don't know why I lied. Who the heck wouldn't be if they found themselves in the basement with two werewolves? I would like to see what you would do in those circumstances. It made me mad that he was calling me out for it, though. It was a jerk move, totally unnecessary.

With Lobo in the lead, we quickly made our way upstairs to the storefront. Sacha perked up when we came into the room.

"Didn't you say you took Rosalie's planner when you were first here?" I asked.

Lobo waited for Doule to come into the room, then closed the basement door. "Yeah, it's at the station in my desk. Couldn't enter it into evidence since they barred us from opening a case. It was a dead end, though, I told you that."

I had been carrying the planner I found the whole time. I lifted it for Lobo to see. "Then how did it get back here?"

Lobo tilted his head to the side, just like I imagined a curious wolf might. "Well, for starters, that's not the same planner."

"Why would she have two planners?" I asked.

"Rosalie kept one for personal stuff and one for business," Sacha interjected.

I arched an eyebrow at him. Why would he offer this information without a bargain? I made a mental note to ask him what rule that answer fell under.

"May I?" Lobo asked, his hand outstretched.

I handed him the planner. He quickly flipped through it to the previous month, then scanned each page slowly, with a finger from top to bottom before flipping. "Okay, this is interesting." He showed the book to Doule.

Doule's eyebrows went up.

"What?" I asked.

Lobo flipped the planner around so I could see. "This is the day before Rosalie and I were supposed to meet up."

"Is that an intersection?" I asked. "Any clue where this is?"

Doule shrugged. "Fourth and Catman. Must be down by the docks. The old warehouse district."

"What would an old lady like Rosalie be doing down there?" Lobo asked, directing the question to Sacha.

The imp shook his head. "Haven't a clue."

Lobo growled.

"I really think he doesn't know," I said. "Are you going to go down there and check it out?"

Lobo closed the book and slipped it into the back pocket of his jeans. "I am. Doule, I found this on her board. Can you run it for me back at the office?" Doule took the torn sheet and nodded. "Lanie, I'm going to camp out front tonight, keep an eye on the building in case our mystery guest comes around."

I felt an abrupt sense of relief. I had not realized how tightly wound up I was. I guess finding out someone who might have killed your grandmother was now stalking you will do that. The idea of Lobo guarding the building suddenly left me feeling secure. "You don't have to do that. I should be fine."

Lobo shook his head. "It's not safe. Not until we know more about what's going on."

"Okay."

Doule smirked.

Oh no, did I agree too quickly?

"Ah, I almost forgot," Doule chimed in. "Here's the printout of your unsub." He unfolded a piece of paper and handed it to Lobo. "Looks pretty familiar, huh?" Sacha fluttered over behind them to get a good look.

Lobo and Sacha gasped at the same time, the imp flying a few feet higher in the air.

"What? You know him?" I asked.

Lobo twirled the picture around to me. "This is the creep that's been following you? The same one we chased at Free House?"

It was the hooded man, just as I had seen him on the camera. "Yeah, that's him. He's the guy that knocked me over a few weeks ago at the pub too. Why, who is he?"

"That's Rosalie's missing assistant."

13

I didn't get much sleep that evening. Lobo looked so lonely out in his car. I know this because I kept going over to the window and peeking between the blinds at him. I felt guilty. I debated back and forth with myself on whether I should go down and tell him to come up to my apartment. It seemed silly for him to be guarding me from a distance. What would he think of me if I invited him up, though? I did not want to send the wrong message. Smoke drifted out of his car window, the way it does when you breathe outside during the cold. The season was shifting rapidly into late fall. He had to be cold.

This was silly. If I asked him to come up but made it clear it was not for anything risqué, then I could just get some sleep.

Ha! Who was I fooling? I let go of the crack in the blinds and went back to bed. If Lobo was in the apartment, I still wouldn't get any sleep. I would be thinking about him in the next room the whole night, wondering what he thought of me. Remembering the way I felt when his hands touched me, the heat from his body when we danced.

This was stupid. I needed to sleep. When had my life turned into this sophomoric after school special? Last week I was happily arranging flowers. Now my world was dead grandmothers and fae and curses. Ugh. Even worse, what if Rosalie was alive and in some horrible situation? And why did her assistant want to hurt me? And why did my mother lie to me my whole life about who we were? What were we even? I always felt like a human, but what did that even mean? I wished I had some way of getting ahold of my mother. Had she heard of Rosalie's death? I had no way of knowing where in the world she might be.

I told myself I didn't care where she was. More importantly to me was a hope, above everything, that Rosalie was fine and that we would track her down. I had so many questions about my legacy for her. Did she know who put this curse on me? Why would someone curse me to be unable to have sex? It seemed a bit cruel, considering I had never hurt so much as a fly. Well, maybe that wasn't true. I've swatted my share with a rolled-up newspaper or two. But that wasn't something you cursed someone over.

I lay there and thought of the questions I would ask her, and each of them led to more questions. It was enough to make me dizzy.

Eventually I fell asleep. The next morning, I got ready for the day, then made Lobo a cup of coffee and brought it out to his car. He was still awake, staring at my building. I hopped into his car on the passenger side.

"Coffee?"

"Thanks." His voice had that *I've been up all night* coarseness to it.

"I made it black. Figured you're the no-bullshit kind of coffee drinker."

Lobo snickered, then sipped some. "Actually, I prefer mine with peppermint mocha creamer."

I laughed. "What? A serious guy like you? I never would have guessed it."

He grinned sideways at me and drank some more. The coffee was piping hot, but it did not seem to bother him at all. "It was a quiet night. No one came around."

"I figured." I tried to think of what to say next. Something witty would be perfect. *Think, Lanie, think. Fuck.* I waited too long. Now it was awkward. "Do you need to use the bathroom or anything before we go? I know you've been out here all night."

"You're not going to the warehouse, Lanie. It's too dangerous."

"So you'd rather leave me here all alone while you go to the warehouse?"

By the look on his face, Mr. Serious had not thought of that one. He considered it for a minute, drinking the last of his coffee, then handed me the empty mug. "Okay, just run that back inside, and we can head out."

I snickered. "Nice try."

Lobo shot me a wolfish grin and shook his head. He started up the car and pulled out.

It was a nice early-morning drive. Joggers were out, and workers were opening their little shops all over town. I wondered how many of them were fae. Was the entire town? It seemed likely. "How does Drys fit in to everything?"

"What do you mean?"

"She's like, what, the mayor of the town?"

"Kinda," Lobo said. "But maybe more like she's the caretaker of Willow's Edge. Without her we wouldn't have this province. Her tree is at the center of it."

"Like, the town's heart?" I asked, remembering Tae calling it that.

Lobo nodded. "That's a decent way of describing it."

"I could feel it, even when I first got here. Willow's Edge is like no place I've been before. There's this interesting sort of energy that cuts right through the air here."

"That's because this is your first fae province, I'd imagine," Lobo said. "It's different than the human world."

I snorted. "You say it like we're not on the same planet."

"This is Earth, just not the same Earth you're used to. I'm not the best person to describe it. I'm not a professor. Think of it like two circles that are overlapping. Where they overlap is where the two worlds meet. That's where we are, in the fae province Willow's Edge."

The possibility that presented was almost too much for me to fathom. We drove past a birch tree with glowing magenta leaves that danced on the fall breeze. "So it's more than just pretty trees and strange creatures. You're saying on one side there's the human world, like New York City."

Lobo snorted. "Doesn't get more human than New York."

"And on the other, there are lands that are completely fae? What are they like? And they're both on Earth? I can't even picture it."

"Right now I'm more concerned about finding Jalk."

"Yeah, you're right. I guess I just ramble when I'm nervous sometimes." I stared out the window watching the town pass us by.

"I just can't figure why Jalk would do this," Lobo grumbled. "He came on as Rosalie's assistant a few years back. I've never liked him much, but I have to admit I never expected he could do something so violent."

"How do we know he has?"

Lobo furrowed his brow at me. "Lanie, he trashed your apartment and wrote 'You're Next' on your wall. I don't think that was an invitation to join him for tea. The guy's clearly unhinged."

"But what about his hand you found?"

"Rosalie is no lightweight," Lobo said. "She's not one to go down without a fight."

"But why did he try to kidnap her in the first place?"

"You'll get the answer to that soon enough," Lobo said. "We're here."

The area we entered was odd. It was like driving into a black-and-white film. Everything around us was washed in only grey tones. It was a stark contrast to the lush landscape of Willow's Edge. The streets were barren, with no signs of life anywhere. The car immediately jostled as it drove over the uneven pavement. Lobo steered around a large pothole that looked like a meteorite must have hit the road. I could not tell if the empty lots were where buildings used to exist or if they were just overgrown parking lots. The warehouses were massive structures that took up entire blocks. Doors were boarded up. Most windows were broken.

"What the heck happened down here?" I asked. "It looks like a third-world country."

Lobo snorted. "What does that even mean? Silly human phrase for superiority and neglect."

"Human? Aren't we still in Willow's Edge?"

Lobo slowed down and pulled into a tight alleyway between buildings. "Barely. This is the edge of the province. This was what the land was like before Drys moved Willow's Edge here."

Moved it here? How did you move an entire town somewhere? I had so many questions.

Lobo slowed the car to a crawl. "This is it." He grunted, then pulled over and turned off the engine.

I climbed out of the car and shivered. The air was brisk with the promise of snow. I pulled my sweater around me tighter and buttoned the front of it. The air smelled like a garbage dumpster. "Why does it taste metallic?" I whispered to myself.

"Used to be processing plants down here," Lobo said, carefully closing his car door so it did not make a sound. "Mass produced cutlery or bolts or something." Without any explanation, he headed across the deserted street to an alleyway between two buildings. I quickly followed. Something about the place made me sure I did not want to be left alone.

The warehouse's façade was peeling in long thin strips of paint, like curled fingers reaching for the bleak sky. I did not know how it could be broad daylight and yet so lifeless. I peered closer at the paint. It used to be red at one point, but it was like looking through a gray lens. I checked my hand and found my skin to be duller in color too. There was something so off about this place. Willow's Edge felt alive with a vibrant energy. In contrast, the warehouse district was like walking through the town's dying arteries.

"Lanie."

I turned to find Lobo staring at me. How long had I been standing there, staring at the paint?

"Are you okay to continue?"

I nodded. "Yeah, sorry."

"Okay, just stick close to me. There's no telling what we'll find out here. And don't wander off, whatever you do."

He did not have to tell me twice. I huddled close to him as we rounded the corner to a lot that was overgrown with weeds. Stacks of cement tubes used for culverts were interspersed on our side of the lot. Rows of old weathered tires were on the other. In between was a cracked patchwork of weeds and broken ground with the occasional electric pole.

"That's the building over there." Lobo's voice was barely a whisper. He beckoned for me to follow as he slid behind one of the culverts.

We stood there, motionless, watching the building from the edge of the culvert. It was identical to the rest of the structures we had passed, huge with peeling paint and shattered upper windows. An enormous brick chimney protruded from the farthest side of the warehouse, like some dead giant's finger pointing to the blotted sun. We were on the backside of the building, with loading docks for trucks spaced out in even intervals.

Lobo was intense, his gold eyes flicking back and forth across the structure. I tried to do the same. Some of the unbroken windows were covered over with old newspaper from the inside. "I don't see anyone here," I said softly.

Lobo hissed at me. "Quieter than that. Jalk's always had pretty keen hearing."

I nodded sullenly at his rebuke. His hiss wasn't that much quieter than I had been. *I'm not a bull in a China shop.* What kind of fae was Jalk that he could hear that well?

Lobo tensed up. I followed his gaze across the yard. There. One of the loading docks had a door that was lightly swinging in the breeze. Lobo centered his focus on that spot and then sniffed the air.

"He's here."

Lobo dashed across the yard, waving for me to follow. I was not even halfway across the lot when he made it to the building. With one leap he moved from the ground to the top of the loading dock. He paused, sniffing the air again.

"Wait for me," I whispered, knowing canine ears could pick it up.

I stopped in my tracks when he snapped his head around to gaze at me. There was something feral in his eyes that shook me, and he bared his teeth. He hesitated for a moment but then cocked his head to one side, as if listening to something far away. He vanished inside the building. I quickly climbed the cement steps to the loading dock.

Someone screamed inside the warehouse, followed by a crashing sound like shopping carts falling over. Oh no, Lobo had walked into a trap! I ran as fast as I could, and suddenly I was inside the building, standing in front of a makeshift tent. Lobo was wrestling with the hooded man, his knees on each of the man's arms as he pinned him to the floor. When I approached, he visibly flinched, then snapped his attention to me.

"What the heck was that?" he snarled.

I was surprised I could scare him. I shrugged. "Sorry, I'm a fast runner when I want to be." Of course, I had no idea how true that was or why. But I am getting ahead of myself. The warehouse was a disgusting dump, with a second level that was falling into the first floor in spots. Rusty machinery was toppled over. Brick columns dotted the area, some with sad excuses for graffiti on them. Jalk had set up a shanty tent in the center of the main room.

"Please don't hurt me," Jalk whined.

Lobo's growl ricocheted across the empty warehouse. It was powerful enough to make Jalk stop struggling. Once he was still for a few moments, Lobo seemed satisfied. He brought his face inches from

Jalk's so that his sharp teeth were fully visible. "Where the hell have you been, Jalk?"

"H-here," Jalk stammered. "Right here."

"Little liar," Lobo snarled.

"I didn't do nothing, honest," he mewled.

"Then why run from me at Free House?"

Jalk stopped moving. "That was you? Honest to goodness, Lobo, I didn't know. I wouldn't have run if I knew it was you."

Lobo snarled again. "Second lie." He clacked his teeth in front of Jalk's face, causing the frightened man to flinch.

"He's obviously scared to death. Why don't you let him sit up and explain himself," I said.

Lobo kept his face inches from Jalk's, studying his eyes for a long minute. "Okay, I'm going to let you sit up, Jalk. But if you so much as blink, I'm going to tear your throat out with my bare hands."

Jalk whimpered.

Lobo slowly slid off him but remained crouched right at his side. Jalk sat up with a jerking spasm of his arms, gathering his black robes close to his body. Dirty bandaging poked out from one of his sleeves, marking the stub that remained of his severed hand. It was the first time I'd seen him with his hood down. He was a very slight fellow, with a delicate moon face and pale pink hair. He looked like he was born with diamonds where his eyes should be. I immediately understood why they seemed to glow beneath the hood. There was no white to his tiny, rounded eyes. He pulled his hair away from his face, tucking it behind a pointy right ear. Three wooden hoop earrings decorated the lobe. It was the first time I'd seen a pixie in real life. It made me mad to think that all this time I had feared this man.

"Why have you been following me?" I snapped.

Jalk flinched. Then he looked up at me with wide eyes. "Followed you? I only did my duty and delivered the letter."

"Some delivery," I snapped. "You bowled me right over and left me there on the sidewalk."

Jalk looked at Lobo with a worried frown. "No, no. Honest, that wasn't my fault. I didn't know you'd react like that when I gave you the letter. It was something to do with the Rosalie's will, I think. It hit you like an electric shock when you touched it."

"The spell that lifted the veil," I mumbled as I understood.

Jalk nodded emphatically. "Yes, that's right, it was some sort of spell."

"Why'd you trash her apartment, you little runt?" Lobo snarled.

"Trash it?" Jalk grew haughty. "I did no such thing." Lobo snarled, and Jalk withered again, shying physically away from the detective.

Lobo presented the printed picture of Jalk. "It's no use lying to us. We caught you red-handed, you little cretin."

The little man studied the picture in Lobo's hand. Then he turned to me. "I'm sorry about your recording mechanism. I remembered you had it on the ceiling the first night I found your apartment. I had to make sure it was disabled before I left the city a few days later. I figured you would be out of town at that point, so it would be safe. It was just a wee little thing, about this big. You can hardly consider that trashing the whole place?"

I glanced at Lobo. He was looking at me with the same expression. Something was off. Jalk was hardly the mastermind of some heinous plot. The man was scared stiff even by me raising my voice.

"Jalk, I don't understand. If you didn't... Why did you run from me like that at Free House?" I asked.

Jalk looked down at his bandaged stub, then up at me. "You were so scary. Your eyes were all wild. You were pointing at me and shouting like you wanted to kill me."

Lobo lifted his eyebrows and nodded. I wondered how hysterical I must have looked with the prickly pink coursing through my system. "But what about my grandmother?"

"It wasn't me." Jalk whined and clamped his hands over his mouth. His body shook as he broke into sobs. "Please don't kill me, Lobo."

Lobo stood up, his teeth and fingers normal once more. He looked genuinely concerned. "Jalk, I believe you. I've known you for years, and you've always been an annoying little shit, but I can't see you doing anything to harm Rosalie. I'm not going to hurt you, but you must tell us what in blue blazes is going on. What are you doing in this stinking warehouse? Where is Rosalie? Why have you been lurking around Lanie?"

The pixie grew silent. "You're not going to hurt me? You promise?"

"I promise."

When Jalk looked up, his eyes were tiny pinpricks. "Okay, I'll tell you everything I know."

"A few months ago, Rosalie caught wind of an orphan who needed her particular brand of help. He was in trouble with the law in the human world, caught up in some smuggling nonsense they make such a big deal about. Well, somehow his blood ended up getting run, and it triggered all sorts of alarms in those databases the council uses, so they got Rosalie involved."

"Fuck. A changeling?" Lobo grumbled.

"Changeling?" I asked. "Like another werewolf? Why would that be a big deal?"

"Not a werewolf," Lobo corrected. "We're shifters. A changeling is a half blood, a mixture between human and fae. Bad news."

"That sounds fairly racist," I said. "Besides, isn't that what I am?"

Jalk chimed in. "Fae can mate with other creatures from our realm. And sometimes there's a child that's a mix of them. But a human and fae? That's a different story."

"Because they go mad," Lobo explained. "It's not right, upsets the natural order. A being of both realms confuses nature." He turned back to Jalk. "Did this cretin hurt Rosalie?"

"She refused to let me get involved. You know how she is," Jalk whined. "Rosalie has to do everything herself. His name is Brom. She worked with him for a couple of months, trying to cure the blight from his mind. He seemed like a harmless man at first. But something changed a few weeks ago. He went wild. He's killed a few times in your realm." He gestured to me. "But Rosalie, she wouldn't give up on him. Said it wasn't his fault he'd been cursed this way into existence. I tried to tell her to stay away from Brom. He was messing with some dark stuff, I could smell it on him like hot tar. But you know Rosalie."

"Stubborn," Lobo agreed.

"Where is she?" I asked. "Where's my grandmother?" I could feel the tears pooling in the corners of my eyes. I already knew what he was going to say.

"She's dead. Brom murdered her."

I heard my sobbing before I felt it, like a long-protracted sound that came from someone else. I had been so close. All this time I had this voice in the back of my head. I did not want to hear it because to do so would be to embrace hope. Hope that I could finally have a family. I was a fool for hoping, and I knew that in my pitiful soul. I was alone, as I would always be, with no one to love me and care for me.

Lobo was there suddenly, wrapping his strong arms around me. I pressed my face into his chest and let my tears stain his jacket.

"It all happened so fast, Lobo," Jalk insisted. "Rosalie was going to meet with him. He was camped out at that cemetery behind Forest Hill. She was so excited. She said she'd figured out how to make him all better."

Lobo pressed me tighter to him, letting me cry all the tears I had to give. "Take me there and show me where to go, Jalk. I'll take care of the rest."

"I'm sorry, Lobo. He's too dangerous." Jalk's voice changed to a frantic pitch. "He scares me so bad. Much more than you do."

My ears popped as the air pressure suddenly dropped. Lobo let go of me and spun around. Jalk was gone. All that remained was a puff of smoke where he had been standing.

"Damned pixies," Lobo snarled.

14

"Maybe we should leave," I said, pulling my sweater tighter around myself as a chill wind blew down the street.

Before Lobo could respond, Drys opened the door to Free House. She looked like a high priestess in her airy white robe. Golden stitching that resembled the branches of her willow tree adorned the trim of the garment. Her hair was plaited down to her waist in long blonde tresses. She looked Lobo up and down, then frowned. "Why are you banging on my door, Lobo? You know Free House is closed on Wednesdays. I'm resting. Come back tomorrow."

Lobo firmly shook his head. "Can't do it. Lanie needs your protection. She's in danger."

"Oh? I haven't felt any danger." Drys straightened, quickly scanning the street left to right. She sighed. "You better come inside and explain it all to me, then."

I felt really uncomfortable. This was the sort of thing Deedee had done to me time and again, dragging me places where people were clearly not excited to have me.

"I can't come inside," Lobo said, gently nudging my elbow as I walked up the steps. "There are some things I need to do back at the station. Lanie can explain everything while I'm gone."

"You're not coming in with me?" I faltered at the doorway.

"Just stay here," Lobo said. "There's no safer place in Willow's Edge than with Drys." Then he was off, sprinting back to his car.

"Well, don't dawdle in the door all day. You're letting all the cold air in," Drys called, already deep inside the tavern.

It was strange to be inside Free House while it was closed. The chairs were flipped onto tabletops. The candle chandeliers were unlit. Other than the sound of air blowing from a vent somewhere, the place was deadly quiet. I had never felt like such an intruder.

"I'm so sorry to be bothering you on your day off."

"I'm over here, Lanie," Drys called. She sat on the ground beneath her willow tree. The sunlight filtering down through its boughs made her hair and robes glow with radiance and warmth. I still could not comprehend where that light came from. It was a cloudy fall day outside, yet her tree was bathed in clear rays of sunshine. The willow was massive. I craned my neck to gaze up past the wooden beams, but it was just a vaulted ceiling lost between the leaves of the canopy. Drys patted the mossy ground beside her, near an ancient, exposed root. "Come rest with me. Tell me everything."

A myriad of twinkling sprites had flitted about the willow's boughs the last night I was here. Even without them, the tree held motes of light, as if someone had hidden a string of twinkling holiday bulbs amongst the leaves. As I stepped off the tavern floor and onto the circle of mossy ground surrounding the tree, I hesitated. Something felt wrong about stepping on that ground with my soiled loafers. I quickly slid them off and tucked them neatly onto the wooden floor, just at the edge of the tree's perimeter, then stepped inside.

Drys smiled approvingly at me, then beckoned for me to join her.

The ground warmed my feet like a sunbaked beach. The moss was soft and spongy, with an earthy aroma of wet soil. The fear that had been choking me sloughed away in waves. The air seemed alive, and the branches swayed in what I could swear was a sigh.

"You are safe here," Drys reassured me as I sat on the ground beside her. Her eyes were ancient with knowledge. I understood. This was her place of power. She reigned supreme in Free House, so if she said it, then it was so. "Now, tell me everything."

I held no inhibition. My story poured out of me like water dribbling down a creek and then turning into the raging torrent of a river. I walked her through everything from that first night bumping into Jalk in the city to earlier that morning at the warehouse. I let it all spill out, leaving only the curse Tae had discovered to myself. As comfortable as I felt with Drys, there were some shames I couldn't bear revealing.

"Then Jalk disappeared, and Lobo brought me here."

Drys took my hand in her own, then presented me a handkerchief. I was startled to find I had been crying for a while. I had been so lost in the telling of things that the present had slipped away from me.

"It pains me to hear confirmation of Rosalie's death." Drys spoke with the raspy sound of leaves rustling together in the breeze. "I knew your grandmother for a very long time, my dear. She was more than just the Warden to me. I considered Rosalie my friend." She squeezed my hand. I could feel the depths of her sorrow in that touch. I knew enough to stay quiet. It was Drys's turn to share.

"You know, I felt it when she passed," Drys said. "It can be that way for me sometimes, when I am close to someone." She gazed up into the swaying branches and sighed. "Perhaps that's why I distance myself these days. Oh, Rosalie…why get involved with a changeling? It troubles me to hear her last moments were likely filled with terror. When I felt her leave this realm, I only hoped it was a peaceful death. One of old age."

We sat in silence for some time, holding hands and listening to the heartbeat of the tree. Finally, Drys sighed, and as she did, the boughs swayed. She went to fetch some tea for us but bade me to stay put. When she returned, she set a long wooden platter on the ground, balancing it perfectly on the exposed root between us. She poured our tea and handed me a small cup with no handle. I cupped it between two hands, feeling the warmth in my fingertips. I let the smells of chamomile and citrus cleanse me. I was pleasantly surprised when flavors of cinnamon and cloves exploded in my mouth and warmed my throat deliciously.

Drys grinned when I expressed my delight. "This is so yummy. You have this way of making things taste so amazing. I don't know how you do it."

"That's kind of you to say, dear."

"There's something I don't understand. Everything feels so different here. Ever since the veil was lifted, it's like I've been seeing the world for the first time."

"The simple reason for that"—Drys paused to sip her tea—"is because you are."

"But why is the human world so drab? How can it be so much more colorful and fuller of life in the fae realm?"

"We are not in the fae realm, dear. Willow's Edge is a province. We are between both realms, human and fae. There could be many explanations for what you are experiencing, though they are all only tiny truths and not at all correct. Magic is all around you now, in Willow's

Edge. That energy is exuding from the different fae here, as well as our plants and the very air. Another explanation could be that the light bends differently when you are in the lands between realms. This gives a sort of glimmer to things, particularly if they harness magical energy in some way. Or perhaps it is simply because you are looking on things you have never before seen, and this has reawakened your sense of childlike wonder.

"However, I would disagree with you about one thing," Drys continued. "The human realm has much life to speak of. I've often wondered at the way humans live, like meteorites, shining brilliantly as fast as they can because they know, deep down, that soon enough that light will burn out. I understand what you mean about the colors of our world, but do not mistake that there is much beauty to be given in humanity as well."

It gave me comfort to hear Drys speak so of humans. Everyone thus far had spoken with open disdain of them. It appeared things were not as cut and dry as my brain wanted to file them. And I realized that was a good thing.

"It's just…I *feel* things here that I never did before." I shook my head.

That caught her interest. "Like what, dear?"

"Never mind. It's probably exactly as you explained. Everything is so new. I think I've just been in awe all this time."

"No, there's something else on your mind," Drys said, not letting me off the hook. "What were you about to say?"

I could feel myself blush. One day I would learn how to control that reaction. Drys seemed so wise. I wanted her to like me. I wanted her approval. I was so tired of being a wilting flower. Why did I need everyone's permission to just be me?

"When I found out I had a grandmother…I acted surprised, but in some ways I was just going through the motions." It was astonishing to hear my innermost thoughts spoken aloud. "It's like…deep down inside of me I always knew she was out there somewhere. In college I would daydream that one day she would come knocking on my door and tell me I'm not alone after all. And I don't mean some long-lost relative. It was specifically my grandmother that I used to imagine. And now I still have that strange feeling, as if I know she's still here. When the lawyer said she was dead, I went along on the outside, but somewhere inside my soul I did not believe him. It's like I could feel her calling for me."

Drys watched me with an alien gaze.

"I know it's silly. Jalk saw her die. He wouldn't share it with us, but he saw something horrible. There was no doubt in his mind Rosalie is dead."

"But you still feel her out there somewhere?" Drys asked.

"Like I said, it's just a silly fantasy."

Drys stood in one fluid motion and leaned over to press her hand on the willow. She closed her eyes as if she were listening for something. After a few minutes of awkward silence, she pulled away and sat back down beside me. "I don't feel her, Lanie…"

"I know I—"

Drys shook her head to cut me off. "I don't feel her *in this realm*, but that does not mean she's not out there somewhere. You are clearly strong with the Alacore bloodline. It is entirely possible you have been feeling a real link to your grandmother this whole time, despite that despicable spell your mother placed on you as a child."

"Could that really be possible?" I was somewhat dumbfounded. What else did one say when they found out they might have been feeling a piece of their grandmother all their life?

"Do you still feel her now, right at this moment?"

I shrugged. "Sort of. It's like I have a thread pulled out there somewhere. Except it's a much dimmer feeling than it was before."

"It sounds worth exploring," Drys said. "Is there any chance you have anything of Rosalie's on you?"

"Like one of her possessions?" I thought about my grandmother's store. Most of the antiques were too large to casually lug around with me all day. Not to mention dangerous. Her clothes were not exactly my style either. I frowned.

"It would have to be something she was close to. Something she used each day."

My fingers brushed the pendant hanging beneath my sweater. It was strange how it had become a sense of security for me recently. I felt a sudden rush of excitement. "I have this pendant necklace she left in her bedroom."

Dry's eyes widened when I pulled it out for her. She took it with trembling fingers. It was not the reaction I had expected. "Where did you say you found this?"

"It was hanging on her headboard."

Drys closed her hand around the crystal pendant and shut her eyes. She looked so pained that I did not know what to say. After a few moments, a tear trickled down her left cheek. "Rosalie loved this necklace," she whispered.

"It is quite beautiful," I said, just to break the awkward silence.

Drys opened her eyes again, and she suddenly looked very tired. She handed me the pendant and smiled. "You don't understand, dear. Rosalie would never have left her home without this. It is a very old family heirloom. She wore this pendant every day of her life. If you have it now, it is only because it was meant to find its way to you."

I stared down at the azurite crystal horn. The light of the willow made it sparkle in my palm. How could an object find its way to me?

"And with this, we can most certainly see if Rosalie is still out there somewhere."

My heart leapt up at that proclamation.

She held her hands out to me. "Keep the pendant in your hand and press your fingers to my palms."

"What are you—?"

"If some piece of Rosalie is still with us, it stands to reason that you, of her bloodline, have a connection to it. Take my hands, and I will channel your energy to help see if we can find her."

I was so scared I was shaking. Was this like a séance? Pressing my fingers to Drys's hands might as well have been the same as asking me to jump off a five-story building and expect to be saved. Because that was what the hammering in my heart and the sweat on my brow felt like. I decided to take a leap, not physically but mentally. I threw myself into the unknown with abandon.

Drys pressed my fingertips and started mumbling in a strange language. I've read that the police started using a device called an LRAD. It's a sound cannon used for crowd control that fires a sonic wave just slightly higher than what was normal for the human ear. That was what it felt like to listen to Drys chant. It was unnatural to me, wracking my body in spasms of disorientation.

The pendant in my palm heated. That dim feeling of my grandmother bloomed like a flower in my mind. Suddenly a heavy gust of air picked up, billowing Drys's robes like the sails of a majestic ship. I closed my eyes against the growing torrent and tried to stay calm. Something was hiding in the darkness of my mind. Like a candle, steadily moving closer to light the way.

"I can see her," Drys exclaimed. The leaves rustled overhead as if a storm were coming. "Reach out to her, Lanie," she called above the winds. "Embrace the connection between the two of you."

I pressed out with my mind. There was a tiny dot of light. I could feel that connection, a thread that bound us together. Could I tug on that thread? I tried. The point of light exploded into a billion tiny particles, dancing around my mind until they coalesced and there was nothing remaining but white in every direction. It was a pure brilliance that deafened my thoughts until I too disappeared.

I opened my eyes and found myself lying on my side beneath the willow tree. A glade of poppies surrounded me, a rainbow of colors in every direction. I sat up quickly, pulling my knees to my chest. The sky was a spread of magenta and violet with twinkling stars frosted across it like sprinkles.

Where am I? What is this place?

I realized I was not alone. At first, I thought it must be Drys sitting behind me with her back pressed against the willow tree. It took a few moments for my eyes to adjust to that place. A plump older woman with braided violet and indigo hair sat across from me. Her legs were folded and her palms upright and resting on her knees. Pale blue eyes twinkled above a kind and loving smile.

"Hello, Granddaughter."

15

In many ways the police station Lobo called home was much like the human equivalent. The fae constabulary were, after all, based on the human concept of law. It was an older building of brick and mortar salvaged once the province moved to the area. Any human who happened to stumble across Precinct 214 would find the usual signs of bureaucracy, stale coffee, and the sweat of desperation clinging to its walls and floors.

Norbert, the three-armed cuegle working the front desk, shot Lobo a curt nod as he walked by. A pair of seven-foot ogres wearing matching leather vests and tweed slacks came down the hall toward Lobo. *Bodyguards?* Their client was tucked safely between them, a bespectacled fae with wisps of hair curled against the sides of his bald head. His pointed nose was held firmly up in the air as they passed. Lobo moved to the side of the hall without breaking stride, giving room for the massive ogres to march. The closest one snarled down at him, squeezing its gargantuan orange fist until the bones cracked audibly across the echoing corridor.

What are a pair of thugs like that doing here? Lobo wondered, ignoring the slight. It was not unusual for ogres to take on jobs as bodyguards, but that kind of patronage was usually reserved for the upper echelon of fae elite. It took a lot of money to feed and house one of those insatiable behemoths. He decided whatever business they had at the constabulary was well above his pay grade.

The office space detectives used was fairly empty, as usual, with most of the werewolves out and about the province on open cases. Desks piled with paperwork and personal trinkets dotted the larger open room, each set back-to-back in pairs. That way it was easier for partners to work and discuss their cases.

Lobo planned to be in and out before anyone could wonder what he was up to. Things would be much easier to explain that way. Act now and beg for forgiveness later was a motto he enjoyed.

"Good to see you finally dragged your ass in today." Doule was sitting with his feet propped on his own desk, reading a report he had just taken the time to pen. He playfully twirled his quill across four fingers and then back again as he read. He did not bother to look up at Lobo. "Up late with the tourist?"

"What's with the Bobbsey Twins?" Lobo thumbed over his shoulder.

"Who knows? Ogres brought in some representative a little while ago. Been with the chief ever since." Doule slapped down the parchment and crossed out a line with his quill. Then he turned his chair to Logan. "C'mon, man, why you holding out? How'd it go with that girl?"

Lobo thought of Lanie. "She's…confusing." Ever since he met her, she had thrown off his game. At first, he thought of Lanie as nothing other than some naïve city dweller who was about as exciting as watching paint dry. She certainly had the librarian shut-in look down. Then at the club, she had somehow gotten under his skin in a whole different way. Lanie on the dance floor was someone else entirely. He would have thought that was just due to the drink, but her behavior back at Rosalie's shop and again earlier that morning in the warehouse had surprised him. Lanie Alacore was certainly unique. There was something about her he could not put his finger on.

"That good, huh?" Doule smirked.

Lobo opened his mouth to deny it.

The chief flung the door to his office open. He was a red-faced dwarf with a furry barrel chest that he showed off by leaving his top two buttons perpetually open. Thosimir was known as a man with a temper on even the happiest of days. That afternoon he looked like Mount Vesuvius ready to explode. His bloodshot eyes locked on Lobo, and he snarled.

"There's the sack of shit hisself. Happy you could join us today, your highness. Don't scowl at me, ya mutt. Get your ass in here. We need to have a little chat." Without another word, he stormed back into his office.

Lobo shared a worried glance with Doule. They had known each long enough to understand the unspoken, *Oh shit, I'm a dead man walking.* Knowing better than to keep the chief waiting, Lobo rushed into his office.

"Close the damn door behind ya."

"Yes sir." Lobo obediently complied, then stood at attention before the chief's desk.

Thosimir met him with a withering gaze from his seat on the other side of the desk. This was not the worst sign. If the chief was seated, at least that meant he did not yet have plans to strangle Lobo.

"Do you know the kind of shit storm I had raining down on me this morning?"

Lobo assumed it had something to do with the ogres, but he knew better than to attempt a guess. "No, sir."

"Don't play coy with me, Lobo. You've eyes in that thick skull of yours. How could you miss a pair of council thugs waltzing through my precinct? Bad enough I must open the doors to damned ogres, worse yet when they're here because of you."

That took Lobo aback. "What would ogres want with me?"

The chief snorted. "You really thought you could go raising a ruckus at Free House and it wasn't going to come to my attention?" He carefully gauged Lobo's reaction, then snarled in disgust. "You did, you really thought I wouldn't notice. Well, look the fuck out, here comes Mr. Lobo, larger than life to do as he pleases, 'cause he's so much fucking smarter than the rest of us mongrels."

Lobo shifted on his feet. "Chief, you've got me all wrong."

"Because I'm so stupid, of course."

Lobo sighed. This was not going well. "Please, Chief, I didn't intend any disrespect. Things just happened so fast…"

"Explain it to me, then. Tell me why were you bouncing some bloke across Drys's bar like he was a basketball? You have one too many, was that it?"

"It was Sam Usou, that pervert who tricked that brownie girl a few years back."

"The gangbanger?"

Lobo nodded.

"Didn't he get locked up for that?"

"I wish. The council only exiled the bastard from Horacio's Tavern for life. It's all that money the bastard's got. The other night I saw him duping another victim and intervened before it could go any further. I'm surprised Drys complained. She banned him from Free House for life too."

The chief slammed a closed fist on his desk, rattling everything in the room. "Are your ears filled with bricks? Does it sound like Drys to send ogre bodyguards and an uptight fae to my office if she has a problem?"

Lobo counted himself a fool. *Of course not. Drys would summon the chief to Free House and ream him out in person if that was the case. But if not her, then who?* Why would anyone care about him knocking around that pervert?

"And what about you running half-cocked all through Free House that same evening?"

"Ah, the chase. Sir, I wasn't *half-cocked*. A lead fell in my lap, and I reacted, that's all."

The air sucked out of the room in one swift inhale. The chief glowered at Lobo, who realized he could now count himself twice a fool. When would he learn to shut his mouth and think things through before speaking? That was the problem with being a werewolf, with raging fight or flight constantly coursing through his body—impulse control was a challenge. And the chief knew exactly how to rattle his detectives when he needed them to speak. He would press right on that instinct until one of them blurted out their mistakes.

"Did you just say lead?" the chief growled. It was low in the way that said *I'm seconds from losing my mind.* "Tell me something, you absolute thick-headed fuck. How can you have a lead when I don't even have you assigned to any cases right now?"

Lobo took a deep breath. This was not going to be good. "It was a lead on Warden Alacore's disappearance, sir."

The chief moved like a blur. Lobo never even saw it coming as the dwarf's fist planted squarely into his chest. Most fae considered Lobo to be an able-bodied fighter. But when an Alpha werewolf dwarf punched you, you felt it. He staggered backward and bowled over, gripping his chest.

"You were told Alacore was off limits, you daft little weasel. How dare you go behind my back and open an investigation?" Thosimir bared a full row of canine teeth at him, saliva dripping on the floor. Both his arms had transformed into werewolf form, and he raked his talons across his desktop in frustration. They added another row of gouges over the top of a myriad more he had made over the last few years since replacing his old desk, which he had broken in half while raging.

Lobo knew he better speak quickly. He had sorely messed up, not looping the chief into what he had been up to, but if he did not help Lanie, she was as good as dead. He growled loudly, the sound of it reverberating across the room as loud as splintering wood. The office grew still. He had never once in all his years raised his voice to the chief. "The Warden has a granddaughter. She inherited all of Rosalie Alacore's holdings and asked me to help find out where her grandmother went." It was only a half lie. Lanie technically hadn't officially given him permission to help until the previous night. The events at Free House were before that, but it was enough to give the chief pause.

"Alacore has a granddaughter?" His features rapidly shifted back to a dwarf's.

"Yes, sir. She arrived in town just a few days ago. She has given us free rein to delve as deeply as we need to into Rosalie Alacore's affairs."

The chief leaned back in his chair and folded his hands calmly over his lap. "Well, why didn't you say so? If Rosalie's next of kin has requested we open a case, that should give us latitude to explore it, council approval or not."

"Her granddaughter is in danger, sir. Rosalie was murdered by a changeling, and now he's after Lanie Alacore. He left a death threat on her wall."

"A changeling?" the chief's eyes went wide. "How can you know this for certain?"

Lobo went through the events of the last few days, omitting details where necessary but painting the chief the larger picture.

"And we have this Jalk in custody?"

Lobo grumbled. His chest was sore, but he was damned if he was going to let the chief see it. "No, sir. He teleported before I could grab him."

"Likely halfway back to Ruby City, if he knows what's good for him. That puts the slippery bastard out of our reach. Well, from what you've told me, you're completely screwed."

"Sir?"

"I can't let you continue this investigation."

"But, sir, the Warden's granddaughter—"

The chief held up a hand. "I can't let you continue an official investigation into this. I was trying to piece together why Prince Lucien's agents would come here and file a complaint against you. Figured you must have shot your mouth off at one of his entourage or something, like you usually do. Now I understand better. This Lanie Alacore poses a serious problem. She has given you free rein. I suspect they already knew the Warden was murdered by a filthy changeling. Now they see you traipsing around with her, poking your nose in shit that's way above your pay grade, and I'm guessing they don't like it one bit."

"If they know the Warden was murdered, why not dispense justice?"

The chief rubbed his forehead. "Lobo, you've always been as daft as you are clever. You just answered your own question a few minutes ago. If the council dispenses justice, it will have to be a public action. That means it would have to be discussed in an open hearing." He paused, then sighed. "Wow, you still don't get it. We're not talking about one house being involved. This was a Warden. She is not affiliated with any of the four great houses. Why would they send their assassins after this changeling? For a woman who flaunted her position of neutrality in their faces for centuries?"

"Rosalie Alacore was a decent person," Lobo insisted.

"Not saying anything different. In my book, she was one of the best. But she also made an awful lot of enemies over the years. Now, think to the heart of it for a minute. Let the problem marinate in that thick soupy skull of yours. If they publicly decree that a Warden was murdered by a changeling…"

The answer hit Lobo between the eyes. It had been there waiting, lingering somewhere in his denial. "Then they would have to admit that someone as powerful as a Warden can be murdered by someone far lower in class than a pureblood fae."

The chief pointed at him. "There you go. The council is not about to admit anything like that is possible. What, and give the natives ideas? 'Hey, if the Warden can be murdered, what's to stop us from taking out the council?'"

"They would fear a power grab," Lobo admitted. His chest was still throbbing from where the chief hit him. He thought it might not be wise to continue, but he could not shake the image of Lanie sobbing when she found out about Rosalie. "Sir, the girl, though…she's still not safe."

"You're not on any case involving Warden Alacore. I don't care how close you were to the woman," Thosimir shouted loudly enough for anyone in the bullpen to hear. Lobo opened his mouth to speak, but the chief threw up a warning finger. When he spoke next, his voice was a whisper, low enough so even an eavesdropping werewolf could not hear him. "You want to go out there and hunt down a changeling? That's your damn prerogative. Except I haven't heard nothing of it. You do it on your own. That's your fucking job, ain't it? Keeping the province safe from threats inside and out? But if the council catches any wind of it, they'll kill you soon as look at you before they risk letting that information get out into the public."

Lobo slowly digested the chief's words. If he did this and things went sideways, the chief would hang him out to dry in a heartbeat. He understood. The pack's needs came before the individual. What he was about to embark on would flaunt the council's unspoken directive regarding Warden Alacore in their faces. It was a dangerous line to tread.

"Friggin' fae bureaucracy," he growled.

"Hey, watch your mouth. Those fae are who we work for. Plus, they've got eyes and ears all around this station, mine included. Now, nod your head that you understand what you can and can't do and fuck off out of my office. I'm sending you home without pay for making a scene in Free House."

Lobo met the chief's even gaze. They shared an unspoken agreement in that moment. He nodded and turned to leave.

"And, Lobo?" The chief waited until he met his gaze again. "You better be careful out there, lad."

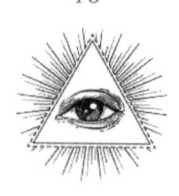

16

"Hello, Lanie."

Rosalie Alacore was radiant. The ethereal light of the otherworldly realm reflected in her eyes like twin sapphires. The crow's feet around those eyes crinkled as she took in her granddaughter for the first time.

"Are you real?" I asked.

Rosalie gave a slight nod.

I looked around us. The willow tree was still there, but Drys and the rest of Free House were gone. We sat in the grass in a radiant light, surrounded by colorful poppies on all sides.

"Where are we?" I gasped.

Rosalie could not take her eyes off me. She was beaming. I had thought she was meditating at first glance, but now I saw large wooden knitting needles in her hands. She was working a ball of yarn without even looking down at her project. "Where we are is not really a place but more of an in between. Like a rest stop on the way to a longer journey."

My heart ached at the insinuation. "You are truly dead, then?"

"Yes, dear. I suppose I am."

"That's horrible," I whispered, tasting a bitter tang in my mouth.

Rosalie shrugged.

"How can you be so calm?" I asked. "If someone murdered me, I would be livid."

Rosalie's smile did not waver. "Lanie, I lived a long, long life. Far more than you would guess possible, compared to human standards. It was grand and spectacular and heartbreaking and beautiful, almost everything I could have hoped for. The time for living was bound to end eventually. And it did. And now, at long last, I get to see my beautiful granddaughter."

Was she saying death was worth it to see me? No, she meant something else, but what was happening was too much for me to wrap my head around. I realized my heart was beating as hard as a snare drum at a heavy metal concert. Something rustled overhead. I looked up in time to see the tiny leaves of the willow drifting down over me.

"We haven't long, dear."

"What's happening?" I asked.

Rosalie took a deep breath before beginning. "Drys is holding the bridge for us. Such a feat is beyond difficult, even for someone of her immense power. Our time together is limited, so I will speak quickly. I am dead. What you see and hear in this moment is the last vestige of my soul, anchored inside the horn pendant I left you, in the hopes you would find me."

"To tell me who murdered you?" I asked.

Rosalie shook her head softly. "My dear, that is as it was. I wanted nothing so much as to see you before I passed on."

"Why didn't you ever come see me before, then?" I whispered, a lump lodging itself in my throat. None of this seemed very fair to me. I was finally able to speak with my grandmother, and apparently it would be over soon. Dried leaves rained down around me as the willow swayed in a growing breeze.

That was the first time Rosalie's smile faltered. She looked wounded and let her knitting needles drop into her lap. "Oh, dear girl, surely you know at this point why that was. But I'm certain it hurts no less for knowing. If it hadn't been for that horrible spell… When I think of all the years we lost because of your mother's nasty little trick and how I could have fallen for it… I was such a fool, and there has not been a day that has gone by since that I have not lived with that regret."

She meant it. Word for word. I could feel my grandmother's raw pain at being kept from me all my life as surely as I could feel my own skin. "Why would she do such a thing to me?"

"That I do not know, child. For I have not spoken a word to your mother since the day the deed was done."

The air picked up with a frosty chill. Dried leaves skittered across the ground in a rustling wave of sound. It matched the static sound in my mind. "Why would she not want us to speak? And why on Earth did she cast that veil on me? I don't understand anything."

Rosalie was growing soft around the edges, like an image losing focus. "No, not yet," she yelled to the darkening sky. Fast as a whip, she leaned forward and grasped my hand. Her grip was tight but not painful.

It was as if my vision cleared and there she was again, whole and complete.

"Lanie, there is so much to tell you," she said urgently. "I know you have many questions and I wish I could answer them all, but that is not to be. I'm afraid you will only have time to listen. Our moment is almost up."

I nodded.

"I have lost sleep many a night trying to understand why your mother did what she did. Now that I see you, it is a bit clearer. You have some other curse hanging over you. I can feel it. Tell me quickly, child, do you know anything about its nature?"

"I can't have intimate relations with anyone, male or female," I spit out before I lost the nerve. I was mortified and knew my face must be scarlet. Telling my long-lost grandmother about my sex life seemed wildly inappropriate.

Rosalie's eyes went wide, but I saw understanding pass through them. Her grip tightened. "Then they are linked."

"What are?"

Rosalie glanced up nervously as the branches shook in the wind. "I don't know why your mother put the veil on you, why she hid the fae realms. But I have a notion it has to do with our bloodline." She was unfocused again, and her grip was becoming softer. She leveled her gaze at me. "Perhaps you were right to worry about my murder. Brom was a good lad, but he's a changeling, and that sort of thing has a way of twisting one's mind. I made a mistake in thinking I could save him. I did not know he had already killed others before we met. And even then…it's not his fault, really, no more than you could blame a lion for eating a gazelle. It is the twisted nature of a half-blood to become a changeling. The change pulls at their mind, breaking it and filling it with chaotic intent. It is the will of chaos that alters them so, that corrupted poor Brom until the good in him was gone as if it had never existed. I could have saved him. I had found a cure to break the curse that pulled his mind apart and filled him with the power of chaos, but I was too late to retrieve it."

I opened my mouth to ask a question, but she gripped my hand and became slightly less blurry. The leaves on the willow were almost gone, and I could see my breath in the cold air. The poppies around us were wilting, spreading apart in the wind like torn paper. We did not have much longer.

"What I found, it is an ancient relic called the sentuin. Lanie, you must retrieve it. I was going to do so, but Brom fooled me. Chaos is an ever-cunning power. To think I fell for it when I imagined the boy was still redeemable. Even now I cling to the certainty that I could have saved him if I had only uncovered the relic's whereabouts even a week earlier. Brom has no idea what my plans were. If he has been following you, it is because he intends to kill you for your blood."

"Why would he want my blood?" I shouted over the wind.

"Our blood is powerful, Lanie. This is an age-old secret our family harbors. I'm afraid that fool of a son of mine shared the secret with your mother. For why else would she—?"

The wind gusted, and it was as if it blew away some of Rosalie. She was suddenly transparent and her words harder to understand. I leaned in close and wrapped my arms around her fading form. I could feel my tears freezing against my cheeks as the harsh wind stung my eyes. "Don't leave me."

"How I wish we had more time together," Rosalie bemoaned, her voice slightly stronger once more. "I discovered where the relic is hidden. You must go to Greystone Chapel. Behind the lion's paw, you will find the sun's broken day. Take the relic hidden there and keep it with you. With this, you can lift the curse on the changeling. Finish what I could not and in doing so keep yourself safe. Promise me you'll do this, Lanie."

She pushed me back to gaze intently in my eyes.

"I will, Grandma. I promise."

Rosalie sighed and loosened her grip. Her kindly smile was back, and her eyes twinkled. "You are so beautiful. I can see you are strong too, inside where it counts. I love you so much, Lanie."

"I love you too," I said, trying with all my might not to cry. Her form was barely there. A wispy ghost of the woman who had sat knitting under the willow. Her hands released me, and her body began to float backwards.

"Wait," I said, snatching her hand back. "The blood. Why is our blood so powerful?"

Rosalie's hands were insubstantial. It was like trying to grab hold of smoke. Her loving eyes were swept away by the roaring wind. Our moment was over as quickly as it had begun. Once more I would be left alone, an empty shell scared of the world around her. Rosalie's lips moved as she answered me, the words swallowed by the storm.

And then she was gone.

I was back in Free House with Drys sitting beside me, gripping my hands. Drys looked as if she hadn't slept for weeks. Her face was ashen with dark bags under her eyes. She let go of me and slid to lay down in the moss.

"She's gone," I sobbed, pressing my hands and the pendant to my face. I felt empty. The world spun around me with curses and unanswered questions. The pendant warmed against my eyelid and then hummed. I pulled it back, inspecting it curiously as it glowed for an instant.

And in that moment Rosalie's last words found me.

17

Human cities always held a particular stink about them. It was like burning rubber and sulfur. Lobo wondered how anyone could ignore such awful odors. One of the abilities werewolves held over other races was their heightened sense of smell, so it came through sharp as a razor to him. He had a hard time believing an ordinary human could not smell the acrid haze that hung over their city. Another stark contrast was the sky. To the average person it would seem the night sky was largely blotted out by clouds. Lobo knew differently. Those 'clouds' were actually smog lingering over the polluted wasteland where the humans chose to dwell.

It was no wonder winter had come early to their realm. His breath plumed in the chill night air. A heavy gust of wind beat withered leaves across the thin layer of snow on the sidewalk. The cold did not bother him too much. And at least this city had some trees still standing, lining the road in intervals in front of each house. It was depressing to see the impact their way of living was having on the land, though.

Forest Hill was one of the larger cemeteries in the area and very old. There would be graves marking lost soldiers from the humans' civil war behind those walls. These days humans did not bother to wall up their cemeteries. The whole business of death had turned into something more akin to a transactional burden than spiritual passage. That was one of the ways he could tell Forest Hill was very old. The wall around the cemetery was six feet in height, masoned expertly with large red stones. The humans would never spend that kind of time and care for their dead these days. Even their modern buildings were sticks and vinyl, easy to destroy.

A car whizzed past, bass music thumping. *At least they have good music,* he thought. He slowed his pace until the car was out of sight around the bend of the road, then scanned the nearby houses. Best to be sure no prying eyes were watching.

It was all clear.

Lobo leapt up to the top of the wall in one springing motion, glanced at the houses again, and then leapt into the cemetery. It was all rough shadows on this side of the wall. That was all the better, for it made it easier to hide should someone spot him, and Lobo had no problem seeing in the dark. This was another gift of being born a werewolf. His boots crunched in the strange mixture of snow and dried leaves that blanketed the ground.

Maybe I should take them off. No sense in giving away his position if the changeling was here. The cold would not bother his leather padded feet. *Yeah, but then the snow will get inside my boots.* He curled his lip at the thought. Lobo hated soggy shoes. He decided against it for the moment.

He lifted his nose to sniff the air. Another way he could tell the age of the cemetery was by the wet earth around him. There was a rot that he only found in cemeteries, the mixture of old bones and decaying wood. There was no one around. He was alone for the moment. He moved deeper into the cemetery, following the gravel path that wound upward around one of the small hills the cemetery was named after.

Alone. That was how he preferred it. Doule had wanted to tag along for the hunt, but Lobo told him the chief strictly forbade it. Normally that would not have been enough to deter Doule, so he shared the fae council's complaints. Even Lobo had been surprised the council would intervene in this. Doule had a healthy fear of the ruling families, and rightfully so. Over the years, how many times had they seen any sort of justice for a werewolf? Never. If the great houses decided werewolves were no longer needed, they would be put down, plain and simple. The fae elite did what they wanted when they wanted.

Werewolves were born and bred for one purpose, to maintain the laws of the fae provinces. Of course, those laws only pertained to the lower-class creatures unless there was some political gain to be had by making an example of a full-blood fae, and even such a rare event took a lot of political maneuvering. He did not envy those chosen for such a task, as it would inevitably lead to that werewolf's disappearance down the line. They were nothing to the winged *purebloods*.

He growled and let a puff of hot air out into the night. Snow was gently falling around him. There was still no scent of the changeling. He followed the path deeper, around a sloping curve, past the statue of an angel embracing a lamb.

That was what made Rosalie so special. The Warden cared for all the creatures in her province, no matter their stature. He had been nothing more than a teenager when Rosalie first came into his life. He had just been coming into his change, and soon he would take the rite of passage and be seen as a man and no longer a child. He was fourteen. The rest of the fae attended a school near his own where they learned subjects such as complex mathematical formulae, alchemy, or magical analysis. His school focused on tracking, hand-to-hand combat, survival instincts, and the like. He was walking back to the pack's den after school one afternoon when he spotted, of all things, a human.

Lobo had never seen a human in Willow's Edge before. They were quite rare. He guessed it must be some warlock or wizard come for supplies. The man was quite unassuming, and most fae might not have noticed him. But Lobo could smell the stink of human all over the stranger. The man cut across the street and down an alley. Before he knew what he was doing, Lobo quickly followed, using his training to stay just far enough behind to avoid the man's notice. The alleyway ended with a sharp turn to the left. He waited at the corner for a second, then peeked around the side. The man was entering a building. *That seems off. What would a human be doing sneaking into a fae building like that?*

His curiosity was thoroughly piqued. He quickly loped to the door and entered. No sooner had he stepped inside the building than someone grabbed him by the scruff of his collar.

"What are you doing following me, you little mutt?" It was the human. His beady eyes glared down past a thick gray beard at Lobo.

Someone in the room gasped.

It was a sweets shop. Lobo's heart plummeted into his bowels. This was exactly the type of place he had been told he was not allowed to go. Only fae needed things like iced treats and chocolate toads. It was a smaller confectionary than the one on Main Street but amply busy just the same. A score of fae dotted the shop, all their eyes turned toward the commotion. He spotted the girl who had gasped, her hands clutched on the arm of a taller fae who stood protectively in front of her, cold eyes glaring at him.

But why was she so scared? That's when Lobo realized, with embarrassment, that he had partially shifted. Thick matted brown fur covered his face and hands. In those days he had little control over when it would happen, like most adolescent boys.

The man shook him again, this time much more roughly. "I said, what are you doing following me, you little shit?"

"I—uh."

"Get out of here, you beast," someone yelled.

A bar of candy hit his chest.

Lobo looked up into the man's angry face. Why had he followed him in the first place? He was just interested in seeing a human.

The taller fae boy tucked his girlfriend farther behind him and spat at Lobo. A gob of phlegm hit him squarely in the eye. "Disgusting mongrel."

Lobo was shaking so hard he might have a seizure. He was not allowed to be here. They were going to kill him. He started to cry, and he heard a couple of the fae laugh at him.

"Hollinger, you get your hands off that boy this instant," a commanding voice cracked through the shop. The storefront went silent.

Lobo was shocked when the man suddenly released him. His face registered a shift from rage to fear in an instant. "But…the flea hotel was following me. A man has a right to walk about unbidden, doesn't he?"

An old woman came around the aisle, a basket of sweets tucked under one arm. Even though she was only half the man's height, she was regal and imperious, commanding the attention of everyone in the shop. "That gives you no right to grab a child and scare him half to death."

The man eyed her incredulously, then licked his dry lips and looked down at Lobo. He patted the boy's head. "Right then, no harm done, eh, *lad*?"

"Just get on with your business and leave the boy alone," Rosalie snapped.

The man flinched as if she had struck him. He quickly scurried away, toward the back of the shop where a tall slack-jawed ent was waiting for him. They muttered to each other and disappeared into the backroom.

A handkerchief presented itself in Lobo's vision. He realized he was also standing with his mouth agape. "Thank you, madame," he said through the choking sob that was still lodged in his throat. His fur was rapidly pulling back inside his body, making it a little easier to clean the spit out of his eye.

"The wolf has no business here," a voice said. It was the tall boy who had spit at him. He stood sulking with his arms crossed. This was a boy used to getting his way. Lobo guessed he must be an upper-elite fae, possibly from one of the great houses.

"Jada, maybe we should just—" the doe-eyed girl behind him whispered, reading the room better than her companion.

"Shut it, Endi," he commanded, refusing to take his eyes off Rosalie and the wolf boy.

Rosalie struck as fast as a cobra, seizing the boy's left ear between pinched fingers. She tugged him down to her height and thrust her face into his. "Who do you think you are speaking to right now, boy? This is how you were raised, to berate other fae? There are no laws permitting you to abuse another creature, just as there are no laws forbidding a wolf from buying sweets."

The girl behind him yelped. However, Lobo noticed very distinctly that the rest of the patrons and the owner had quite pointedly shifted their attention to other things.

"Everyone knows their kind shouldn't be in fae shops," the boy stubbornly said between gritted teeth.

Rosalie wrenched his ear harder. "Then I am sure Jelendeen will be quite proud to hear how her son treated another student today."

The boy's eyes shot wide. He might not have feared this old woman, but the sudden threat of his mother being involved was a different story. "You know my mother?"

"What kind of Warden does not know her people?" Rosalie asked.

"I—uh—I didn't know." The boy loosened up entirely. She released him.

"What, that you were talking down to the Warden of Willow's Edge, or that you were behaving like little prat? You should not be spitting on someone who will grow up to keep you safe in this province, you foolish child."

The boy stood there worried, shifting between Rosalie's withering glare and Lobo. Without warning he gave a tiny yelp and ran from the shop. A few of the patrons laughed at his retreat. The girl looked

Alacore's Apothecary

frightened, but she gave Rosalie a quick bow before following her boyfriend out of the shop.

It all happened so fast. Lobo stood dumbfounded.

"Are you okay, lad?"

He nodded sheepishly at this grand woman who had just saved him. "I'm sorry to cause so much trouble, madame. I wouldn't have come into a fae shop had I known. The human was just so…"

"Interesting?" Rosalie smiled with a twinkle in her eyes.

He nodded.

"Yes, they really are," she said. "Quite dangerous too."

He did not know what to say to that. He bowed and handed her back her handkerchief, embarrassed that he had sullied such fine cloth. "I better take my leave now."

Rosalie's hand was on his shoulder in a heartbeat, but it was gentle and warm. "Listen to me, lad. There is nowhere in Willow's Edge where you don't belong just as much as any other creature. This is the whole point of the provinces, a crossover between all cultures. Don't ever let anyone tell you any different. That kind of talk is not about you, anyhow. It's a reflection of their inner cowardice and ignorance."

Lobo was stunned. He knew full well that werewolves were at the bottom of the food chain in the fae class system, nearly as low as trolls or goblins. But this amazing woman was telling him that was not the case. He felt uplifted for the first time in his life. Emotions swelled inside him, and it was wonderful and terrifying at the same time. Behind her, the shop owner nodded his head in agreement.

Rosalie wiped a tear from his eyes with a maternal energy that soothed his nerves. "Now, why don't you pick out a treat while you're here? C'mon, it'll be on me."

That was how he had met Rosalie Alacore. She was an amazing woman. He'd stayed close to her all his life; through military academy, when he first joined the constabulary, and even as he became a detective. She had so much wisdom to share, and he loved her as if she were his own blood.

And now she was gone.

There was a void in his heart that no other pack member could understand. Rosalie had taught him that he was not a lesser creature. She had shown him the true value of an education, which had nothing to do with degrees. It was the value of life and the moments we all have to experience it; it was the beauty of the world and all its creatures, no single one of them greater than the other. That was a very dangerous thing to know in his world. As he grew older, he realized Rosalie's behavior was not isolated. There were a good many fae who felt similar, but she'd left her mark on him in more ways than he could count. He would do anything to avenge her death.

A gust of wind blew against his face. He realized he had tears running down his cheeks as they froze in the chill wind. The scent of oiled feathers slapped his senses.

It was the changeling.

This was the same peculiar odor he'd smelled in Rosalie's basement. He had not thought it wise at the time to share that with Lanie. She was already spooked enough. She was too new to their world. *Evidence that confirmed the killer had recently been in her basement would've more than she could handle,* he reasoned. Then again, maybe he was underestimating Lanie's courage. *She did run like a bat out of hell after Jalk at Free House. She's not exactly a wilting flower.*

The night was quiet other than the faint sounds of cars periodically driving by on the road skirting the cemetery. Even with snow falling it was odd not to see any signs of wildlife. Especially as the snow was dropping much earlier in the season. Not even rabbit tracks marred the surface of the snow. The wind had blown in from the northeast, so he followed it, sniffing the whole way. A row of mausoleums edged a frozen pond, skirted by a copse of tall birch. The trees were bare huddled shapes in the darkness, their branches clattering in the wind.

He crouched still, listening to the night.

Nothing stirred.

Lobo grunted and kept on the move, following the odor to its source. *No, Lanie might be scared, but she's no coward. There's a big difference.* After what had happened to her apartment in the city, most fae would have tucked tail and run. Instead, she had made the decision to return and confront the evil.

Lanie was very much like her grandmother in that respect. It was for that reason he needed to protect her from herself. She was bound to make bad choices as she leaned further into their world. He cursed himself for thinking about her again. He needed to be focused purely in this moment.

The changeling was a dangerous entity, a formidable foe. No sense in making it easier for him by daydreaming about a girl. Even if that girl did smell as good as Lanie.

He grinned. It was an odd aroma that she carried around her, like jasmine and ivory mixed with some sort of unfamiliar floral scent. At first he had thought it must be some human perfume he had never smelled. The longer he spent around her, the more he realized it was just a peculiar odor she carried. For Lobo, it was intoxicating. He pictured her laughter as she danced with him at Free House. It was a warm memory.

A twig snapped.

Lobo froze in place and snapped his head around toward the sound. The brush shuddered just past a nearby mausoleum. He extended talons from his fingertips. Was he really fool enough to daydream right into a trap?

A doe burst from the brush, prancing right across his path. Another, smaller deer shot out after it. His stomach rumbled at the sight of them. *Ugh, I should have eaten before coming out to the human lands.* His appetite was always worse when away from the province. One of the deer spotted him and stopped in her tracks. His mouth filled with saliva. It would be so easy to chase her down and sink his teeth into her throat. Hot blood and tender meat. *I haven't had a good hunt in a while.*

He snapped his fingers. "Scram, you idiot." There was no time for such indulgence.

The deer scampered away after its companion. When they rounded the pond, they veered off course. Their destination was clearly the line of trees that marked the end of the mausoleums, where the path ended. Instead of taking a straight line to them, they halted, then sprang between the nearest stone structure and zipped down the hill toward the entrance to the cemetery.

What's got them so spooked? Lobo narrowed his eyes, focusing on the mausoleums. He slipped out of his boots, tucked his socks inside each, and left them beside a weathered gravestone. He moved like a phantom through the snow, his padded feet scarcely leaving a print as he soundlessly darted for the copse. His stomach still growled. The odor of oiled feathers was stronger near the mausoleums. He carefully studied their stone roofs and the narrow alleys between them for signs of lurkers.

The changeling's odor was like a line of smog he could almost see, like looking at the air above a steaming kettle. It centered around the mausoleum at the end of the path, on the farthest side of the horseshoe pond. A carved stone above the entrance marked it as Family Smith's. Nothing special about that name. The mausoleum was like most others along the row, probably crafted by the same mason. It had a vaulted stone roof attached to a cubic structure, with two decorative columns on either side of a brass entrance. The metalwork of the door had a verdigris patina to it, the shiny brass long faded to a whitewashed green. The glass between the metalwork was intact. He leaned in closer, then recoiled. The changeling's odor was as strong as a slap in the face.

The door had an old lock built into it. *This place must be as old as the early 1800s. There's no way I can pry open an ancient lock like that.* He tried anyway. The door lever was coarse to the touch, like scraping a chalkboard. It turned with a slight squeak, and then the door popped outward. He paused for a moment, listening intently to the air. There was only wind and the dull pitter patter of snow drizzling against the stonework.

If he's in there, he hasn't heard me yet.

Lobo slipped inside, slick as a fox, and closed the door gently behind him. If the changeling came around while he was inside, he did not want to spook him with an open door. The air inside the tomb was dank, with stacked drawers on either side of the main area. One of the drawers stood ajar, its massive stone panel hanging straight down to the floor. The bones were so long decayed that they smelled more like old books than rotting flesh. Tombs like this were built for wealthy merchants, a grand gesture to mark their end in hope that someone would remember them. No doubt the same family had given a large sum of money to the church, hoping to secure their path into heaven. Lobo shook his head at the foolish notions of humans.

The stone floor had no markings of anyone recently passing through. A layer of dust coated the stonework, and only his bare feet disturbed it. He growled. This was the wrong place. No one had stepped inside this tomb in years.

Then why do I smell that bastard here?

He followed his nose to the corner of the vault, just beneath a small stained-glass window depicting praying hands. The shadows of the corner turned out to be more than that. There was a gaping hole in the stonework floor, large enough for a man. He leapt down into it.

It was a short drop, just enough to fit inside crouching. His eyes adjusted to the complete absence of light. *Nothing natural-looking about this hole,* he thought. *But if someone dug it, where did all the dirt go?* He turned in a semi-circle before he saw the tunnel. It was slightly shorter than the depth of the hole. The changeling's odor permeated the air inside it. He had to move on hands and feet down the burrow.

Lobo had never been too fond of tight spaces. He swore he could feel the hundreds of pounds of soil pressing down over him. If the tunnel caved in, he would be stuck here for good. Not even Doule knew where he had run off to. He would be trapped here to suffocate or starve to death, whichever came first. *But Lanie knows where I went.* That reassured him. Lanie was stubborn. She would not let the precinct turn their back on him. He was certain of that.

He crawled through the corridor for some time, so far that when he glanced back, he could scarcely see where he had jumped inside. The one thing that kept him moving was that the scent was getting stronger. It was mixed with something else now too, something unnatural.

Finally, he came to a dead end. It was mystifying. The last thing he expected to find in the ground underneath a cemetery was a cobbled stone wall. He pressed against the wall, but it was solid. Sweat beaded on his brow, despite it being ice cold underneath the earth. He had a dizzying sensation that the area was thinner somehow. That defied logic as well. He needed to get out of this hole.

Lobo frowned and looked up. Sure enough, the tunnel ascended parallel to the stone wall. Something dimly lit the area above. He leapt upward and kicked his padded feet onto the wall. Bracing his back against the dirt tunnel, he shimmied up the chute until the stone wall gave way to an opening.

Lobo slowed his progress, studying that new hole and listening intently. Just as before, nothing stirred. *Something's crackling up there, though. A fire, perhaps? And the tunnel's definitely brighter.* He shimmied up to the hole and then grabbed hold of the edge. He flipped his body so he hung there in the air. With a little effort, he pulled himself up enough to scramble out of the hole and drop onto the ground of a room.

No, not a room, he thought morosely. This was more of a den, a ramshackle hovel dug into the ground. The area was wide. It smelled horrible, so much that he had to cover his mouth and nose with his hand. The bones of animals and humans alike were scattered all around him. Straw, string, clothing, shoes—they were all bound together in a large funnel to one side of the space. Lobo had seen funnels like that before, but they were used by spiders. Candles lit the area, with deep rivulets of wax dripping along the walls, around the den, and on the floor. A faint breeze flickered the candlelight.

We're closer to the surface.

A fire pit was dug in the center of the den. A wet headless corpse lay beside it, chest down. It was not Rosalie. *How many people has he killed?* The changeling had to be stopped. There were the remains of at least a dozen people in the den, not all of them human. *He's hunting fae. But why? For the sick pleasure of it?*

His eyes caught the glint of light on glass. The den was much taller than the tunnel. He stood upright with a stiffness spreading through his joints. The top of his head brushed against exposed roots hanging from the dirt ceiling. He skirted a mound of soil and found wooden shelves. *There must be some other way into this den. There's no way this guy dragged these shelves down that long tunnel and up the narrow dirt chimney.* Glass jars rested on the shelves. He recoiled from their contents.

What's he been doing, dissecting people?

His stomach lurched. That was a strange sensation. Lobo, like most adult werewolves, had a stomach of steel. It should take a lot more than some eyeballs in a jar to make him feel so queasy. He shook his head and felt the room spin on its edge.

What's going on? Why do I feel so sick?

A pungent odor beneath the stench of remains and changeling stung his nostrils. He waved his arm as if to ward off the stench and hit something on the dirt ceiling. At first he thought it was a root. Then it came flopping down on his shoulder. Lobo pulled it off him and stared dumbly at the item in his hand, trying to place it.

Why can't I think straight? I know what this is. It's...it's... His mind trailed off. What was the word for it? He had seen images of it so many times; had even smelled some in military school. It was used to make shifters like him very sick. But that would only be if he was foolish enough to ingest some. A small handful like this did not pose any real threat. His head felt so muddled though, like someone had stuffed cotton in between his thoughts. Then it hit him.

This is wolfsbane!

He snapped his head upward with a sudden realization. That was not exposed roots above him. The ceiling was lined with row upon row of hanging wolfsbane. That much of the toxic stuff in such a small area, with so little room to ventilate, could be very dangerous.

He turned just as the changeling sprang out of its funnel, just like a spider ready to strike, half-man, a swarm of oily feathers like a nightmare. It was too late. He had walked right into the trap. Lobo lunged sideways to avoid the blow. It glanced off his ear. He growled triumphantly a second before the other side of his skull cracked into something solid.

The dirt floor against his cheek was the last thing he felt before the world swallowed him.

18

My grandmother's last words echoed across the void, buoyed on the mystical currents flowing through the pendant that had tethered us together. "Protect the blood of the unicorn."

She might as well have been speaking Latin for all that meant to me. Drys, however, was floored by the revelation, for she heard Rosalie's words as well. "I always suspected." She shook her head in wonder. "But to hear it uttered aloud is astounding."

"I don't understand," I said. "Where is this unicorn supposed to be?"

Drys stared at me pointedly.

I scoffed. "You can't mean me. Do I look like a horse to you? That's silly."

"Yes, as *silly* as my tree or the little imp in your store," Drys murmured. She was too tired to argue the point with me, already curling in a fetal position around the roots of her tree. To my amazement, some of the roots slithered around her protectively. Her face was weathered, drained of all color. Meanwhile, her willow was as radiant as ever, and a halo of light settled around her sleeping form. The tree was healing her. I don't know how I understood this, but in my gut, I knew it was so.

I grabbed Drys's throw blanket off the bar table and draped it over her.

"I will never forget what you did for me today," I whispered. It was selfless. That one glimpse of my grandmother was all I was ever to have. There are times in life where you just know what is happening will stay with you forever, leaving an indelible mark upon your being. Rosalie had thrown the veil wide, allowing me to see my birthright, the fae folk and magic that surrounded my mundane world. Now she had also given me a path toward understanding how to fix my curse. What I'd just experienced was equally confusing and wonderful.

Many thoughts swirled around my mind. Why would my mother try to keep my heritage from me? She had never been the most loving or open person, but she hardly acted as if she hated me. Who could do such a thing to their own daughter? Was Rosalie right, did my father's bloodline have something to do with it? I did not know how to come to grips with any these mysteries and soon fell asleep against the willow.

It was very late in the evening, well past midnight, when I woke. Drys was still resting beneath the tree. The wrinkles and strain were gone from her face, erased like a bad dream. I placed a hand on her tree, feeling the heartbeat of the willow thumping beneath my fingertips. This really was a miraculous place, and I wanted to learn so much more about it.

I stayed at Free House through the night, until Drys finally awoke. She seemed mildly surprised to find me still there.

"I didn't want to leave until I knew you were alright," I said.

That pleased her. The roots receded back into the mossy soil, and Drys stood, flattening out the wrinkles in her robes. The old woman was gone. She was a strong, powerful Viking warrior once more.

"Not quite," she said, as if reading my mind. "I'm rather weak right now, to tell the truth, but it's nothing I can't recover from in the next week or so." She placed a hand on my shoulder and met my gaze evenly. "Thank you for that gift, my dear girl. It was lovely to see Rosalie one last time. My boughs are filled with light and laughter at the knowledge that you were able to meet her, even if it was brief."

"It was amazing," I said, trying not to tear up. There was such a power to Drys. You could feel it in the air around her, like static electricity waiting to snap. Her emotions were sincere to the point of being palpable. I was starting to understand what Tae meant when she said Drys was the heart of Willow's Edge.

"Well, be a dear and find somewhere comfortable to lounge. It is time to get Free House ready for tomorrow's business." She disappeared in the back for a bit, then came out with a tray of glass mugs.

I walked over and leaned on the bar top while she hung the mugs on hooks above the ice trough. "What did my grandmother mean by that unicorn's blood nonsense?"

Drys tilted her head as if it were her first time hearing those words. Astonishment riddled her face as the memory came back to her. "Oh my, I had completely forgotten." She suddenly burst into a smile of utter happiness. "The blood of a unicorn. How marvelous it is."

"Yes, but what does that mean?"

"It means you are descended from unicorns, Lanie. Which is both a wonderful and dangerous legacy."

I felt my forehead wrinkle.

"Unicorns have not been seen in the lands of fae for centuries now. Your kind are believed to be extinct. And that is how it must stay. You must never tell another living soul this secret. It is far too dangerous."

I snorted. The whole thing was so ridiculous.

Drys hung the last mug and leaned over the bar. She tapped my nose as if I were a baby she was trying to get to focus. "I know what you are thinking. 'Silly old lady Drys, I don't have a horn on my forehead, and I don't go around prancing on four feet.' Yet you know very little of your heritage, Lanie Alacore. For example, what if I told you that once upon a time dragons and unicorns were as real as the wood you're leaning on? They were some of the great and powerful forces of our world, the embodiment of death and life, bound together in the everlasting cycle of the cosmos. But there was a terrible war between the fae and the giantkin that sought to conquer our realm. As the riftwars grew dire, the people looked to bolster their power and so began to hunt down and slay the dragons. With the power they gained from dragon blood, they overcame the invaders. Alas, after the war was over, those who had sought the dragon's power became bent and twisted beings. They could not stop their destruction, and so there were fae who took it in their minds to turn their designs toward the unicorns. For surely with the blood of unicorns, they could counteract the blood of dragons."

"Except the unicorns were gone. No one knew what happened to them. They just disappeared. Some conjectured that the unicorns were bonded to the dragons and could not survive without them. Others say they left our realm for lands of peace in other worlds. Either way, the gravity of what had been done hit our people. The cost of that power was too great. We had wiped out the bloodlines of dragon and unicorn. It is said that Queen Titania wept, and all those across the realm felt her sorrow and lamented. For they realized what a horrible mistake they had made, breaking the bonds of that eternal cycle. Never again would the fearsome dragons fly overhead with roars that could shake valleys. Never again would anyone glimpse the majestic unicorn and know what purity felt like. It was a stain on the fae, one that can never be erased. If anyone ever found out you hold the blood of unicorns…it is far too great a risk. There are too many who would not be able to contain their greed. They would desire that blood, covet that power. It is no surprise Rosalie kept her secret so closely guarded all these years."

"I wonder how Brom, the changeling, discovered her secret?"

"How this changeling found out that Rosalie had the blood does not matter. The important thing is that he must not be allowed to share that secret. He must be stopped. Rosalie's blood would have bestowed him a great power." She shuddered. "A cursed man like that is dangerous enough. Let us hope he does not figure out how to unlock the blood's true potential before he can be stopped. Even worse is if one of the great houses hears about your existence. If the blood of a unicorn were to fall into the hands of one of the ruling families, life as we know it could forever be altered."

"But it's just my blood."

"There is no power in either world as strong as blood magic. Naturally that depends a great deal on the blood being used, but all the same."

"Well, why don't I have four legs, then?" I scoffed. The whole tale seemed ridiculous and overly superstitious.

Drys shook her head, clearly irritated with me. "Does your friend Lobo always walk around looking like a wolf? Do I amble about as a willow tree, trying to serve beverages?"

"No, but—"

"Lanie," Drys said firmly, "do you trust me?"

It was a serious question. At my core, from the moment I shared the experience under the willow with Drys, I knew that I fundamentally trusted her. "I do."

"Then you must hear me when I say absolutely, under no circumstances, should you tell anyone about this. No one can know you have the blood of the unicorn. Ever."

I gulped. She was serious as cancer. As ludicrous as it all sounded, this was real. I believed Drys with all of my heart, no matter how much it scared me to accept it. "I understand."

She sighed in clear relief. "Excellent. Now, if you'll excuse me for a moment, I have some work to do. Make yourself comfy while you wait for Detective Lobo to return."

Lobo. I checked the clock behind the bar. It was already six-thirty in the morning. The entire night had gone by with no sign of him. I had a nauseated feeling in the pit of my stomach. Lobo went in search of the changeling, but he did not know the killer had some of my grandmother's blood or even the importance of that. If it was as potent as Drys believed, then he would be at a serious disadvantage. I needed to warn him.

No, wait. How could I? I had no car and no way to get to the cemetery he had gone to. Lobo didn't use a cell phone did he? What could I possibly do to help him? Guilt stalked me like a specter of death. It was an ill feeling of helplessness. *He's only out there searching for the killer because of me. I have to help him. I can't just sit here cozy and warm while he risks his life to keep me safe. Think, Lanie.*

The relic! I thought, remembering my grandmother's words. She wanted me to retrieve a relic she'd discovered was hidden at some church in town. Whatever it was, she was sure it would help stop the changeling.

The front doors to Free House opened. I felt lighter, for an instant, expecting Lobo to come walking through the door. Instead, it was a dwarven barmaid. She was the same one who had served me the prickly pink a few nights before. She was yawning as she stepped inside, then stopped with wide eyes when she spotted me.

"What are you doing in here?" It was more of an accusation than a question.

"Hi, Bob." I rushed for the door. "Please tell Drys I said thank you for everything and that Lobo came to pick me up."

The dwarf frowned and glanced around the bar. It was obvious she was looking for Lobo, but I had no time to chat. Drys needed to think I was alright, otherwise she would never let me leave. I was past the dwarf and out the door in a heartbeat.

I needed to find that relic.

It was a short walk to the antique shop. Those birds foolish enough to linger as early winter set in were chirping as the sun rose. I felt about as insecure as I could, even in broad daylight, and kept checking over my shoulder. I had to remind myself that Lobo's absence could mean many things. He was not exactly the most reliable guy when it came to commitments, after all. For all I knew, he was back at his police station, chumming it up with that sly partner of his.

A few minutes later I learned that was not the case. Doule was waiting for me in front of the store, wearing that lopsided grin of his.

"What are you doing here?" I tentatively asked as I crossed the street.

"Looking for my partner," Doule said.

"He went after the changeling yesterday afternoon. I haven't seen him since." I tried to search Doule's eyes for some sort of reaction. "Should we be worried?"

Doule frowned in contemplation, and then his attention was taken up by a car pulling to the curb behind me. It was the local cab. Deedee stepped out, beaming in the morning light. She was wearing a floppy sun hat that she held on her head as she stepped up to the curb.

"Oh wow, look at the welcoming committee I get." She winked at Doule. His grin grew wider as he took her in. I almost groaned. Lobo was out there, likely in trouble, and these two were flirting.

"Why are you here, Deedee?"

I didn't mean it to come out as abruptly as it did. Deedee shot me a wounded look that would have normally made me wince at my faux pas. "Didn't you get my message? I came in on the early train. I figured we could take a stroll down Main Street, maybe check out that little bistro before we go over the realtor's info."

This time I did groan. I had one hundred percent forgotten Deedee was supposed to come back to help me with the sale of Grandma's property. With everything going on, selling the store had been filed into my least-kept worries folder. I rubbed my eyes, realizing how tired I suddenly felt. The cab driver plopped Deedee's suitcases on the curb and waved goodbye.

"Did you forget I was coming?" Deedee asked, looking like a wounded deer.

"Sorry, I've been really preoccupied. Things have been hectic here," I said. "Honestly, I wouldn't have been able to contact you anyhow. I've gotten zero cellphone reception."

Deedee arched her brow and smirked, looking pointedly at Doule. "I don't mind you being *preoccupied*."

"Just come inside, both of you," I grumbled. I unlocked the storefront and held the door for them, then entered last.

Deedee's brow was furrowed as she took in the store. I had gotten little done in the time she was gone. She looked cross with me, but I was certain it had more to do with forgetting about her arrival than my ineptitude with cataloging the store. I did not care either way. All I had time to think about at that moment was Lobo. He was in danger, and I needed to get that relic to stop the changeling.

"Why aren't you with Lobo right now?" I asked Doule.

"That detective from the day we got here?" Deedee asked.

I ignored her and waited for Doule to speak.

He shrugged noncommittally. "He told me not to intervene. Geez, don't look so mad. There's a bunch of politics going on right now back at the station. It's tough to explain. Anyhow, he's a sturdy motherfucker."

"And yet you're here looking for him, worried," I said, cutting through Doule's bullshit. He was just as concerned about Lobo as I was.

"Is someone going to tell me what's going on?" Deedee asked brightly.

The office door opened, and a bedraggled Sacha came out. He climbed onto his stool and rubbed his eyes, taking in our little gathering. "Nice, the hot one's back." He waggled his eyebrows at Deedee.

"I spoke with Rosalie," I said.

All eyes turned to me as the air was let out of the room. "She's alive after all?" Deedee asked.

"No. My grandmother is very much deceased. It's wicked complicated to explain, but I did speak with her before she moved on. There's a relic called the sentuin. She was hot on its trail before Brom got her."

"Brom?" Doule asked.

"The changeling, that's his real name. She thought she could heal him, but his change happened faster than she anticipated, and he turned on her before she could finish the job. Anyhow, I need to retrieve this relic so we can stop Brom from hurting anyone else. She told me I could find it at the Greystone Chapel."

Doule's eyes lit up. "Alright, let's go get it right now."

I thought the werewolf would give me a hard time. It was ingrained in me that people never listened to what I wanted, so I guess I always expect a kickback when I speak. Sometimes I don't speak at all because I already know that's what will happen. Having Doule join me would be a huge relief. "Oh good, I don't know where the chapel is, and it would be good to have someone strong by my side."

"I'm coming too," Deedee said excitedly.

Shit. Look at her with her silly sun hat when winter is setting in. She's dressed for a weekend trip. Deedee has no idea what kind of danger she's just dipped her toes in. I knew there was no way I could allow her to come. "Absolutely not," I said resolutely. "It's far too dangerous out there for you. In fact, I don't even think you're safe here."

Deedee retaliated with hands on her hips and a condescending grin. "My little Lanie. Are you sure you're not overreacting a little? It wouldn't be the first time."

I was *not* sure. And she was right, there were plenty of times I had been wrong and thoroughly earned the title of a worrywart. Knowing this did not stop me from seething with annoyance and her unintended belittlement. Not because she was right but because I realized I would neither be able to bring her along nor leave her alone at the shop. Not only was she in danger if the changeling came for me, but her flippant dismissal of the situation put her at even greater risk.

"You can't come. I don't have time to explain it all, Dee. I wish I did." Before she overcame her shock and could respond, I turned to Doule. "And you can't come either. I need you to stay here and keep Deedee safe in case that cretin come around."

Doule did not like that idea at all. "You wouldn't last five seconds if you ran into him out there."

I threw my arms in the air in exasperation. "What do you want me to do? I can't leave Deedee alone, there's no way. And I can't just sit here with a thumb up my ass while Lobo is out there in trouble. Now tell me where this chapel is so I can get moving."

"I'll go with you."

Neither of us contained our surprise to hear Sacha utter those words. He hopped over the counter and fluttered over to me on his leathery wings. I could see in his eyes that he was serious. I had seen Sacha get mildly annoyed, with the fangs and spitting fire. He would make a great companion to keep me safe. I could feel Deedee stewing behind me and wanted to get out of there as quickly as possible.

"Fantastic. That settles it. Sacha will be my bodyguard, unless you think an interdimensional daemon isn't up to the task."

Doule was already nodding. "Just…if there's trouble, get out of there. Don't try to go toe-to-toe with a changeling."

I snorted. Fighting was the last thing I would dream of doing. I tossed my apartment keys to Doule. "Keep Deedee safe. If anything happens to her, I will rip your hands off and feed them to you."

"Lanie, are you really going to leave?" Deedee whined. "I just got here."

"I'm sorry, Dee," I said. "I don't have time to walk you through this."

I headed out of the store as fast I could, my adrenaline pumping. Sacha was right beside me, fluttering his little bat wings to keep up. His leathery skin glistened in the dawn light. "You really know where this church is?"

Sacha looked strange without his customary cigar dangling from the corner of his mouth. There was a seriousness to him that I had not seen before. "I've been around town plenty with Rosalie."

"I thought you couldn't leave the shop?"

"I'm not too partial to sunlight. Us daemons tend to be weaker in the daytime. Give me a nice full blue moon like we're having tonight anytime. That makes for a walloping punch of power. Anyhow, I can go anywhere my master allows."

I stopped in my tracks. What he had just said was important. Sacha had decided I was his new master. I did not want to hold that kind of sway over any living creature, no matter how much mystical mumbo-jumbo tradition backed the dynamic. "I'm not your master."

Sacha hovered beside me. "Rosalie is gone from the land of the living. You are her sole heir, inheriting all her contracts, possessions, and clauses. Now I belong to you."

"And if I broke that agreement? If I set you free?"

A flash of incredulous disbelief passed over him. "You mean release me from service?"

I raised an eyebrow. It was the best serious face I could make.

Sacha shrugged. "I'd head straight back to the fiery pits and say good riddance to this world."

It was not what I expected him to say. Also, hell was a real place? That opened up so many more questions for me, but there was no time for them.

I needed to get the relic. I could feel time running out as surely as I could feel the air getting colder around us. There was a strange gnawing in the pit of my stomach, and intuitively I knew the source. This was *my* magic. It was telling me something horrible was going to happen if we did not find that relic soon.

If I released Sacha from his bondage to me, I would be defenseless out there in the open. I suddenly felt how absolutely exposed and helpless I was. But keeping him was wrong on so many levels. I would never be able to live with myself, chaining another being to my service. It was a lot to weigh. I made up my mind.

"Show me where the church is."

Sacha grinned. "As you wish, *Master*."

19

Deedee was stunned. In all the years she had known Lanie, she had never witnessed her behave with such callous disregard. She stood with her mouth agape, watching her best friend walk past the storefront windows with the tiny man Sacha in tow. *How can she treat me like this when I came all the way out here just to help her? Like I'm some second-class citizen.* Even worse, Deedee was left in the store with a man she'd never met before. A charming one, but a stranger nonetheless. *Kinda sucks being left alone with some guy you never met, huh?* she thought, realizing the irony of it. *Maybe this is payback for all those blind dates I sprang on her.*

"I don't like this store," Doule said. "We're too exposed. Let's head up to Lanie's apartment. At least that way you can relax a little."

"I guess I have nothing better to do," Deedee muttered.

Doule grabbed her suitcases and headed outside. At least he was a gentleman. He locked up the storefront, then motioned for her to follow him to the apartments. The stairs were narrow and creaked with age. A faded green rug had once adorned each step, but years of traffic had left the fabric worn to the point of nonexistence in the center. Kind of like Deedee's life these days. *Old and worn out.*

Even with the suitcases, Doule zipped up the steps. *Must have to stay in really good shape to be a cop,* Deedee thought, admiring the way his slacks fit snugly around his bum.

Doule paused on the landing at the top of the steps. He looked at Lanie's door then at the other apartment. "You know what, I have a different idea," he said, knocking on the second door.

She caught up to him as he knocked a second time. "You know who lives here?"

Doule muttered something under his breath when there was still no reply. He handed Deedee one of the suitcases and fished around in his pants pocket. "Yeah, she's a friend of mine." He pulled out some jingling keys on a chain and flipped one into the lock.

Deedee raised an eyebrow as he opened the door and held it aside for her. "Must be one hell of a friend," she teased as she slid past him.

The apartment was dark, but she could tell they were in a living room. A strong perfume lingered in the air, mingled with a pungent incense. It was pleasing to her senses, and she felt the tension unwind from her shoulders. Doule locked the door and called for his *friend* as he probed deeper into the apartment. "Tae? Anyone home?"

Deedee plopped down on a couch that swallowed her with cushions. It was love at first touch. She could picture herself curling up in her pajamas among those cushions, with a flannel blanket, an earl grey, and a good movie. "That's odd," she said, "there's no television."

"Guess she's out," Doule replied as he came back down the small hallway. He looked troubled. "What was that you said?"

"The television?"

"Oh, most of us folk around Willow's Edge don't really go for that sort of thing."

"You mean fairy folk?" Deedee said, just to see his expression.

He grinned at her. "Ah, I wasn't sure if you knew about us or not."

"Lanie tells me everything," Deedee said. As the words left her lips, they felt sour. It would be obvious to this Doule character that this was not entirely true. Not after the way Lanie had behaved downstairs. The whole thing was so out of character. She wanted to be mad, but she could not shake her worry that Lanie was in trouble.

Doule went to the window to peek through the blinds. He muttered something under his breath again. She could tell he was not going to be any fun. "You're obviously worked up about your friend. Can't you just call his cell?"

His shoulders slumped. "We don't really use those much either."

"Are you allergic to technology?" Deedee teased.

"It's not that. In fact, in some ways you'll find a few of our cities are more technologically advanced than their human counterparts. But your type of tech—especially cell phones—the magic in fae lands tends to mess with it."

Deedee frowned and pulled out her phone. The top corner showed a red X over the signal strength. *So Lanie wasn't just making excuses.* She felt guilty for doubting her. "Do you know your *friend's* Wi-Fi password?"

Doule snickered and opened his mouth to answer.

"Let me guess, you don't use the internet either." She groaned. What kind of a weird community was this, where the people pretend to be fairies and live like the Amish? This was going to be a miserable morning. "How long do you think Lanie's going to be?"

Doule shrugged. "The Greystone's pretty close by."

The room fell quiet. Doule was deep in thought and began pacing back and forth between the living room and open kitchen area. She wanted to turn on a lamp, but he said it would be better not to draw attention to someone being home. Deedee sat there with nothing to do but stew, flipping on and off the screen of her useless phone. The only sound was a clock ticking somewhere in the apartment. Doule's tension was getting to her.

He finally broke the silence. "I should be out there looking for Lobo."

Deedee shrugged. "Then why aren't you?"

He nodded absently and resumed his pacing. She found it deeply irritating.

"You're kinda sketching me out with all your tension. Why don't you just go find your buddy and make sure he's alright? Like you said, Lanie's close by. She'll be back soon, right?"

His eyes brightened, but then he met her gaze and frowned. "She asked me to keep you safe."

Deedee scoffed at that. "I have been keeping that girl safe since the day I met her. I doubt some psycho is going to attack me in broad daylight. Besides"—she reached into her handbag and pulled out her 9mm pistol—"I'm not some helpless little girl." She waggled the pistol toward the ceiling to make her point.

"Well, then," Doule grinned. "You don't mess around, huh?"

"Why don't you hurry and get your friend? I bet it's a misunderstanding and he's fine. Then get your sorry ass back here so we can go get a drink, eh?" It was not the best pickup line, but in her experience anything would do. Guys weren't exactly complex creatures. Deedee could bat her eyes and say pretty much anything to drop their pants. Fae or whatever they wanted to call themselves, Doule was no different.

He shook his head ruefully. "Girl, you're definitely trouble. Listen, do not leave this apartment. And if you hear anyone go into Lanie's apartment next door, then find somewhere to hide, quick. Don't answer this door and don't make any noise. If Tae comes home, just tell her you're a friend of mine and explain what is going on."

"Your girlfriend won't mind you dropping some random chick off in her home?"

"She's not my girlfriend," Doule corrected. "She'll take care of you, though. Tae's good people."

Deedee waved a hand in the air. "Just hurry and get it done."

Doule headed out straightaway. "Lock the door behind me," he said before slipping out to the stairwell. Deedee got up and headed to the window. She parted the blinds slightly. It was bright outside, a stark contrast to the dimly lit apartment. Doule came out and hopped into his car. She watched him slide it away from the curb and drive down the road, then sighed.

The apartment was so quiet. The clock ticked away. What the hell had Lanie gotten herself into? She could still hear the acid in Lanie's voice before she left. They were going to have to talk about that. Deedee did not deserve that kind of abuse, and it was no way to speak to your best friend.

I never should have left her here all alone with these weird people, she thought. Maybe she deserved a little of this treatment, to be honest. At the end of the day, she wasn't going to stay mad at Lanie for one transgression after years of friendship. There was no one in the world she cared for more. Lanie was like family to her, her only family, even if she was prone to overreacting at times. Deedee was just happy she was okay.

A woman pushed a stroller past the building. She could hear her whistling a nursery tune amid the infant's giggles. Why was she in this creepy dark apartment when she could be out there in the sun? *This is all nonsense. I've seen Lanie get worked up over nothing so many times I've lost count.* Yeah, but those were over things like being late for an appointment or worrying about having to talk to a guy. Today's Lanie felt different. She really believed there was someone out there waiting for her.

Deedee shivered. What was she doing here in some stranger's apartment? *I'm going outside to wait for them.*

A floorboard creaked behind her. She spun around. No one was there. The door to the apartment was open. *Great, now I have to explain to this woman why I'm here.*

"Hello," she called, closing the blinds and dashing for the living room. "I'm Doule's friend. He said I could—"

The words died in her throat.

A man stood by the couch. The light of the stairwell should have illuminated him. Instead his features were bathed in shadows darker than the room around them. "I was starting to think the wolf would never leave," he said.

Her purse sat on the end of the sofa several feet away, the butt of her pistol sticking out of it.

The changeling's smile cut through the darkness.

20

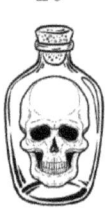

Greystone was an unusual sight. Then again, what wasn't these days? I had seen only a small section of Willow's Edge at this point. There was Free House, which was filled with light and energy, then the warehouse district on the outskirts of the province, which was eerily devoid of color and life. Greystone Chapel was neither of these things.

Apparently Willow's Edge is not always in the same spot. Don't ask me how that works. All I know is every so often, when the need strikes, the entire province moves, like a bubble sliding across water to escape encroaching pinpricks. When the province moves, so do the fae who enjoy living between the two realms. It is a bit like occupying a town. They take over the buildings and improve upon them, adding their own flourishes and fauna to their new land. Each house we passed was unique. At first glance they were just ordinary homes you would find in any upstate New York town, but there were touches of fae if you looked more closely. Oddly shaped extensions built onto existing structures, a tree house in the front yard that looked fit for royalty, lush gardens of brilliant flowers I had never seen before, or even mushrooms as large as me with colorfully spotted caps. One home had a wide pond in the front yard with a domed canopy over it. I had no idea what most of these additions were for, but they all felt appropriate in their own way.

Then there was Greystone Chapel. It stood in the middle of a quaint and quiet neighborhood, jutting from the earth like probing fingers of a buried god. It had a vibrancy that lived somewhere between the stark warehouse district and the brilliance of Willow's Edge. Gargantuan grey blocks of stone made up the chapel, stacked in a neo-classic design to reach an arched zenith. It was the sort of building that would stand for centuries. The chapel was closer to the size of a small cathedral, with a long row of steps leading to three vaulted entryways. I knew in an instant that this was a survivor of the previous human town that became

Willow's Edge. Greystone had a peculiar quality, as if it was overlayed onto the world around it like an amateur Photoshop project.

"How is it still here?" I asked.

Sacha curled a lip to expose two fangs as we approached the chapel. "Places like this have a power of their own."

"Churches?"

"Not all of them. Greystone is old enough to have memories of its own. Even the fae can't shake powers rooted this deeply. There's a saint entombed inside the altar. He was a powerful cleric. The caretaker is a direct descendant of the same family, though he doesn't know it. The blood bond between them is strong, and not even Drys's magic could shake that sort of thing."

"Does he—?"

"Know about the fae folk?" Sacha snorted. "Not a chance in hell. If that fella knew those folk existed, he would be out starting a holy crusade to exorcise them or something."

There was a smaller stone cottage to the right of the chapel, which I assumed was the priest's home. The lawn had been turned into a wide vegetable and flower garden. Several six-foot-long raised beds divided up most of the area, with a row of tall hedges boxing it in, except for a wide arched entrance. We were in luck. The priest was tending his garden. He wore robes that would look more at home on a monk, and his head was even shaved in a tonsure. *Maybe he is a monk?*

I paused at the archway. "Can you talk to him? You know, cause you're a daemon and all."

Sacha chuckled. "I ain't going to blow up in a beam of light for talking with some granddad what owns a cross. He's just some bloke out begging the dirt for food."

"Oh, right." I chuckled, feeling silly.

"Now, get me in that church there, and that's a different story. Place as old and powerful as that's liable to leave me a puddle of piss." Sacha was kinda hard to read sometimes. His face was deadly serious, but there was this fiery mischief behind his eyes. It was like watching an actor who was trying not to laugh, so I couldn't tell whether he was being serious or not.

"Right. Well, let's not go in for a prayer, then, eh?" I said.

It felt odd to step onto the church grounds. A tingle shot up through the soles of my feet, right past the loafers. It was not unpleasant, like an electric jolt, but more like a firm message that I was now on hallowed ground. Sacha was still flying, with tendrils of smoke coming from his nostrils, so I knew magic still worked here. The world looked overly focused, and I gaped in awe at the garden, instantly feeling a pang of loss at my own destroyed beds back in the city.

"His name is Father Willem," Sacha muttered.

"Good morning, Father," I called toward the raised bed he was working in.

"Huh?" He jerked his head up from the dirt, eyes wide behind Coke-bottle glasses. His gaze switched between me and Sacha, then relaxed. "Oh, ho there, my child. You gave me quite a fright."

"I'm sorry, I didn't mean to sneak up on you."

He put both hands on the raised bed to help support his weight as he stood. Father Willem was a skinny old man. It was a wonder his halo of hair was still so dark because he looked and moved like someone about to be a hundred. "Heavens, no worries to be had." He brushed the dirt from his knees. "What brings you to my lovely garden this fine morning?"

"This is Rosalie Alacore's granddaughter, Willem," Sacha said abruptly.

The priest stopped to study me for a moment, his eyes working over my face in recognition. "Ah, so it is, so it is. And goodly met…" He lifted an open hand, prodding me to finish his sentence.

"Lanie, Father. My name is Lanie."

He gave a curt bow. "Lanie. I am sorry to hear about your late grandmother. Rosalie was a dear, sweet woman, given in God's grace. I have no doubt she has returned to his pastures, in blessing and light."

Sacha snickered, and I elbowed him to stop. If Father Willem noticed, he was not letting on. He had a bit of a nutty professor vibe to him.

"I assume you've come to set up her funeral arrangements?"

Funeral? Oh my, I had not even thought of that. I felt my face turn scarlet. It had never crossed my mind to set up some sort of service for her. From what I always understood, funerals were about closure. I'd gotten all the closure I needed the evening before, saying goodbye to her under Drys's willow. "Oh, uh, we already did that," I lied. Wait, was lying a sin? I tried to remember the commandments. And if it was, did it cost more Hail Marys if the lie was to a priest? "It was in the city."

Father Willem frowned thoughtfully. "That is a shame. There are a good many parishioners who would have liked to say their goodbyes, I am sure. She has been sorely missed at Sunday Mass."

Another surprise. "My grandmother came here for services?" I glanced at Sacha. He shot me a slight nod. The idea of it was so strange. She was a fae who kept a daemon in her shop and yet attended church services? The people around here were so odd. I would have to ask Sacha how any of that made sense.

"Every Sunday, never missed a beat. Rosalie always came early and helped me with the garden. She had a proper green thumb, that woman." He looked downcast, hands on his hips as he surveyed the garden beds around us. "I don't know what I will do without her."

"Maybe we should have a small service here," I thought out loud. It was exactly the type of commitment I found myself regretting the moment I made it.

"That would be splendid. A memorial service, at least," Father Willem beamed. "However, if that's not why you came by…?"

He was leading again. This Willem was cleverer than he appeared. "I was hoping to walk around the chapel a bit. My grandmother mentioned she liked to come here to think. There was one statue in particular she enjoyed. Something about a lion crest?"

"Yes, of course," Father Willem said. "Rosalie loved to walk the hedge maze. The congregation planted it back in 1880. There's all sorts of statues back there. Very lovely." He pointed to the back of the garden. I had not noticed the opening in the long row of hedges before. It was uniformly sculpted as an entrance into the maze.

"That must be it," I said. "Do you mind if I go back there?"

Father Willem bowed slightly and closed his eyes. "We all mourn in our way, my child. Please feel free. The house of God is your house."

"Thank you," I said, eagerly walking that direction. Something struck me just as I was about to enter the hedges. I stopped and turned to find Father Willem retrieving his trowel from the grass. "Father?"

He smiled at me.

"I'm going to be living in town for a while. Would you mind terribly if I came by from time to time and helped you with the garden?"

His eyes lit up. "Oh, that would be splendid!"

I felt warm inside. The garden was so beautiful. It was like it looked back at me and promised to fill a hole in my heart. "Great, thank you. And maybe when I come by, we can talk about my grandmother's memorial service."

"What was that horseshit about?" Sacha grumbled.

"What do you mean?" I asked as we turned the corner of a hedge row. The hedges were higher than my head and the maze itself much deeper than it looked from the garden. It was an impressive place. The hedges formed a long angular maze like I had only seen in movies. Every so often we would come to a statue marking either a split in the path or a dead end. It was unnerving to have to find my way through it with Lobo's welfare hanging over my head, but fascinating all the same.

"You're going to have a service for her *here*?" Sacha scowled.

"Does this maze seem a little large to you?"

Sacha shrugged. "Stupid fae magic. Someone's extended it. Poor dopey Willem probably doesn't even realize it. He's always lost in his own head."

That made sense. I wondered if it was my grandmother who had performed the magic. "I was surprised to hear she went to church every Sunday. Isn't that odd for a fae?"

Sacha zipped ahead and looked right then left. "They can do whatever they want out in the provinces. To a degree. You go to a fae city in the realm and start spouting Jesus this, God that, and you'll find yourself headless quick enough. But come out here to the provinces and anything goes so long as you keep your mouth shut. Fae don't like to have others' shit rubbed in their faces, especially when it comes to human religions. There are lots of Buddhists in Willow's Edge too."

I laughed at the idea of someone like Lobo meditating. "And the—what are they called—the ruling families, they just let that sort of stuff slide?"

"I think they figure it's better to have the weirdos out in the provinces where they can keep tabs on them than in the realm," Sacha said distractedly. "You know what? Let me fly around and try to find this damned statue."

It was a good idea. I felt silly we had not thought of it earlier. In seconds he zipped over the top of the hedges and away. The sky was already getting overcast with dark clouds. *Stupid storm clouds,* I thought glumly. *That's going to ruin the view of tonight's blue moon.* I frowned and instantly wanted to slap myself. *Who cares about a storm?* I needed to stay focused on what was important. A breeze was picking up, rustling the hedges around me. I looked over my shoulder, down the long row, trying not to picture a man stalking me. The hedges blotted out their corners in lean shadows. *Maybe it wasn't such a good idea to split up.*

"Found it," Sacha called over the hedges.

I sighed with relief and hurried toward his voice. A few moments later he came flapping overhead. "Just follow me," he beckoned, keeping above the hedges as he guided me along.

I rounded a corner to find a dead end. For a second I assumed Sacha had made a mistake. Then my eyes adjusted to the shadows and saw the effigy at the end of the row.

It was a squat rectangular structure, the bottom two-thirds bricked up. The top of it housed a recessed marble alcove, with the statue of a woman resting on a pedestal. I could make out better details as I approached. The statue and alcove were sculpted from a single piece of marble. It was amazing work. There was a small worn plaque below it, riveted to the brickwork.

"Saint Apollonia," I read aloud. "Is this the saint buried inside the chapel?"

"More like stuffed under the shrine," Sacha corrected.

"I wonder what her story was," I said, running my fingers over the statue's face. Sacha plopped down on the stone bench and produced a cigar from somewhere I'd rather not think about. Apollonia's face was serene, staring down at the ground. One hand was held up in blessing, the other clutching a baby to her breast. Wait, not a baby. It was an animal, a lion cub. When Christianity initially spread, it incorporated many local beliefs, explaining them as God's miracles. What kind of symbolism was at play here with a mother nurturing a lion? Did it have anything at all to do with the fae or was it just happenstance that my grandmother found what she was seeking around this statue?

Sacha cleared his throat. "Well, is this what you were looking for?"

I was glad for his distraction. My mind has a habit of falling down rabbit holes at times. I stepped back to take in the whole picture. "Was this the only lion statue you found?"

Sacha blew out a plume of cigar smoke. "The only one."

I tried to recall my grandmother's exact words. *Behind the lion's paw…break the day.* I felt the statue again. The marble around the lion and Apollonia's arms was smooth, all made of one piece. "There's no secret compartments here," I grumbled. I felt all around the statue a few more times, even reaching into the alcove and rubbing the marble of her back.

"Think you blew it?" Sacha asked candidly.

"Ugh, I hope not," I groaned. "But probably."

"She say anything else?"

I backed away from the alcove, feeling antsy and a bit cranky. I really needed to get some sleep to get rid of the headache pressing around my temples. "Just that the way is behind the lion's paw. But I searched the whole statue, there's nothing there."

"Huh," Sacha grunted.

He was annoying me with his cavalier attitude toward our dilemma. "Wait!" There was a faint etching of a sun on the inside wall of the alcove. An idea struck me. "She said something about being past the break of day too. What if the answer's more literal than I'm thinking? Instead of behind the lion's paw on the statue, it's *behind* the lion's paw."

Sacha frowned. "You lost me."

I quickly circled the statue to look at the back of it. There it was. More than halfway down the stand was a brick with a slight discoloration to it. Could I be right? I grabbed it, slipping my fingers into the surrounding grout. It pressed inward with a shudder. "It's loose," I exclaimed triumphantly. Sacha leapt off the bench and flapped over the statue. "You see, right here," I said, trying to get a better grip on it. "If I can just jimmy it out a bit…"

The brick slid a millimeter forward then suddenly snapped back in place. I yelped, feeling my fingernail pulled with it and torn in half. I sucked on my finger, hopping up and down. "Fuck my life that hurts, fucking bitch mother cocksucker."

Sacha laughed hard at my show.

"It's not sunny, you little weasel. I mean funny," I snapped, pressing the remains of my nail firmly in place. I did not even want to look at the damage that was done.

"Settle down, toots," Sacha said. "I'll show you how it's done." He raised a hand for me to see, then tensed his knuckles. Blackish-red talons popped out of each fingertip. He pressed them easily into the grooves around the brick and shimmied it free. He dropped the brick to the ground with a shit-eating grin and offered the small open space to me like Vanna White.

"Thank you," I muttered. There was a small bound cloth inside the opening. I quickly untied it and let the side fall over my palm. I almost forgot about my throbbing finger when my eyes landed on the relic. I knew at one glance the item in my hand had some sort of power. I could feel it in my gut again, just like before, except stronger.

It was a piece of a branch, as scarlet as blood. The tips were slightly translucent even in the cloudy light. It looked like when you wake up to find the trees frozen over with a thin layer of ice. Except there was no ice, and the relic was warm to the touch, almost like it had been recently heated over a fire.

"That's pretty cool." Sacha grinned.

"We did it," I said, smiling back at him. "Now we can help Lobo stop the changeling!"

Sacha snapped his head around. "Uh oh."

I was about to ask what had spooked him when I saw the shadow above us.

21

I heard it like a whistle whining through the air. The shadow flew overhead, then abruptly crashed into the hedgerows at the end of the lane. I thought I must have lost my sanity because it looked exactly like a crow. Except I've never heard of a crow the size of a grown man before. Then, to further my disbelief, I noticed a cloud of black feathers fluttering around where the thing had crashed.

"What the hell was that?" I gasped.

Sacha put a hand on my shoulder, tugging me to the side. "Time to run, toots."

I looked at him, my mouth opening and closing but nothing able to come out. The hedges rustled where the shadow had fallen.

"Run!" Sacha shouted.

The sound of a daemon scared struck me like lightning, jolting me into a sprint. I turned and ran but stopped as quickly as I had begun. "Oh no, it's a dead end."

The path out of this section of the maze was the other way, to the left of the crashed shadow. My feet turned to lead. I suddenly realized how foolish I had been this entire time.

I was not built for a fight. I had never even had an argument with another girl let alone gone toe to toe with a man-sized flying crow. Why did I ever think I could do this without Doule? I looked to Sacha for advice just in time to see him zip over the hedge on flapping wings. My heart squeezed inside my chest, and I suddenly felt dizzy. Sacha had abandoned me.

"Laaaaanie," a voice from a nightmare trilled. It was wet, like oil coated the man's throat. Shivers ran down my spine.

This isn't real, I denied, grasping at straws in my mind. I must still be asleep back in the city. All of this was some horrible nightmare that I would chalk up to eating day-old pizza just before bed again. I was frozen to the spot. The hedges rustled as the man spilled out of them. I was too afraid to turn and look directly at him. If I did that, then he would be real, which meant that I was about to die.

"Don't be a shy little shit," he giggled. It was the first time I learned someone could mix laughter with such a deep-rooted hatred. "There's nowhere for you to run. Be good now and get over here."

My body moved without my control. I found myself suddenly facing him. He stood at the end of the path, hunched forward. Black oily liquid dripped from lacerations around his forehead and hands. Crow feathers adorned his arms and protruded from a tattered black T-shirt. They were growing from his body. His eyes were like tiny pieces of charcoal, beady, penetrating, mocking. The brilliant white teeth of his smile could cut glass, starkly contrasting with the shadows that seemed to cling to him. All of that was horrifying enough—I mean, I could barely wrap my mind around what I was seeing as it was unfolding before my eyes—but it was the knife in his left hand that demanded my attention. It was a curved dagger, like the blade was a snake that had frozen in place. Dried blood stained it.

"What do you want from me, Brom?" I whispered. There was no doubt in my mind this man was the changeling.

His eyes lit up with gleeful, murderous intent. "You don't know?"

"I've seen you before," I said, recalling his face. I had mistaken him for a homeless person back in the city just outside my apartment building, dipping into my alley.

"Liar, liar, pants on fire." Brom waggled a warning finger at me. So he hadn't seen me that time. That bolstered me a little, to know this fiend was not as omnipotent as he seemed. "Come over here."

"Why?"

"I want to talk with you."

"Is that what the knife is for? Talking?"

Brom giggled. He ran his fingers over his face as it turned upward to the sky. He was babbling something. "She's a funny one, Rosalie, your slut of a granddaughter."

"Don't you ever say her name," I yelled. Red-hot heat burned behind my eyes.

Brom flinched. He blinked repeatedly, staring at me as if he had never seen me before that moment.

"All she wanted to do was help you, you miserable prick," I continued. He staggered back a step as if struck. "How could you betray her like that? How could you hurt someone so kind?" I heard my anger turning to a sob and hated myself for it. "I could have had a family, but you took that all away. Now I have nothing."

That slight change of tone was enough for the changeling to recover. "You fae." He spit black oil into the grass. "You strut across this earth like you're the only things that matter. Turn your pointy noses up at all the other flesh bags, go around making monsters and then turning your back on any responsibility you have toward them. Look at you. You're pathetic. You have everything in the world, anything you want, with your fae magic. You talk to me about having nothing? Try living on the streets for half your life, selling your body for just enough money to feed your little sister. Then watching her die because you couldn't do more to take care of her."

He began slowly closing the distance between us. His knuckles turned white each time he emphasized a word and gripped the dagger tighter.

"Then, voila, you're eighteen and suddenly your body is changing. Not puberty, not manhood, not that. You're turning into a circus freak. And why, *Lanie*? Why?"

I took a step back, slapping my spine against the statue alcove.

"Because I was weak! One of your kind spent his seed in my whore of a mother, knowing I would turn into this. They didn't care. Why bother with a half-breed? They strut around like their shit don't stink, but they're the foulest of them all." He snarled. "You have no idea what having nothing feels like."

"She wanted to help you," I repeated. It came out as a mewling sound as fear threatened to choke me.

Brom snarled wetly. "Your grandmother was an uppity bitch. Do you know what she wanted to do to me?"

"Heal you," I whispered. He was only ten feet away. I knew with no uncertainty that I was going to die. That's a horrible feeling. The idea of that terrible dagger cutting in and out of my flesh almost made me pee my pants. My whole body was shaking. I could barely keep hold of the stick in my right hand.

"*Heal me?* Rosalie wanted to maim me. She wanted to strip away my power!" He was worked up into a deranged frenzy.

Wait. What stick? Where did I get a stick? My mind raced to remember the significance of it, but even as I tried, I saw Brom blur. His shadowed form sprinted at me with dagger held high.

A red smear cut across the air, zipping over the hedgerow. I heard Sacha's shriek. There was nothing human about it. It was the sound of a daemon battle cry.

Brom was taken completely by surprise. Sacha's talons tore across the top of the changeling's skull. He threw up a warding hand, swiping the dagger, but Sacha was already flying over to me. He grasped my collar and pulled me. "I said run damnit!"

I sprinted past Brom, who was just recovering from swiping at the air while Sacha zipped in at him again. Brom screamed in rage as Sacha tore a jagged line across his chest.

I was at the end of the row, turning the corner, when I glanced back. Brom was chasing me.

Sacha was hot on his heels but struggling to keep up suddenly. I rounded the corner, the edge of the hedges scraping my forearm. I felt so heady, dizzy with the adrenaline flooding my body. I blindly ran through the maze, trying desperately to remember the path we had taken. Close behind me, Brom screamed in frustration, and Sacha snarled. My legs pumped harder. If I did not get out of that maze, I was as good as dead.

Right. Left. Straight. Keep moving.

Brom's snarling frustration grew farther and farther away. I was gaining ground! I scrambled around a corner.

Right into a dead end.

"Shit, fuck, no." I rushed back, certain the changeling would already be barring the way. He was nowhere to be seen. The maze had grown as quiet as death.

I slowed my pace to a crawl. Something was incredibly off. *Where did they go?*

The hedges to my right burst open. A shadow lunged through them, bowling me over into the grass. I dropped the stick, grappling with Brom's weight as we rolled across the ground. His crow-like talons dug into my arms. In a flash he had me pinned to the ground, a knee on each of my arms beneath him.

Oh no, I panicked, finally remembering the importance of what I'd held. *The relic. I dropped the relic!*

"Fucking little bat," he snarled. Sacha had done a good job of cutting up the changeling's face and arms. Oily black liquid dripped from the wounds. Fresh blood also dripped from the upraised dagger onto my face. I stopped struggling.

"Sacha…" I gasped.

Brom giggled like only a madman can, his eyes lit up like a jack-o-lantern. "Stuck him good. I've never killed a daemon before. It was like stabbing a little piggy."

"You son of a bitch," I screamed, bucking my lower body as hard as I could.

Brom could not hide his look of shock as he flipped over me. That was his problem. He was too cocky. Never in a million years did he imagine I could overpower him.

I rolled over and scrambled on hands and knees across the grass. Brom grabbed my ankle and wrenched me back just as I was about to grasp the relic.

"Feisty little unicorn," he growled.

I kicked my legs hard, trying to shake him off.

The hedges burst open again. Sacha's red shape howled out of them. He smashed headfirst into the changeling's forehead, knocking the cretin backward and off balance. Brom slammed down on his rump, blinking as he tried to regain his senses. Sacha tumbled into the grass nearby. A thick gash ran across his side, dark brownish-red blood spurting out of it.

"Sacha!" I cried as I kneeled in the grass, my fingers atop the relic.

Focus came back into Brom's face. He quickly followed my gaze to the imp lying limply in the grass near him. "Damnable abomination getting in my way. I'll send you right back to hell." He punched Sacha hard in the temple. The little imp whined but did not move. He had used the last of his strength to catch up to us and knock Brom off of me.

"Stop it!" I screamed, pulling myself up to hands and knees.

Brom took delight in that. He raised his dagger. "You want me to stop? Fuck no. I'm going to stick this little piggy right between the eyes this time. I think an imp head will look nice in my den." He snapped his hand out and down, fast as a pecking crow. The dagger flashed through the air.

"No!" I howled with a fury I've never felt before. The world lit up with color. A shimmering bubble of it burst from me. I felt it let loose from my core, radiating outward in every direction. The force field slammed into Brom, tossing him aside like a leaf. The bubble of colored light, prismatic like a rainbow against liquid, kept tumbling him backward, straight through the corner of the hedge wall before it finally burst. All I could see of him around the corner were his legs, which slapped down onto the ground where he landed.

What. The. Actual. Fuck?

Some sort of magic had ripped out of me. It was gone, but my body felt energized and radiated a quickly dimming light. Brom's legs were not moving. *Is he dead?* I wondered in horror. I had a lurching sensation in the pit of my stomach and suddenly puked all over the grass.

How did I do that? What was it, even?

Sacha moaned in pain. I scrambled over to him on hands and knees. I rolled him over. His skin was cold as ice and his face a sickly light purple. "Sacha," I cried, tears pooling in my eyes. "Oh no no no. What do I do? How do I save you?"

"Too late for all that, love," he rasped, then shocked me with a weak smile. "Bastard sure was surprised when I clawed him, though, eh?"

I sobbed hard, running my fingers over his clammy forehead. "Yeah, you got him, Sacha. You saved my life."

"Rosalie would be proud of me," Sacha whispered. The light was fading from his eyes.

I was suddenly flooded with anger that burned me from the inside out. Why did this have to happen? Sacha never even should have been here. If I was not such a stubborn fool, rushing headfirst into these situations, then he would still be alive. No, not just that. I had tethered him to me as his master, no better than some of history's worst fiends.

"Sacha, I was wrong," I sobbed. "I'm so sorry. I never should have kept Rosalie's contract. You never should have had to fight that *thing*."

Sacha placed a cold hand on my forearm. He gave me a weak squeeze. This imp, on his deathbed, was trying to comfort *me*. It was more than I could bear. I ugly cried. He was trying to say that what I had done was okay.

"It's not okay," I demanded. "Sacha, I release you from your contract. I am not your master." At least I could give him freedom in his final moments. I didn't know what Sacha had done to make Rosalie trap him, but no one deserved that sort of captivity.

Sacha's eyes were two empty pockets of flame. His mouth gaped. The air around us grew blazing hot as a seam opened in reality. It was a slit at first, black as the abyss, then gaping hungrily like a mouth. Flickering flames spilled from the vortex. Tendrils of fire wrapped around Sacha and pulled him into the opening.

For a moment I thought I had done something horribly wrong. But Sacha was smiling. He mouthed the words *thank you* as he was pulled inside the portal. Then the seam sealed itself, and once again the air was still. I closed my eyes and cried. At least Sacha's last memories would be of freedom. He was home now, where he belonged.

Brom mumbled something. His legs twitched. I had half forgotten about him until that moment. I had never hated anyone or anything as much as I loathed the changeling. He had taken so much away from me. "No more," I vowed to myself as he stirred.

I rose shakily to my feet and retrieved the relic. "My grandmother was going to use this to help you," I said as he groaned on the other side of the hedge. "I never got to know her, but from what I could see, she was a damned saint to want to save something like you."

I came around the corner of the hedge. Brom was dazed still, trying to lift his head to see me. "I see her folly, to ever think something like you deserved her mercy in the first place. Hold still now, I'm going to do what she wanted to, even though I hate you with every fiber of my being, and perhaps because I know doing this will hurt you far more than anything else I could do."

I had no idea how to use the relic. I held it like a divining rod searching for water as I approached him. It tingled in my hands as it neared, hungry perhaps to be released against him.

Brom's eyes popped open. He shimmied backward, his hands and feet clawing the grass. "Keep that thing away from me!"

I was going to tell him why I would never keep the relic away from him when he suddenly stopped and seized a glimmering object from his pocket. I hesitated, thinking it was his dagger. Brom flipped the cork off a glass vial and drank what looked like blood all in one move. I felt a connection to the blood as soon as the cork was released and knew it came from my grandmother. His cuts rapidly healed in front of my eyes.

Brom vaulted upward from the ground like a twirling dervish, wide black crow's wings sprouting from his arms.

And then he was gone.

Fled like a coward. But he would be back.

I squeezed the relic, feeling its magic reassure me. Next time I would be ready for him.

22

Okay, it was false bravado. I'm no bold and brave heroine looking to face a serial killer with a stick.

I was a bedraggled mess by the time I returned to the shop. My hands would not stop shaking, and I felt like I had gone ten rounds with Mike Tyson. Who was I fooling? It was more like one round. Maybe even twenty seconds; he's a big dude. Sacha was gone. I was hollowed out. If I had listened to Doule, Sacha would still be alive. How could I have ever thought I knew the best course of action to battle a chaos magic infused madman? A week ago I was arranging bouquets for a wedding. I felt weaker and weaker as the adrenaline wore off.

My grandmother's building loomed ahead. Every time I'd entered that shop Sacha had been around, waiting to be a pain in my ass. The idea of walking into that shop without him was too much for me to handle. But then I saw the front door and my heart stopped. It was propped open. A bare foot was sticking out of the gap. I surprised myself by running toward the store instead of away. I pulled the front door open, rattling the hanging bell.

It was hard to recognize Lobo at first. That was how badly beaten up he was, lying face up on my floor. His hair was matted with mud, and his jacket was missing. The shirt underneath was torn on the sides and back as if he'd been attacked by a lion. I knelt beside him to get a better look at his head. A nasty bump the shape of an egg adorned his crown, with dried blood mixed into the mud. He was as still as a corpse. I was afraid to touch him. He looked dead.

"Lobo!" I yelled.

His closed eyes twitched, and he mumbled something incoherent.

"Oh, thank God your alive. I can't understand you." I gently moved the hair out of his face. His warm golden eyes peered at me, and his body tensed.

"Have to get back…to Lanie," he babbled.

"You're here, Lobo. I'm here." I caressed his brow. He was feverishly hot. I looked around the shop. "We better get you off this floor. Hang on."

The only thing I could think to do was get him some water. I was weird like that. One time in college a girl in my dorm fainted right in front of me. Low blood sugar. My first instinct was to get her water. Same as when Deedee cried over a man she'd broken up with. Always lead with water.

I hopped up and ran around the counter to the office. There was a sink in that room. Sacha's belongings were strewn across the floor. My stomach churned at the vivid reminder of what I had just lost. How many people would the changeling take away from me? I rinsed out a ceramic mug and filled it with cold tap water. The room was blurry. I realized I was crying. I looked down at the mug. I was letting it overflow with water back into the sink.

What had my life become? For the first time I admitted to myself how much I liked the werewolf in the other room. *My heart can't take it if I lose Lobo too.* No, not just liked, wanted. *I want to get to know him. I want him to know me. I look forward to hearing his stupid grumpy voice.* There was something right about the way Lobo made me feel, like no one ever had before. And now he was lying on the floor, dying.

No. I demanded the universe not let that happen. After all I had been through, I was not going to lose Lobo too. I slapped the faucet handle off, still staring down into the mug. *When the changeling drank Rosalie's blood, it healed him in seconds. Could my blood have the same properties? Drys said it was powerful...*

My tears fell into the mug as I wondered at that possibility. The water inside bloomed with a soft glow. It was hard to tell where it was coming from through my blurry vision. A spectrum of colors rippled over the surface of the water, and a tendril of smoke spilled over the lip of the mug.

This was my magic!

I felt the relic vibrating in my pocket as if in agreement. That was when I knew. I could feel it with every fiber of my being, as surely as I could feel my lips and my fingertips. Magic flowed through me. It was cut off by whatever curse had been laid over me, but the relic silenced that curse, allowing me to access my birthright. I knew what my purpose was. A feeling of brilliant elation washed over me at the epiphany. I was born to be a protector. A healer. At one with the world.

I raced into the storefront, careful not to spill a drop of the water. "Lobo, I need you to lift your head," I said, crouching down close to him.

He opened his eyes a fraction and craned his neck so his head was slightly lifted and mouth open. His lips were parted with a gash where he had been kicked in the face. I poured the water slowly, dribbling drops on his cheek until my aim found his mouth.

Spots of his skin glowed faintly, marking where the liquid was absorbed. Then the tiny spots radiated in waves across his whole face. Lobo's eyes shot open. His mouth worked hungrily to slurp up the water I poured. Suddenly he was sitting up, wrenching the cup from my hands. He gulped down every drop. When it was gone, he licked the rim and the side like a child clearing a plate of spaghetti. Finally satiated, he leaned back and sighed. I watched in awe as the deep wounds on his chest rapidly closed until they were unmarred skin.

"It worked," I said with delight.

Lobo snapped his attention like a stirred puppy, first around the room and then to me. "When did I get *here*?" he asked, as if roused from a dream.

"I just found you. What happened to you? It looks like you've been dragged through hell," I said, wincing when I remembered where Sacha had just gone. "You were in pretty rough shape, but I used my magic to heal you."

"The changeling," Lobo thought out loud. "I found where he lives. It was underground, but it was a trap."

I shuddered, imagining being anywhere underground with that fiend. "You're lucky to be alive, then."

"I am," Lobo reluctantly agreed. "I must've escaped and found my way back here." He paused to frown. "I feel amazing. How did you do that?"

I shrugged, suddenly embarrassed. "Let's talk about it later. You stink. Anyway, I want to make sure Doule and Deedee know we're okay."

That confused him even more. I rapidly filled him in on all he had missed as I led the way upstairs. We were both surprised to find the apartment empty.

"But where could they have gone?" I asked, worry gnawing away at my insides.

"If your friend is with Doule, then she is in good hands," Lobo insisted matter-of-factly. "I would trust him with my own children. If I had any. Don't scowl, I'm telling you he won't let anything happen to her."

He was very convincing. Call it werewolf ego. I felt it prudent not to point out how badly beaten up he had been only a few minutes before. "Go wash up," I ordered. "You're stinking up my apartment."

Lobo chuckled. It was the first time I saw him truly happy. His smile had a sharpness to it, like he was embarrassed to be happy. It was better than the brooding detective vibe he tried so hard to give off. I thought his smile looked cute. "Fine. I'll wash up. Some thanks I get for trying to save your life."

"Your thanks is hot water and free soap," I teased. "The bathroom is right through there."

Lobo snickered. He paused at the bathroom door. "Lanie. I'm sorry to hear about Sacha. I'm not saying he wasn't a massive pain in the ass, because if you knew some of the stunts that imp has pulled over the years... Still, the little rascal didn't deserve to go out like that."

I could feel my bottom lip trembling, so I gave him a nod and ducked into my bedroom. The bathroom door shut. I wiped away the tears before they could become a torrent. Sacha was in a better place. It might not be where I would want to go in the afterlife, but the look on his face as he was pulled back to hell was sheer happiness. *Either way, it was kind of Lobo to say that.*

The first thing I wanted to do was secure the relic. I needed it close by in case the changeling came for me again. The problem at the chapel was that I kept dropping the darn thing. My fingers probed my grandmother's crystal between my breasts. It radiated energy that I had never felt so strongly before. This was more of the relic negating my curse. I was open to the universe in a way I had never been before. A thrill ran down my spine at the possibilities. I pulled the stick from my pocket to marvel at its surface. It was shaped like the tip of a branch, with a forking section at the tip. Why did it look like ice sealed the wood? Was it even wood? There were no grains or splinters, no peeling bark, yet I was certain it was from a tree.

The shower water kicked on in the bathroom. I shook my head. The relic had me mesmerized for a few moments. *I better be careful around this thing until I can figure out how to use it to permanently break the changeling's curse.*

A ball of twine sat on my grandmother's dresser amongst her things. I brought it into the kitchen, cut a section off with scissors, and used it to secure the relic to my necklace, overlapping the crystal horn. I felt its presence even stronger pressed against my naked skin like that.

I heard Lobo drop the soap into the tub, and I remembered the way the bathroom looked. *Oh no, it's a mess in there.* My dirty clothes were on the floor, and the trash bin was still full from when my grandmother lived here. *And there's no more towels.* I hurried to the closet and to my delight found a stack of folded towels. They were soft, like pressing your face into a teddy bear, and smelled like clean cotton. The bathroom door was still slightly ajar, steam slipping out into the open apartment.

I slipped in and set the stack on the sink. "There's a towel here for you," I said, quickly picking up the clothes from the floor in a bundle.

"Thank you," Lobo said.

I turned to go and realized, to my horror, that there was another aspect of my grandmother's bathroom I had forgotten. The shower curtain was completely transparent. I remembered being uncomfortable taking a shower, worried someone might walk in on me. Now I had done exactly that to Lobo.

He had his back to me, facing the showerhead. Water trickled in rivulets down his muscular shoulders and back. His skin was dark, tanned, and strangely hairless. I'd expected he would have tufts of fur, but he was smooth as a marble statue. I followed the flow of the water down to his round ass and felt a stirring inside of me.

Lobo must have sensed it. He turned to face me. A mild look of shock quickly passed over his face. I know what he was thinking. I was the last person he expected to be a Peeping Tom. I was the good girl, the one you became friends with. There was nothing sexual about Lanie Alacore. Except now there was. His eyes met mine, golden orbs that stared into my soul. The corner of his mouth quirked into a smile. I was breathing heavily. He gave me a slight nod.

My eyes traced down his chest and over his chiseled pecs. Finally, some hair on him, but not grossly. It was normal *I am a hot fucking stud* hair. A little around the chest, a trail of it leading downward. His abs were more like an eight pack in between defined obliques that pointed down in a V. He ran soap across his chest as I watched, then across his ribs, over each little muscle there.

I was wet. It was the first time I'd felt that way without any inner alarm. It was the relic. If it lifted the curse on me while I wore it, then could I…?

Lobo began to wash lower, and I could see that he was as excited by my voyeurism as I was. I sucked in air, wondering what he would feel like inside of me. Wanting him. I blushed. He looked like some Adonis out of a Roman myth. What would he think of plain old me if I was naked and exposed in front of him? Would he want me the same way?

"Right," I broke the tension. "I'll be in the other room when you finish up."

I quickly retreated to the living room, walking in a circle, trying to think. The shower turned off. I panicked again and ran into the bedroom.

Am I really going to do this? Did I just invite him to have sex?

The door creaked open behind me. I could smell his clean body across the room. I glanced over my shoulder. Lobo wore a towel around his waist, his wet body still steaming from the hot shower. He closed the distance between us in a flash, then hovered just behind me, our bodies inches apart. Heat radiated off him. I took a deep breath, feeling heady with anticipation.

Lobo slid his hands around my waist from behind and pulled me closer. His wet body was solid muscle and dampened my shirt. His breath was hot on my neck. "Is this what you want?" he whispered. I could feel his hardness pressing against me.

"Yes," I said breathlessly, leaning back against him.

His lips danced across my neck from behind, lightly sucking and sending shivers down my throat. Teeth playfully nipped at my earlobe. I craned my head back to meet him and pressed my lips to his. They were warm and strong. Sharp stubble tickled my cheek. Lobo's tongue explored my mouth, running across my upper lip. A wave of heat crashed through me as I met him with my own. We tasted each other as his hands stroked up and down my ribs and circled my waist. I moaned. It was a sound I had never made before, and it astonished me so much that I stopped.

Lobo stopped too. He turned me slowly so I faced him, his golden eyes locked onto my own. "Do you want to stop?"

I shook my head sheepishly. This was all so new to me. I could hardly believe it was really happening. I wanted Lobo in a way I had never wanted anything else before.

He smiled and pushed me down to the bed on my back. His powerful hands wrapped around my ankles. He lifted them up so my skirt slid over my belly, exposing my panties. His rough hand slid up my thigh, massaging me as he slowly worked his way to my panties. He pressed his thumb against me, through the lace, the slightest of grazes that sent a shiver of pleasure up my spine.

"Does that feel good?" he asked.

I pursed my lips, my eyes closed tight, and nodded. Lobo chuckled mischievously then kissed my thigh. He worked me with his lips, up and down one thigh then hovering over my panties, his thumb delicately sliding across my pussy, tracing me through my panties, before moving his mouth to the opposite thigh. He was teasing me. I bucked my hips up to meet him, urging his mouth to give me more. This time when he hovered over my soaking panties he pressed his lips to them and sparks of electricity worked through me. I felt swollen and tingling with need. I tugged my panties to the side. His breath was hot on my pussy lips. He kissed my slit, working his lips and tongue over the lips from top to bottom until I wanted to scream. Then suddenly he buried his face between my thighs.

His mouth worked across the tender flesh of my pussy, licking and sucking. The graze of his teeth sent tingles through me. Each probe of his tongue was ecstasy. "Oh fuck," I moaned when he suddenly sucked on my clit. His finger slid ever so slowly inside of me. Something warm let loose at my core, and I pulled the sheets to my face. His tongue traced my pussy as another finger entered. He pressed something inside of me that made me feel like I would explode. It was amazing. I had never felt such pleasure and I wanted more. I could feel his urgency held at bay. His fingers worked in and out, faster and faster, pressing against all the right places, as his tongue grazed my tenderness. It came quicker than I thought possible, a wave of euphoria from the center of me rippling outward in pure bliss. I moaned loudly as I was wracked with the first orgasm I had ever experienced.

Lobo chuckled triumphantly, and his lips switched to kissing my thighs once more. So this was sex? I could not believe what I had been missing all these years. I stroked the relic where it hung around my neck with silent gratitude. Lobo kept kissing my thighs, then moved back to tease and lick me once more.

"Oh no." I shimmied away, farther onto the bed. "Now it's my turn. Come over here."

Lobo happily obliged, dropping the towel to the floor and standing beside the bed. He presented his cock to me with a mischievous grin. I had seen and read enough to know what I was supposed to do. I stroked the bottom of his shaft with my fingertip, and he shuddered. I could see his longing as he watched me. I wrapped my hand around his hardness and looked up at him. I wanted to watch him watch me. I gently swirled my tongue around the swollen head of his cock, then licked the sensitive skin from the base to the tip. I took him in my mouth, and it was his turn to moan. His fingers grasped my hair tightly. I gagged, and he backed off, letting me explore him. He moaned again. His hands found the back of my head and pushed deeper. I pulled back and laughed.

"I can't," I giggled, embarrassed, "not like this." I patted the bed. "Come lay down here with me."

Lobo eagerly climbed into the bed. I grabbed his wrist and kissed his palm. There was a fantasy I had always dreamed of, and I wanted to try it. I eyed the silk scarves hanging from the headboard then looked to Lobo. He bit his lower lip and gave a slight nod. I led his hand to the bedpost and tied it with one of the scarves. Lobo grinned, watching me work as I bound his other wrist.

I stepped off the bed and let my skirt fall to the floor. His eyes studied me with a fierce hunger. I slipped off my wet panties, then pulled my shirt over my head. Lobo's eyes lit up with a feral intensity. He approved. I snapped my bra off and watched as his longing grew. He studied my breasts and bit his lower lip.

I crawled onto the bed, then straddled his hips with my naked thighs. I rested myself on his hard cock, teasing it outside my pussy, grinding against his hardness as I let it slide just between the lips. Radiating waves of pleasure shot through me as his shaft rubbed against my clit. I bucked my hips against him, pressing our bodies together. Lobo craned his head up, eager to taste me. I brought my nipple down to his lips and let him lick then suck. It was a delicious sensation. I rocked my hips back and forth, rubbing him against my lips in aching pleasure. His cock was fully awake, throbbing to take me. It was heady to see the impact I could have on him. I switched breasts, letting the other rub against his coarse stubble before finding his lips again.

"Kiss me," he whispered.

Our lips locked together, my hunger fully grown. We explored each other with our tongues as I bucked my hips, grinding against him. I finally broke off and then started peppering his chest with kisses. I wanted to explore every inch of him. My tongue found his nipples, and he squirmed in delight. My lips and tongue traced a path down his muscular chest, across his ribs, down his navel. Locking eyes, I took him in my mouth and felt his body spasm with pleasure.

"Oh, fuck," he moaned. His arms flexing as he tugged against the restraints.

I was drenched with anticipation. I wanted him inside me. I brought my body up, hovering my wet pussy over him. Our eyes met again. We both wanted this so badly. This was my moment of freedom. The world and all its misery could go to hell. I was free to do as I wanted for the first time in my life.

I lowered myself onto him, feeling his cock slide inside, filling me. It ached in the best way possible. I slowly guided it all the way down to the base, then let out a long moan, unable keep my eyes open. Lobo gave a slight thrust, and it set me loose. We worked together in a fervor, giving and taking, thrusting, and pumping. Our lips locked tightly as we fell into a rhythm together, my hips rocking furiously, starving for more. That steady pleasure was building up to an explosion inside of me. And suddenly it hit me, another wave of ecstasy.

A brilliant light spilled from my open lips and down my naked flesh, cascading over Lobo. When it touched him, he howled with pleasure. He let loose inside of me, spilling himself into my core. Spectrums of color danced around the room as I tilted my head back and let the ecstasy engulf me. More than just my sexuality was freed in that moment. All of my magic rippled between us. It was pure bliss.

We lay together with my head against his chest, two sweating bodies, breathing hard. Lobo laughed. "You are an amazing person, Lanie." He kissed my forehead.

"That was wonderful," I said, kissing his chest in return.

Lobo chuckled.

"I like it when you laugh," I said. Lobo always seemed tormented in some way. To hear him laugh was a sparkling refreshment.

"Yeah? Well, I think I like everything about you," he confessed playfully. "I have since the day we met."

I squeezed him with a hug. The relic pressed against my breast, caught between us. I had never felt so much happiness as in that moment. I understood now why Tae was so upset when she saw someone had bound me with a curse. How could anyone have deprived me of this all these years? It was beyond cruel. Now that I had experienced it, that moment of complete connection with another, the fulfillment of my desires, a way through the void of intimacy that had shackled my true spirit for over two decades—now that I knew what it felt like, I could never go back. The relic had freed me.

I frowned. What would happen when we used it to stop the changeling? Was it a one-time use sort of thing, to permanently break a curse? The implication of that hit me like a blow to the head. *I can't go back to that life of imprisonment,* I thought in a panic. It was staggering.

"Are you okay?" Lobo asked, feeling my body tense.

"Yes, of course," I lied, sliding off of him. The revelation left me feeling exposed. I was quickly aware of my nakedness. I covered him with the blanket as I left the bed and got dressed.

What if it is a one-time use? Somehow I knew that it was. The core of me understood this magic. If I used the relic to break Brom's curse, it would have served its purpose and the magic would be gone. Whereas if I used it as a charm kept on my person, it would negate my own curse as long as it existed. I could figure out how to use it on myself to permanently lift my own curse.

How could I choose between those two options? I had just felt a freedom I never knew possible. My magic, my sexuality, my happiness, they all seemed to hinge on breaking my own curse. Now that I had tasted of that fruit, how could I ever go back? How could I give that up to stop the changeling?

"No," I said aloud, shaking my head. "I won't." *I'll keep the relic until I can figure out how to use it to break my own curse.* "We'll have to find a different way to stop the changeling," I whispered.

"We will," Lobo promised, unaware of my inner turmoil. I realized he had no idea about my curse. My face turned scarlet. I could never tell him. My shame was too deep.

The sound was so foreign to me that at first I stood there transfixed. It was like a fire alarm or a movie suddenly turned up really loud. It was coming from somewhere deeper inside the building.

"Who is that?" Lobo asked.

My mind clicked into place as I recognized the sound was a scream and it was growing louder.

"Tae?" I gasped in recognition.

23

Once my mind registered that Tae was screaming somewhere in the building, I sprang into action. My feet moved of their own accord toward the sound, to my distress. Had I been thinking clearly, I would have freed Lobo first. I flung my apartment door open.

Tae stood in the hallway, halfway inside her apartment, both hands over her mouth. She had stopped screaming, but everything about her body language told me the trouble was not past. I reached for her shoulder, and she jumped away from me, deeper into her apartment.

"It's just me," I reassured as I followed her inside with upraised palms.

Tae's eyes were wild, flicking between me and the center of her living room.

The world tilted awkwardly, leaving me in a state of delirium. There was no way what I was witnessing could be real. These things were stories, the stuff that happened to other people. This was surely a nightmare.

A chair had been placed in the center of her living room. The back of it faced the door. I did not need to see Deedee's face to know she was the person sitting, her wrists bound by wires to the arms of the chair. A pool of blood surrounded the legs of the chair, staining the carpet around her bare feet. Her blonde hair was spattered with black oil and blood.

"Deedee!" I screamed as I ran around to face her, already dreading what I would see.

Her face was swollen, with large puffy purple flesh around her eyes and torn lips. Lines were etched into her throat from where the changeling had tortured her. I could picture him strangling her until she passed out, then waking her to do it all over again.

Tae pulled me back, pinning my arms at my sides. I had not even realized I was in a state of hysteria, screaming in denial at the sight before my eyes. She pushed my head to her shoulder, but I could not turn away from Deedee, broken and bled out. Tae's hands stroked my hair, her voice cooing at me to calm.

"You know this woman?" she asked.

"She's my best friend," I sobbed, suddenly remembering how awfully I had treated her earlier that day.

Lobo was shouting from my apartment. I could not register what he was saying. My mind was spinning in circles. "She can't be here, not like this. I left her with Doule. He would have kept her safe. He had to. I told him to make sure of it."

"What about Doule?" Tae stiffened. She repeated the question, but I couldn't think straight. Not with Lobo still shouting. Tae used her hands to make me look directly at her. "Lanie, what about Doule? Is he okay?" She frowned. Her attention pulled to the building hallway. "Is that Detective Lobo? Why is he shouting like that?"

Oh my god. Lobo. "Doule was supposed to keep her safe. He was with Deedee." I tried to explain as I pushed away from Tae. I did not want anyone touching me.

"Doule," Tae called, sprinting deeper into her apartment. She was opening and slamming doors, calling his name in a panic.

I ran back to my apartment. Lobo was thrashing on my bed. His hands had been replaced with talons and fur, and a wolf's snout protruded from his face. He locked his golden eyes on me.

"What the—"

"Lanie, you have to get out of here," he snarled. "He's got me…ugh…he's coming."

I nodded. "Okay, okay, let me think. I'll untie you, and we can get downstairs."

Lobo howled and struggled on the bed. "No, damnit, listen to me! He has me. The bastard must have—" He howled in pain. His body rapidly transformed back and forth between werewolf and human as he fought against the changeling's grip. I could see it, black swirls of shadow circling his naked chest. "He's controlling me. I won't let him. I can't. No! Run, Lanie. Run!"

I did not need to be told twice. Lobo's transformation was horrifying, but the urgency in his screams was even more so. I bolted out of the apartment. "Tae!" I was suddenly aware of how dark her apartment was. I slowed only a fraction. "Tae?" Deedee's still body mocked me. Lobo let out an agonized howl. How long could he fight against whatever hold the changeling had?

Tae ran out of the bedroom hall into the living room, her eyes wild. "What is going on?"

"The man who did this." I gestured to the chair. "He's coming back."

Tae gaped at me.

"We have to go," I urged.

Deedee groaned.

Tae slapped a hand to her mouth.

"Oh my god," I gasped. "She's still alive."

"Run, Lanie, run now!" Lobo's howl was monstrous.

"Help me free her," I pleaded.

Tae grabbed a pair of scissors off the floor. There was dried blood on them. She snipped the wire where it met the armchair. We scrambled against blood and oil to maneuver Deedee's limp body. Time went by in a jumble, but we headed down the stairs, propping Deedee's half-alive body weight between us.

A window inside Tae's apartment burst apart, and something heavy thudded onto the floorboards. I screamed and lost my footing. The three of us tumbled down the steps. I hit my head on the door at the bottom and then had Deedee's weight land on top of me. Tae was the first of us to find her feet.

"Are you okay? Lanie, look at me." She kneeled to help me pull myself from underneath Deedee.

"I'm fine. Just had the air knocked out of me." My elbow flared with pain. I looked at it and felt chills. A gash oozed with blood. Luckily, it looked like nothing that would need more than a Band-Aid and some Neosporin. I looked up the narrow stairwell at how far we had fallen. "What about you? Are you injured?"

Tae shook her head. "We were damn lucky. But what was that sound? It was like glass breaking."

The changeling answered her question by stepping out onto the landing of the dark stairwell, black crow wings where his arms should be, his face wreathed in shadows. "Little fae bitches have a spill?" His smile cut through the darkness. "You should really watch where you're walking."

"Goddess alive, what is that?" Tae screamed.

Lobo's howl was bloodcurdling. It was the sound of a hungry wolf calling for its master. There was nothing human about it.

I felt my blood boil. "I'm not scared of you. Come down here so I can finish what we started earlier today, you coward."

"So you can poke me with that little stick of yours?" Brom grinned. "Sure. Why not."

I held my breath.

"Just let me get my good buddy the wolf to come with me," he said. "I wouldn't want him to miss out on a good time."

"Oh shit," I muttered.

The changeling popped into my apartment.

"Who the fuck was that?" Tae asked again.

"The changeling. And he's going to free Lobo."

Tae's face screwed up in confusion. "Good. The detective will stop that creep."

"Shit. Double shit," I cursed. "Help me get Deedee up. He's got some spell over Lobo, controlling him."

Tae's eyes were wide. We pulled Deedee up off the stairs and moved outside the building. A white and red shape laid past the threshold. It took a moment for me to register that it was one of the owls, broken and discarded. Brom had snapped the poor creature's neck clean around.

A car door shut nearby.

"Doule, you bastard," I yelled. "You were supposed to stay with Deedee."

He froze in place, taking in the scene. His mouth dropped when he saw Deedee. "I went to find Lobo."

"Did you leave this girl in my apartment?" Tae snapped. "You can forget about our Wednesday nights."

"I-I..." he stammered.

"Just open the damn car door and get us the fuck out of here," I yelled as we shuffled over to the cruiser.

Doule quickly opened the door. We maneuvered Deedee until her top half flopped onto the backseat. She groaned in pain. "Lanie..."

"Shhh, save your strength," I said, stroking her hair. "We're going to get you to a hospital."

The door to the apartments burst open. Lobo roared as he tore through it, wooden splinters and glass flying in every direction.

"What the fuck?" Doule said. "Lobo, I've been looking everywhere for you, man. Why are you naked?"

Not why are you running through a closed door? I thought. Clearly Lobo was the brains of their operation.

Lobo took one look at his partner and charged him. He tackled Doule hard enough to bounce the car sideways into the street as they hit it. I was knocked forward over Deedee's body. Another window exploded on the second floor, and the changeling landed on the car hood.

Tae screamed and bolted for the storefront door, which was still propped open from earlier. I screamed Deedee's name. It was all my fight or flight could think to do in that moment. Lobo was pummeling Doule with his fists—around the shoulders, in the chest—all while Doule held his arms over his face and tried to stagger away.

Brom hopped off the cruiser and peered inside. The moonlight spilled off his face, a mask of murderous glee. "Hang tight, little Lanie. I'm going to help the succubus bitch out while you wait for wolf boy to collect your blood. I wouldn't want her calling that dryad bitch." He glanced at the fighting werewolves then back. "He shouldn't be long now."

Brom skipped across the sidewalk like a playful child and disappeared inside the store. My heart was beating so hard I could feel it in my throat. I looked at Deedee. She was out cold, her breathing shallow. She was going to die soon if I didn't get her help. I heard Tae's scream inside the building. She would fare no better at the hands of that butcher.

A new howl cut the night air, and the hairs on my neck stood on end. Doule had transformed. Lobo's back slammed against the front passenger window in a spray of glass. I threw an arm over my face and quickly crawled over Deedee to the other side. I turned the handle and threw my body against the door then spilled headfirst out into the street.

I found my hands and knees, scraping my shin on the pavement. The werewolves were brutally tearing at each other on the other side of the car. I peeked inside the driver's window. There were no keys hanging in the ignition. Of course not. That was the sort of thing that only happened in movies.

Tae screamed inside the store.

I have to help her.

I shimmied around the front of the car, pausing at the bumper to look at the wolves. They were a jumble of fur and talons, biting and tearing at each other. I knew if I looked at them too long I would lose my nerve, so I closed my eyes and dashed for the front of the store. A tiny squeal escaped my lips.

Lobo roared when he saw me, his prey. I turned in time to see him lunge for me, a snarling mouth of canine teeth and splayed claws. I threw my arms up over my face and screamed. I was getting good at that. Doule caught his partner's ankle and tugged him backward, and they both fell onto the sidewalk.

My insides turned upside down and threatened to escape my body. I dry heaved as Lobo's jaw hit the cement with a loud *thwack*, like wood snapped in half. Doule, in full wolf form, crawled over his back on hands and knees and planted a furious blow into the back of Lobo's skull.

"No!" I screamed, startling Doule. "Oh my god, don't kill him."

The murderous intent faded from Doule's eyes. He nodded slightly to me, shaking off his wolf form. It was a mistake. Lobo spun on the ground, throwing Doule sideways into the front of the store. His body hit the woodwork below the picture window. I watched in horror as his eyes rolled to whites. Lobo was already on his feet, growling. Saliva dripped from his curled lips when he saw me. He really wanted to kill me. I'd heard a lot of guys personalities changed after sex, but this was ridiculous.

I threw the door open and ran inside, even as he charged in for the kill. Damn the changeling to hell. Lobo hit the door hard, shattering the glass. I was only halfway across the store when he came inside. I scoured the shelves of antiques. *Shit. Why didn't I spend time figuring out what the hell kind of magic these things can do?* Could I risk using one without knowing what it did?

Lobo leapt on top of the shelf between me and the door. His shape was outlined by the hanging lamps outside. A dark, hulking menace with golden eyes peering down at me snarling.

"Lobo," I managed through trembling lips, "you don't have to do this."

His eyes tightened, and he leapt. I scurried out of the way as his body hit the floor, thrashing claws raking the shelves. I screamed as I ran for the counter. There was nothing back there. Nowhere to hide.

The basement door was open, the bookshelf pushed to the side. Tae must have run down there. Lobo must have sensed my thought. He leapt again, clearing the distance in an instant and blocking the door. Tae screamed downstairs. He cocked his head to the side, listening to her.

"Lobo, please," I pleaded. "You have to snap out of it. I need you."

He lowered his head, growling through clenched teeth. There was no sign of the Lobo I knew in him. Whatever spell Brom had wrought was fully controlling him. I realized nothing I said or did would get him to come back. My hand clutched around the relic at my chest. It was used to stop curses, but something in my gut told me Lobo's mind control was rooted in something else.

I was trapped and helpless. My only options were to run or die. Tae shouted something below, followed by a crashing sound. Lobo turned toward the noise for a second.

That was all I needed. I spun and sprinted for the front door. My heart fluttered at the ruin he had made of it. I could not picture how I was going to get past the bent frame and shards of hanging glass, but I had to try.

Lobo howled and leapt after me. He covered half the distance in one bound and was already in the air again. The picture window to my left exploded inward. A shard dug into my shoulder and spun my path sideways. The shards of glass were led by a leaping Doule, coming in like a hell hound. Lobo turned just in time to meet him head on. They collided and smashed into the floorboards, sliding across the room into the shelving.

"Hide in the basement," Doule shouted in his bestial werewolf voice.

I did not hesitate to alter my course. In seconds I was through the open doorway and tugging the shelving closed. One of the werewolves slammed into the door on the other side, almost knocking me backward. It was like witnessing a struggle of titans.

A glimmer of light caught my eye. The outline of the doorframe radiated softly in one corner. I felt it calling to me. This was my grandmother's magic. I could feel it in the same way I used to feel her out there in the world, waiting for me. A part of me reached out to it. There was a gossamer edge to the thing around the door, and I touched it. In an instant we were connected, a thin line of rainbow light triggering the protection dweomer.

Rosalie had set this up to keep the basement safe in case she ever needed to take shelter. The spell swirled around the door, which rapidly grew as if it were a living tree sped up through time. The bark thickened, wedging into the corners, sealing and strengthening the door. When the spell ended, I let out a deep breath. Finally, a moment of safety. A moment to think.

Tae shouted something from deep inside the cellar.

That was when I remembered who else was down there with me.

24

The past two weeks flashed by Lanie in a whirlwind. It sounded like the werewolves were breaking the entire building apart upstairs. The basement was as dark as it had been the first time she entered, with only a dim light in the stacks. Rows of silent shelves shot to her left. She listened intently, trying to place where Tae and the changeling had gone through the sounds of snarling wolves and shuddering floorboards above.

"It's no use," she thought. The only way to hear better was to move deeper into the basement. She clutched the relic at her chest for courage and stepped forward, one foot after the next, until she was around the corner of the nearest shelf.

The corridor opened up before her, past the rows of shelves. She slowly shuffled forward, holding her breath and listening for some sign of Tae. She crept past the stacks, slowing at the opening to each new row to peer into the shadows, searching for some familiar shape. Her eyes landed on a rounded shoulder. It was a crouched man. She gasped, shuffling sideways into the wall. He did not move. Her eyes adjusted, tracing the silhouette again, and she sighed.

It's just a stupid drum kit.

She felt foolish. She had seen the drums on her last trip down here. Then again, could one be too cautious when it came to blindly chasing after a homicidal maniac in a dank basement? *No*, she decided, thanking her brain's reflexes for staying on edge. *I would rather look like a fool than let that slimy bastard slice me open.*

The shelves rattled as something slammed into the floorboards upstairs. It felt like it was directly overhead. Dust rained down around her from the ceiling. She paused to crane her head and listen. The struggle upstairs had stopped.

Calm footsteps overhead walked across the storefront to the basement door. She heard the doorknob turn, creaking ever so slowly. Her heart caught in her throat. *What if the spell doesn't hold?* She remembered how easily Lobo had torn through the door to the apartments. Behind her, around the stacks and up the steps, the door rattled. She could hear her heart beating, thumping in her ears. The door rattled harder. Lobo howled in frustration. The hairs on her neck rose, and she quickly fled the stacks, deeper into the basement.

I don't know how long that door can hold. She frantically swept the corridor with her gaze. *If I can make it to the changeling and break his curse first...* But how? She slowed her pace, remembering she did not even know what to do with the relic to make it work.

Lobo began to beat and claw the door with his fists. She stifled a yelp and sprinted past the chicken wire rooms.

The wider space of the main basement opened before her. It was the room with mounds of rubbish organized around wooden columns that supported the old building. The word *hoarders* flashed across her mind once more. *What was my grandmother doing with all these things?* She frowned. *I'll never know now that Sacha's dead.*

A lone light remained on in the wide open space, an exposed bulb above Rosalie's old work area that swayed back and forth. A man stood nearby, hunched in his own shadows that swallowed the light. Only his eyes and teeth gleamed in its reflection.

"My my, you are full of surprises, aren't you, little Lanie Alacore?" he mused. He was pressing his heel on something that ground apart on the floor. When he moved his foot, she saw it was Tae's cellphone, ground to pieces. So much for calling for help.

"Where is Tae?" she demanded, clutching the relic where it hung on her chain.

He enthusiastically shrugged. "She's a slippery one, the little succubus. No matter, she was only a delightful diversion. It's momentous we get to spend some quality alone time together. Why waste the opportunity pining after a fae whore when I can play with you instead?"

"Big talk," Lanie said. "We both know you have no power over me."

The changeling opened his wings wide, blotting out the light and throwing her into darkness. She quickly scanned around herself, trying to find where the changeling had gone. Lobo pounded furiously on the door above. The changeling's voice came from all around her. "You think yourself so clever. I'll admit, you did have me for a fraction of the teensiest moments. But you revealed your hand, and now I know your limitations." For a moment she caught a glimpse of his wings, stretched through the shadows, oily feathers splayed like talons around their edges.

"I don't blame you," he continued. "Really it was that bitch you call a grandmother who was at fault, abandoning you like that for so many years. That's ironic, isn't it? How alike we really are after all."

"I'm nothing like you." She gritted her teeth in denial, gripping the relic even tighter through her shirt.

"No? Abandoned as a child by a family who never wanted you? Left as a freak, to survive the world on your own, completely ignorant of what you really are? None of that sounds the teeniest bit familiar?"

His words struck home, hard. Lanie loathed the parallels. "You're a devil. I would never kill another to make myself stronger. You can't do anything to me, anyhow," she said, eager to change the subject. "I have the relic."

Brom's form froze, a sleek black shape blending into the darkness around him. His eyes tightened, and his penetrating smile grew wider, almost like a Cheshire cat in its ridiculousness. "You think you can stop me with a twig? Do you know how many of your kind I've consumed? Each one of them thought themselves unstoppable. And each one gave unto me their sacrifice, that I might bestow upon myself their strength." The shadows retreated back inside his form, revealing the basement room once more. The changeling stood across from her with a curled lip. "I have more tricks up my sleeves than you can count, soon to be dead girl."

Lanie opened her mouth to denounce him, then froze. Brom mocked her, opening his mouth as well. Except *his* lips just kept stretching, unhinged like a snake, into an unearthly visage of a gaping maw. She heard them first, their wings fluttering. A murder of crows spilled from his engorged mouth. They were a cloud of black wings and shrieking caws, spiraling out of his insides and aimed directly at her.

She threw her arms up over her face as the first crow swooped down to slash at her eyes. She batted it away with her forearm, surprised how heavy a bird could be. They surrounded her, cawing and clawing, their beaks pecking her scalp, their talons raking her arms. Lanie swatted one away, and another was already there to make her bleed.

She stumbled blindly sideways and slipped on one of Rosalie's mounds of newspapers. They spilled over her as she hit the floor, which was actually a good thing. The crows tore at the newspapers, trying to get to her body. Lanie shimmied underneath the mound. A crow flew directly into the space between papers to peck at her from the front. She snatched hold of its neck and squeezed, snapping its bones. All the crows cried in agony at once. Before she could celebrate, another was already there, tearing a newspaper aside to peck at the back of her neck.

"Get away from me!" she screamed. In that moment something unhinged inside of her. She lashed out in pure panic. A bubble of brilliant light exploded from her core.

Newspapers and crows went flying in every direction, caught in the whirlwind of her spell. She watched the closest crow's trajectory. It slammed into the ceiling, disintegrating into a spatter of black oil. Suddenly the crows were gone. Black feathers fluttered to the floor all around her. The shadows were still. The world was quiet, as if nothing had ever happened. No sounds of werewolves beating down doors, no homicidal maniacs taunting her. Just sobbing.

Lanie stood, pulling feathers out of her hair. A woman was crying somewhere in the basement. Somewhere close by. Her eyes adjusted to the shadows around the edge of the room. It was Tae, with her back to her, huddled on the floor beside a wooden column. Her shoulders trembled as she tried to muffle the sound of her sobbing, with her face pressed into cupped hands.

"Tae?" Lanie said.

Her shoulders stilled. "Lanie? Is he gone?" Her voice was muffled by her hands. She snuffled through her tears.

Lanie ran over to her, scanning the room left and right as she did. "I don't know. Maybe?" Other than the sound of her footsteps and Tae's sobbing, the building was deadly silent. "I think he is. Probably got spooked and ran away like at the church."

"Are we safe now?" Tae sobbed between her hands, too scared to look back at Lanie.

Something moved on the other side of the room, dark flesh glistening off the lone light. Lanie froze, throwing an arm out to ward

Tae. The flesh moved, ducking out of the shadow of a wooden column. It was another Tae, wide-eyed and shaking her head. She urgently motioned for Lanie to run.

From the other side of the basement came the sound of wood severing and splintering. Lobo was making his way past the barrier.

Before her mind could even process the trap she had stepped in, Lanie was turning back. Brom coiled upward like a striking viper, throwing off his disguise as Tae, his skin melting in waves of oily pitch to reveal the truth. His hand snatched her throat and lifted her from her feet.

"Such a stupid little cow," he laughed. She was shocked by his strength. Who had he murdered to steal it? It didn't matter. Those were questions for the living. She was dead now. Brom wrenched her up and then slammed her face down into the floor. She barely got an arm up in time to block her forehead from cracking like an egg on the cement. Either way the wind was knocked out of her.

Brom was on her in an instant, straddling her with his thighs. She flailed, trying to fend him off, but he headbutted her. Lights flashed across her vision. She tasted copper in her mouth. Blood ran down her lip as she lay there in a daze. She groaned in pain.

Lanie willed her magic to attack the changeling. Nothing happened. She tried to reach for it inside of her, but her brain stung like her skull was filled with hornets. She could not think straight. She barely had access to her magic. There had been no time to learn how to harness it. She wanted to cry.

"Tut tut," Brom chided. "I told you yesterday, you should have just come to me. Everything would have been so much easier. Why fight the inevitable? Why cause yourself so much pain?"

Her blurry vision was clearing. Brom had a dagger in his hand, his deadly curved blade. The same one he killed Sacha with. "I'll take my time now. First I'll take your eyes. Those are the best. They taste sweet and pop like grapes filled with jelly." He touched the tip of the blade to her exposed throat. "Then I'll slit you open from here to your groin, but only enough to pull your skin back. I need all those unicorn organs. A fresh harvest to preserve. Oh, think of the wonderful things I'll accomplish with all your power, Lanie."

"You get off of her!" Tae screamed, tackling Brom from the side. He laughed as they tumbled on the floor together. He stabbed at her with the dagger, but Tae was fast on her feet, springing from the floor like a rabbit and racing back for Lanie. She pulled Lanie up to her knees, but then Brom kicked her legs out from under her. Tae hit the floor with wide eyes.

The humor was gone from Brom's face. He curled his lips and kicked Tae's prone body. "Meddling little slut."

Lanie's hand was on human hair. But whose was it? She realized she had fallen into a mound of Rosalie's creepy porcelain dolls. She gripped the doll's feet tight and leapt at Brom. The porcelain head shattered on the side of his skull. He looked at her stupidly, then crumpled to the floor clutching his temple, where a jagged piece was stuck.

Tae was back on her feet in a dash. Lanie was shocked by her tenacity. "Hurry, while he's dazed. Let's get out of here," Tae insisted, pulling Lanie's arm.

They'd made it halfway across the wide area, skirting the mounds of rubbish, when Lobo stepped into the room. His golden eyes reflected in the lone light, seeming to glow in the darkness of the basement, stalking Lanie with a ravenous intent that was the furthest thing from the man she knew. He staggered in on bare feet, clutching his ribs with his right hand. Blood oozed between the matted fur of his taloned fingertips and his left arm hung limp at his side. Doule had not made it easy for him, that was for sure. Lanie shuddered to think what Lobo's partner might look like, lying upstairs somewhere.

"Get out of the way, wolf," Tae did her best to sound imperious.

Lanie tried to pull her back. "No, don't go near him."

Tae shrugged her off and pointed her finger at Lobo. "Stop it this instant, detective. You work for us."

Lobo backhanded her with his right hand, tossing her across the room like a ragdoll. Tae hit the floor, knocked out cold. He turned his attention back to Lanie, saliva dripping from his snarling snout. Lanie backstepped away from him as he staggered closer, until she was pressed up against one of the wooden columns.

"Lobo," she said, her voice coming out as a hoarse whisper. "It's me, Lanie. You don't want to do this. I know you. Fight against the spell."

Brom spit something on the floor, cursing as he rose. "Save your breath," he snapped. "The wolf belongs to me, body and mind." He dangled a thick section of Lobo's fur, wrapped in twine with herbs and arcane symbols. "Isn't that right?"

Lobo looked at his master and nodded curtly.

"You see, just like the good pup he is. Now, Lobo, fetch that stick from the little bitch."

Lanie gasped as Lobo thrust his hand at her throat. Claws snagged her shirt, tearing it open down the middle. The necklace dangled between her cleavage. He swiped at it, wrenching the relic away and tearing the chain loose. Lanie felt her magic pulled back inside the dark hole of her smothering curse. The air was ripped from her lungs and she staggered sideways at the loss.

Her grandmother's pendant fell to the floor. The crystal horn tinkled like bells as it hit the cement, and dazzling blue light spilled out of it.

Lobo froze, his snout curling down in a frown that reached his eyes. He gazed at the horn. The light twinkled in a circle, dimming and gathering back inside the crystal horn. Its light danced off his eyes. Lobo's body softened, and his expression altered.

"Rosalie?" he said breathlessly, confused.

Lanie's heart froze. If she had any chance of surviving, it was in this moment. Without thinking, she ran her cut hand over Lobo's mouth, smearing her blood on his lips.

"What are you doing?" Brom demanded. "You're powerless without the relic. Even I can see that."

"I may not have any power, but my blood does," Lanie retorted.

Lobo looked up at her with soft eyes, utterly confused.

"You do not have to bow to his will, Lobo. Let my blood release you." She dragged her hand from his lips to his chest, feeling his heart beating furiously beneath the leathery skin. She wrapped her arms around him tight and focused everything she had into her will to free Lobo from the spell. It was all she had left. It had to work.

"Lanie?" Lobo looked around the room, his wolf face rapidly becoming human. "Oh no, what have I done?"

She squeezed him tighter to her, pressing her face against his body. His skin was hot as a blazing furnace. Lobo pulled her in and brought his face down to her hair. "Fight him, Lobo. Don't let him control you."

Lobo nodded, his face buried against her forehead.

"No!" Brom shouted angrily, holding Lobo's braided fur aloft. "The wolf is mine! He will do as he is bidden!" Swirling shadows emitted from the changeling's mouth, smoky tendrils of pitch black probing the world. Lobo's body grew stiff. He pushed Lanie slowly away from him. She could see the inner battle he fought to maintain control. But then his eyes turned entirely black, and he staggered back away from her.

"You will do as I say, wolf," Brom commanded. "Bring me the relic. Now."

Lobo howled, fighting against the changeling's hold, his good hand clutching his temple. He shook his head, snarling, and clawed his own face. Then he grew still, snarling but no longer fighting. Tears ran from Lanie's eyes to see him in so much pain.

Brom laughed triumphantly as Lobo walked toward him in a trance, eyes black pools devoid of will. "Did you actually think you could stop me?" he asked Lanie. "In my hands the relic will be insignificant, easily disposed of. Meanwhile, I will make sure to let your boyfriend watch as I dissect you and your little succubus friend."

Lanie did not know how she could have ever contemplated keeping the relic for herself when someone like Brom existed. It was an immensely selfish thing to use it for herself. At least she'd had that one moment though, that second of freedom, the possibility of a life all her own and the memory of being held in Lobo's arms.

"Yes, give it to me," Brom said, stroking Lobo's head tenderly as he reached out for the wolf's offering.

Lanie felt her magic coursing and pumping, channeling through the universe and into her body.

Lobo opened his hand to reveal nothing.

"Empty?" Brom muttered before Lanie's light flared, washing the room in a blinding solar flare. The heat of it dried his oily blood to his forehead, and he gasped as he took in the sight of Lanie Alacore.

In her bloody hand she gripped the relic, where Lobo had placed it during their embrace. Waves of light cascaded out of her, throwing back

Brom's screaming shadows into oblivion. Lanie closed the distance between them and slammed the relic against Brom's chest.

"I call on my ancestors' blood to seal this abomination. Take him to oblivion where he belongs!" she screamed over the deafening roar of the light.

The skin around Brom's chest bubbled sickly as the relic siphoned the curse from of his body. He staggered backward away from her, clutching his chest where the relic remained embedded, continuing to do its work. Tendrils of shadow tried to wrap around him, to resist the light, but Lanie's magic and unicorn blood coupled with the might of the relic would not be denied.

The changeling screamed as he fell backward, and the light enveloped him. Then, as quickly as it had arrived, the light was gone, leaving behind a whimpering Brom clutching his chest.

"My powers. My strength. What have you done to me? It's all gone. This can't be."

A snarl cracked through the basement. Lobo stood, clear-eyed, panting and flexing over the changeling.

"No! You must not, I control you." Brom shook his talisman. "I am your master."

Lobo leapt on him in a flurry of fangs and raking talons. Lanie could not watch as the werewolf tore Brom apart, though she did not feel bad for him for even one second. She turned away and staggered over to her grandmother's desk for support. Her magic was gone, suffocated by the curse that riddled her soul once more. It was an unbearable agony that left her empty inside. As hollow as she felt without it, she knew she had done the right thing.

The changeling would never harm another living soul.

25

My storefront has two massive windows. One of them is boarded up right now. I hung the Help Wanted sign in the other.

A lot of things happened after the changeling's attack. Drys made sure we were taken care of. It was quite a scandal when we all showed up at Free House that evening, battered and broken, not to mention carrying a dead human. Lobo said it was necessary. If everyone saw what happened publicly, then the council couldn't cover it up. People needed to know what had really happened to Rosalie.

Miraculously, no one died that evening. I got off the easiest, with some scrapes and bruises. I mean, those bruises are a shade of yellow and purple that would look better on markers than my skin, and they hurt like bloody hell, but that's nothing compared to my friends. Doule looked like someone had put him through a meat grinder, that someone being Lobo, who, as it turns out, suffered a dislocated shoulder, three broken ribs, and a healthy smattering of stitches. Tae ended up with a minor concussion. Surprisingly she didn't blame Lobo, even though he caused it. He had to live with the knowledge he had been controlled by the changeling's spell, and that seemed a worse burden to carry. I think we were all just happy to be alive.

Deedee suffered the worst of it. Thankfully, she's alive, but she's not waking up. Drys says it looks like a coma. The worst damage was done to her mind, and it's going to be a while before she recovers. I go by Free House once a day to visit her. Maybe if she hears my voice, it'll help her find her way back to me. I miss her so much.

I try not to think about what Lobo did to the changeling, though I am not sure I will ever be the same after that night. I can't say Brom didn't deserve it. He was a despicable man. I wonder how things would have turned out if Rosalie had managed to get to him first. I felt so completely different holding the relic for even a few hours. I was so free and open to the universe. Would it have been like that for Brom? How would he have lived his life without the chaotic pull of being a changeling? I suspect Rosalie would have ensured he lived a better one. However, then I never would have met Tae or Lobo or even poor Sacha. I never would have found this amazing community of fae and realized the world is more magical than I ever imagined.

I've decided to stay in Willow's Edge. It's funny considering everything I've gone through, but this feels more like home than any other place I've been. And there are still a lot of questions to be answered about the fae. I know I'm part unicorn, but what else am I? And why did my mother hide this realm from me? My grandmother was Warden of Willow's Edge. What does that even really mean? Since I announced I'm sticking around, everyone seems to think I'm taking over Rosalie's mantle as Warden, so I guess I better figure it out soon. Above all those questions, one looms larger than life. Why was this curse put on me and how do I remove it?

Because I *will* destroy this curse. I've tasted freedom. I can never go back to a life with my head in the sand after that. To accomplish this, I am going to need money. The antique shop was badly damaged in the attack, and there are a lot of repairs to make. We managed to fix the upstairs windows to our apartments, but that pretty much dried up my funds. There is good news, though. All my jarred and labeled herbs and oils are still intact. That is just as well, since I've decided there is no way I'm running an antique shop.

Nope. Big rebranding coming for Lanie, folks. Rosalie's Antiques will soon become Alacore's Apothecary. I've already planned out where I can build my garden behind the building, and Father Willem has even offered to let me take clippings from some of his plants. Soon I'll be doling out custom poultices and herbal remedies of my own making. I can't wait to open shop!

For the first time in my life, I can say I'm excited to see what comes next.

Epilogue

The battered door to Alacore's Apothecary opened with a jingle from the new bell I'd fished out of the basement. I was resetting a loose panel of wood to the floorboard behind the counter, trying to repair some of the damage done to the shop.

"Sorry, we're closed," I said, wiping the sweat from my brow. "Grand opening's next week, though. Tell all your friends."

"And how is it you're going to feed me if you ain't even making any flippin' money?" a familiar voice chided.

I thrust myself to my feet, dropping the hammer as I gaped at my patron.

Sacha sported a smart business suit to match his sharp grin. In his hands he held the Help Wanted sign. "I hear you're looking for a new business partner."

Michelle Murphy

Author's Note

Hey there! How are you doing after all that? That was a crazy ride at the end, right?

Poor Lanie was totally screwed by someone, wasn't she? (I know you caught what I did there) At least she finally got to fulfill her fantasy and had her first real climax before she threw it all away to save the day.

Can we just pause for a moment to acknowledge the fact that Lanie is a freaking unicorn? That juicy little bit was so hard to keep a secret. I want to know what you think about that and everything else in the story. Join my reader group to hang out with me and other readers and chat about spoilers, subplots, favorite characters, and theories.

It would mean the absolute world to us if you could please drop onto your favorite site and give us a review of Light's Awakening.

Keep reading for a sneak preview of Book 2 Light's Lost, and pre-order your copy now!

1

Charlie had no business being in that alley alone at night. The waning winter air chilled her skin and left her throat feeling raw. Behind her, the walls of the building thumped from the heavy bass inside, echoes of the dance club.

The backdoor to Free House closed, muffling its light and laughter. Blots of melting snow piled in the corners of the tight alley, around the corral of the trash dumpster and against the building where it turned toward the road. A dead rat stared up at her, its body spread halfway out from underneath the dumpster.

"You see? I was right, my dear," the man with her cooed. His words pulled at her mind like plucked harp strings. They were rich and melodious; the sort of sound angels must make when they laugh. "Isn't it the most beautiful night for a stroll?"

Glassy eyes stared at her from beneath the dumpster. She blinked at the rat, in a daze, trying to make sense of something just beyond the perimeter of her understanding.

"A stroll?"

The man's slender fingers stroked her arm, turning her ever so slightly toward the lip of the alley. "Among the flowers, my sweet. That's where we'll frolic. Can't you see them, there at the end of the alley? How exquisite. Row upon row of gardenias and poppies. And there, you see, a hedge of lilacs? Their perfume is intoxicating. Feel yourself fall into its heady embrace. They are all of them inviting us to visit."

Why was she doing this? She did not want to be out here alone with this beautiful man. The dead rat's eyes implored her to turn back. *You're not safe here. Go inside where it is warm.*

"I don't know," she mumbled, turning back toward Free House on wobbly legs.

The man laughed. He wasn't worried, for he possessed the mirror and with it control. It was a small hand mirror of hammered silver, quite unremarkable to the layman. The glossy surface rippled with his desire. The mirror was old magic, outlawed these days. He lifted it to her eyes, so she could see what he wished. The imagined fields of flowers opened before her.

"You see, my love," he murmured. "Off we will go on our adventure, over the hills and into the valley of spring. Surely you have never wanted to go anywhere so badly?"

He watched her eyes glaze over as the spell regained control over her, fogging her brain with his will. Her body language changed all at once. Suddenly, she stood straight and confident. Charlie coyly chuckled. She stroked his broad chest with her delicate fingers.

"I told you we should go," she insisted, as if it had been her own idea all along. "I don't know why you're acting so strange."

He tickled her chin and laughed. In an instant she bolted away from him, trapped in his illusion, straight down the alley toward the road.

"Come on, silly," she called back. "Last one to make it to the top of the hill is a peasant."

He relished watching her for a few minutes, enjoying the spectacle of the girl frolicking among imaginary flowers. She danced and twirled in a circle, letting the illusion of sunlight warm her face, her delicate lips smiling, her soft supine form folding with the wind. She was beautiful. And now she was his.

He pushed the mirror back into his shirt pocket and gingerly followed her, already wondering what Charlie's lips would taste like once he stole them from her pretty little face.

2

"Thank you, Lanie," a woman with a doe face said.

I do not mean to say she had demure features. Isa is a regular of mine, and she literally has the nose and ears of a deer, with a soft-tufted pelt covering her body. She's a talking deer person. How cool is that? I get to meet all sorts of interesting fae like her these days … because my life rocks now.

About three months ago, my world was drastically different. I used to spend my days working long hours at a florist, tucking myself as far back in the shop as I could manage. I scarcely interacted with anyone back then. Most nights I would stay late in order to avoid declining a drink with my only friend, Deedee. After work, I would scuttle home to tend my rooftop garden, my absolute happiest place, then eat dinner alone and fall asleep either watching television or with a book hitting my face. That really was the bulk of what each day looked like. Lanie Alacore hiding from society. Alone.

Everything changed when my grandmother Rosalie died. Not only did Rosalie bequeath all her worldly possessions to me, but she also gave me the greatest gift of my life. She lifted a spell my mother had placed over my mind. That horrible spell kept me from seeing all the amazing things around me, places and people I should have been attuned to, since I, too, am a fae. Well, more aptly, a unicorn. That is, I have unicorn ancestry in my blood. This means I have deep mystical powers I must keep absolutely secret. Unicorn blood is supposedly one of the most powerful forces in the fae realm. I wouldn't know too much about it, since I can't access my own power thanks to my curse, but I had a taste of it for one evening. It was amazing. My grandmother's warning about our bloodline wasn't just lip service. The last person who found out about my lineage put my best friend in a coma. My friends and I almost died trying to stop his murderous rampage. So, we don't talk about unicorns around Alacore's Apothecary.

That's what I named my new business. It's so exciting and sometimes I have to pinch myself to make sure it's all real. I run my own apothecary! We sell poultices, herbs, crystals, unguents, and even the occasional elixir. Most of what I have to offer is behind the counter, on tiered shelves with jars and vials displayed for all. Each container has been carefully labeled, and all my ingredients are of the finest quality.

Word of my shop is slowly spreading. It seems I have a knack for growing, finding, and mixing the right ingredients to help those in need. It's ironic because Deedee used to tease me that I was going to end up joining one of those MLMs for essential oils. Now, I actually do prescribe them. Except, mine are infused with a bit of magic. I've noticed that no matter how much this curse blocks me from accessing my inner magic, a bit of it seems to seep out when I'm lost in thought over my workbench crafting remedies for my customers. It's not enough to make any major difference, just a trickle. But that trickle is something that gives me hope. Even better, I've found these amazing rose petals that help me harness a teensy bit more of my magic.

I found them when I was walking the hedge maze behind Greystone Chapel a few weeks ago around dusk. The rose petals glowed faintly with a ghostly blue light that drew me to them like a moth to a flame. They stopped glowing once I picked them, but I could feel their magic like it was calling to me. I've found grinding a tiny bit into what I'm doing helps the magic locked deep inside me leak its way into my craft. It pains me to know what's lurking beneath the surface of my curse is far more powerful. I almost wish I never experienced its release during my brief time holding the relic, yet I'm glad I know what waits for me.

It would bother me more, but of one thing I'm certain – I am going to break that curse. One way or another, I will figure out how to free myself from its bondage. And in the meantime, I still get to help others and meet friendly doe-faced women like Isa.

"I hope you feel better soon, Isa," I said as she left the store.

My shop was practically destroyed a few months ago. I removed the debris of broken shelves and shattered antiques from the storefront. With Lobo's help, we repaired what we could around the building. Luckily, we were able to replace the windows upstairs and fix the front door, but that pretty much dried up any savings I had left. The glass picture window on the left side of my shop is still boarded up, which doesn't look great. It's not exactly screaming *Fresh new apothecary that you simply must check out!* People like to shop somewhere they feel is successful; because if you're successful, there must be a reason for it. Customers want to discover what that reason is, with a subconscious hope that some of it will rub off onto them. I think we can make enough money in the next couple of months to replace the glass. I still have some antiques on the remaining shelves in the shop. If Deedee was still around maybe I could sell them in the city. I felt sick to my stomach when I thought about what she must have gone through the night the changeling attacked.

Deedee's not going to be in a coma forever. She's the strongest person I know, I told myself. I realized over the last few weeks that I'd relied on Deedee to sort out my problems for too long. From now on I needed to take care of things on my own. I would find a way to remove the curse on my own. Then once it was gone, I could possibly use my unicorn magic to heal her and help her wake up.

I'm not going to be able to sell those antiques on my own, not even in Manhattan. They're an eyesore on the apothecary. If I had space in the basement, I'd store them down there for now. A cold shiver worked down my spine. Memories of crows and shifting shadows snuck up on me. I didn't like to think about the basement.

The shop door clinked closed on its springs as Isa left. I was able to replace the bell above the door with one I found in the basement. I like the way it sounds when people come and go. Less opportunity for someone to sneak up on me as well. That morning I felt lighter than air, so happy I thought I might be able to solve all the world's troubles with one of my salves. My life had certainly changed a lot in a short amount of time, and I loved it.

"Why are you smirking like you just swallowed a lizard?" Sacha asked from his stool where he read his newspaper.

Sacha said he read them because he wanted to catch up on world events. He was on year 1922. It was a good thing he was a fast reader. He always had his head buried in one of those dingy old newspapers while he 'worked' the counter.

"Who would smirk after they ate a lizard?" I snickered.

"A demon," the little winged imp said.

"How can I explain it? For once in my life, everything is perfect."

"Whoa, there." Sacha's eyes flared a fiery red to match his skin. He dropped his paper on the checkout counter and scowled at me. "What are trying to do, jinx us? You don't just throw around the P word like a cursing sailor, damnit."

I could only laugh at his reaction. "Sacha, you worry too much."

He scowled and opened his mouth to berate me, but I was saved by the bell of the door opening once more.

"Mr. Anders, it's lovely to see you today," I beamed, purposely cutting the imp off. Mr. Anders was a lovely old tephyr. A fae with three arms.

Mr. Anders tipped his cap to me. "And a good morning to you as well, Miss Alacore. It is certainly an exquisite morning to be out and about."

"I have the remedy to your troubles all set to go," I said, retrieving a parcel from underneath the counter. "Just lay it in your pantry and the ants will stay away." I handed him the wrapped sachets I'd prepared the evening before.

"Oh, wonderful." He smiled, folding the wrinkles around his eyes. He paused to inspect the packets through his thick spectacles. "It's rather early in the season for them to be out scavenging my larder, you know. But what kind of poison is this? It smells so lovely."

"No poison, just a little concoction I came up with. It's a bit of a few things: cayenne, mint, even some coffee grounds." *And a little of my magic of course, to seal the deal.*

"Well, whatever it is, if it works half as well as that honeysuckle tea you sold me last month, I should be pest free soon enough." Mr. Anders took a polite bow before turning to leave.

I'm not sure how he managed to look so dapper in his out-of-date tweed jacket, but he always had an air of sophistication to him. His third hand stuffed the sachets into his breast pocket.

Sacha snickered as the old man opened the shop door to leave. "Coffee grounds to get rid of ants," he grumbled. Mr. Anders did not seem to notice, as he was held up at the door chatting with another patron who had just arrived.

"What's your problem with my ant repellent?" I asked.

Sacha is three and a half feet tall with dark red skin. He's bald, loves wearing clothes that look like they're from a 1920s gangster film and has tiny leathery wings. He was smoking a cigar of his own creation as usual and still reading his newspaper when he snorted at my concoction. He's grown increasingly more annoying over the last week.

"We've got a busted window and no money." Sacha puffed a ring of smoke. "And you're over here peddling *coffee grounds*."

"What? They work," I said defensively. "It'll definitely keep the ants out of his pantry."

Sacha grumbled. "I don't doubt it, Lanie. Everything you make seems to punch the ticket alright. It's just ... we need to drum up more business than *coffee grounds for ants* before we go destitute."

I rolled my eyes. He was right as much as he was wrong. "We're not exactly starving."

We were making enough money to stay fed and clothed at least, but that was about it. There was no overflow coming in to save away for a rainy day. Although, I discovered one of the truly amazing things about living in Willow's Edge was that there was no electric or water bills. Utilities were something fae handled in a more communal fashion. Everyone put a fair share into a communal pool based on their earnings. Appropriate amounts were doled out to the fae who ran the mill and so forth. I'm still clueless as to how the tree lanterns appear every night, but as far as basic necessities were concerned, Willow's Edge was covered. It was all very socialist and yet not at all. Living in a fae province was deeply confusing business.

"A happy afternoon to you, Miss Alacore."

Chulie was a tiny woman, just under three-feet tall. Other than her diminutive size and exceptionally large eyes, she looked fantastically like any other human. However, she was not a human, she was a brownie who'd come into my shop several times in the last month and was quickly becoming a regular.

"Well, what a lovely day it is indeed, Mrs.... ma'am." I had no idea what her last name was. I almost winced, waiting to see if she noticed my slip. "Do you need a restock of your joint medication? It's awfully quick to have gone through that entire vial already. I can make it stronger if you need."

Sacha grumbled. He was clearly unimpressed with how quickly I veered away from his confrontation. What the heck else was I supposed to do? We had a customer. Plus, I hate to argue, especially when the other person is right.

Chulie glanced sideways, as if she was trying to find a thought taped to the side of her head. "Not so much in the need of potions today, dearie."

I was going to point out that the unguent I had made her was not a potion, but her demeanor was odd, like a dog waiting to be told it can lie down. Some of the fae had very strange ways about them and how they communicated. We stood there in silence for a few moments.

"Well? What is it you want for fucks sake?" Sacha snapped, cutting through the awkward silence.

Chulie's whole body twitched, and she spun about to flee the store. Sacha grumbled, and I held a hand up for him to settle down.

"Chulie, please don't leave," I called.

The diminutive brownie's retreat faltered to a standstill. I would be lying if I said her skittish nature didn't annoy me. But this was a business, and we needed all the customers we could get, as Sacha had pointed out only moments before.

"You came here today for a reason, right?" I said, slowly coaxing her back to the counter. "Sacha didn't mean to frighten you. He's just a world-class grouch."

Chulie shot him a nervous glance, then frowned at me. "He's a demon," she said, as if that explained everything.

"Yes, he is, a daemon to be exact, and he's also my business partner. Don't mind him though; his bark is worse than his bite," I said with a wink.

That was a lie. I had seen Sacha rake a serial killer's face open with his talons. Probably best skittish little Chulie didn't hear about that, though.

"Now, why don't you tell me what it is I can get for you today?"

"Well, since you asked," Chulie spoke slowly, unraveling her words like bundled yarn. "It's about the bazaar. I mean, I was wondering … that is, I was hoping …"

"Bazaar?" I didn't mean to cut her off. I do that sometimes, blurting out the first thing that springs to my mind. I had lived in Willow's Edge for four months and this was the first time anyone had mentioned anything about a bazaar.

"It's a huge marketplace in the fae realm," Sacha said, folding his paper and setting it on the counter in front of him. He was suddenly very interested in our conversation. His eyes practically lit up with attention. Sacha is, by nature, an aloof person. To see him showing that much interest in anything made me all the more curious.

"Well, it was. You see, that is, your grandmother Rosalie, she would take things to the bazaar for me when she went every so often like," Chulie said. "And I was wondering if you could, if you would be a dear, deliver a package maybe, to my cousin, Bertie."

"Well, I've never been to the bazaar," I said.

Chulie's face dropped. She looked so distraught, I thought she might start weeping. "But Rosalie, she was the Warden. And now you're the Warden, I think. People are saying as much around town. Every end of the month the Warden goes to the bazaar. And you, being her granddaughter, and the new business, the shiny jars and vials, surely …"

"Yer ramblin' toots," Sacha cut her off. He was smiling despite himself.

The shop door popped open with a jingle. Lobo, my … well, what was Lobo? He was a detective for the province. Also, a werewolf. All werewolves are police for the fae provinces. Tae, my succubus friend and neighbor, told me it was for that purpose that the Court of Shadows created them in the first place. We never officially declared what *we* were, but I considered him my boyfriend for the most part. Even if he did try to rip me limb from limb while he was under the spell of a madman. Live and let live, right?

"Afternoon," he grumbled.

As you can imagine, werewolves prefer to be out and about at night, although his mood isn't generally much different. He's a bit of a grump. Lobo always walked with a certain swagger that said he didn't give a shit about anything around him. The way he marched straight past Chulie to come around the counter and plant a kiss on my cheek was no more brazen than anything else he did in life.

I blushed as his lips and stubble grazed my tender flesh. Chulie's eyes grew so wide they looked ready to pop. I always liked the way Lobo smelled, like aftershave and cloves.

I giggled despite myself. "Hey, hun. I'm with a customer."

Lobo looked around the shop. When his eyes landed on Chulie, she wilted. He snickered. "I'm sorry, ma'am. I'm afraid sometimes I only have eyes for Lanie here. Please forgive my intrusion."

Now it was Chulie's turn to blush. I had to hand it to Lobo. Sometimes he could be just as charming as he was gruff. She averted her gaze from him, staring at the floor instead.

"Oh, young lovers. It is a splendid sight to behold. I'm sure you're both proper and decent in the way of our Queen's honor."

I did not know what any of that meant, but I nodded along with her. "Chulie, tell me more about this bazaar you mentioned."

Confusion clouded Chulie's oversized eyes. "Miss Alacore does not know? It is the Warden's place to attend these things, not a lowly brownie like Mrs. Etune."

Ah, so that was her last name. I repeated it three times in my head so I wouldn't forget. "What do you know about this?" I asked Lobo.

"Once a month folk come from all around the realm to hock their wares at a giant outdoor faire," he said. "It's called the *bazaar*."

"That sounds amazing," I said, turning my attention back to Mrs. Etune. "But I still don't understand why you would come to me. This is an apothecary not a postal service. I wouldn't know the first thing about the bazaar. Besides, why don't you just deliver the package to your cousin yourself next time you go?"

Sacha snorted. "It's not exactly a place some folk can get to, Lanie."

I did not understand, and it was making me agitated.

Sacha rubbed his fingers and thumb together under the counter where Mrs. Etune could not see.

"Oh, money," I stupidly said aloud, instantly regretting it when I saw Mrs. Etune's cheeks turn scarlet. "Please don't feel embarrassed," I quickly said. "Things are tight here as well. Why, we haven't even made enough to fix our window yet. See? If the bazaar is expensive, I'm in the same boat as you."

Lobo cleared his throat. "Actually, as Rosalie's heir you would have a free pass whenever you want to visit. It's a perk of inheriting your grandmother's Wardenship."

There was that title again. Things had been so hectic since I arrived in Willow's Edge that I had yet to find time to learn what being a warden even entailed. I wasn't even sure I wanted to inherit that title. Running the apothecary was more than enough to keep me busy and happy.

Sacha snapped his fingers together, creating a little spark of flame that dissipated in a puff of smoke. "The mutt's a genius. Why didn't I think of it before?" He glowered at me briefly. "Probably on account of you starving me to death."

"You're hardly starving to death," I admonished. "I feed you the same as I eat every day."

"Leaves and berries." Sacha stuck his tongue out in disgust. "Not even scraps fit for a rabbit."

"It's called a salad," I groaned. "And I only served it to you once. How many times do you want me to apologize?"

"Doesn't matter," Sacha said. "The point is Rosalie used to go to the bazaar all the time. Quite the regular she was. Think the old bat even has a stall there for the shop."

"A stall?" I gaped. "Why is this the first time I'm hearing about a stall?"

Sacha's stomach emitted a loud growl, as if it was an empty echoing cavern. "Case in point," he said, flicking his rounded belly beneath his shirt and suspenders. "An imp needs to eat if he's going to be expected to think proper."

I rolled my eyes and ignored Lobo's chuckle behind me. We both knew full well Sacha made his stomach do that.

"If you go to the bazaar, you might be able to unload some of those goods in the corner," Lobo said. "Probably turn a pretty profit."

"Then we can get the window fixed," I said excitedly.

"And buy some steaks," Sacha agreed.

"Do you really think I can get in for free?" I asked Lobo.

"It shouldn't cost you anything to travel and enter the bazaar," Lobo confirmed. "All you need is Rosalie's Warden permit."

"I know where it is," Sacha said. He hopped off the stool and scurried into the office. It was one of the few occasions I've seen the little demon so excited.

The old antiques glared at me from the opposite end of the store. What looked like someone else's trash was actually a mixture of magical wares procured over time. I knew my grandmother peddled the enchanted artifacts, but I thought that business was done strictly through the shop. Except, in the months I had been there, no one had come by to inquire about them. I dared to hope the bazaar would be more promising. Could we have finally stumbled upon a solution for our financial woes?

"Well, then, Mrs. Etune," I said. "It would be my pleasure to deliver your package to your cousin."

She beamed and handed me her little package. I took it with my mind already drifting off to dreams of all the money I might make selling the antiques at some big fancy bazaar. I felt that I owed Mrs. Etune a debt of gratitude for telling me about the bazaar and the delivery of one small insignificant looking box seemed like a poor trade.

If only it had dawned on me at the time to ask what exactly was in that package.

3

That weekend, I embarked on my adventure to the bazaar. I left Sacha behind to run the apothecary, much to his chagrin, and brought along my new friend, Tae. Tae is a succubus who lives in the apartment across from mine. We've only known each other a short time, but we've been through some serious shit together and I think it's created a sort of bond between us. She's fun to be around, and she doesn't make me feel like a burden. Plus, she knows everything there is to know about all the different fae. Lobo and his partner, Doule, dropped us off at the train station. We only brought one stack of merchandise, but Sacha assured me it was valuable enough to make the trip worthwhile.

"You said the bazaar is in the fae realm, right?" I asked Lobo as two treants took my parcels from him at the loading platform.

Lobo grunted. He's a real conversationalist.

"Well, then, how is a train supposed to get us there?" I continued. "It's not like we're taking a daytrip to Pennsylvania."

One of the treants handed him the ticket for my belongings. Lobo leaned in close enough for me to smell his aftershave and slid the ticket into the front pocket of my blouse. "Relax and enjoy the ride, babe. You'll see everything soon enough." He tapped the pendant I wore round my neck. "And don't lose this. You'll need to present the sigil at the gates to be allowed free entry."

The pendant was the Warden's sigil that Sacha recovered from the office. It was a pink crystal obelisk with runes etched across its rough surface. I had tied leather twine around it in a weaving pattern to keep it in place, and I wore it along with the crystal horn my grandmother had left me.

Standing there in his arms, watching the tree people load the train, steam billowing out from the tracks, I felt both anxious and excited, like a child who knows tomorrow is the first day of school. That wild expectation was muddied only slightly by the disappointment that Lobo could not join us.

He seemed to read my mind and nudged my chin with his rough fingers. "Don't be glum. I'll be out first thing tomorrow morning once my shift is over."

"It's not fair you don't get any vacation time." I pouted.

Lobo chuckled. "Imagine that. A werewolf taking a vacation."

We both smiled, and he kissed me. Something about the way he did it so abruptly made me flinch and stagger back. It wasn't the first time something like that had happened between us. Ever since that horrible night with the changeling, I'd found myself jumping at shadows. I swiftly corrected my knee-jerk reaction and grabbed his arms to pull him back toward me. I didn't miss his pained expression, though he quickly tried to hide it.

Good job you big jerk, I thought. I knew in my heart it wasn't Lobo's fault that Brom had gotten ahold of his mind. Try telling that to my brain. It's only fair my body reacted to a memory of a murderous Lobo chasing me, all claws and teeth hungry for my blood.

The last thing I wanted to do was take off for the fae realm leaving him feeling shitty, so I rewarded him with a deep kiss. His stubbled jaw tantalized me where it grazed my skin. He pressed me to his chest with his powerful arms, and for a moment I was able to pretend everything was normal in the world. I lost myself in his embrace, each of us exploring the other with our tongues.

I gently pulled away, breaking the spell before my body thought more was going on. No sense in blacking out on the train platform in broad daylight. I was still cursed, after all, and if I allowed myself to get too aroused, the curse would sense it and punish me. Lobo had no idea about my curse. I'm embarrassed to admit I couldn't bring myself to tell him about it. I told myself at the time that it was none of his business. The curse was my problem to deal with alone. What a crock of shit that was. That little secret didn't make things easy between us.

"I wish you could come tonight instead," I said, gazing up into his golden eyes.

"No trains to the fae realm run that late." Lobo smiled. "Anyhow, time passes differently over there sometimes, so pay it no mind and try to enjoy yourself. And stick with Tae. No wandering off on your own to explore."

It annoyed me when he started treating me like a helpless child. "Of course."

Tae signaled it was time to go. I finished saying goodbye to Lobo and waved a thanks to Doule. It was great to know the two of them had stayed so close, even after trying to kill each other that night. Doule, like myself, had completely forgiven Lobo for any transgressions.

"You're sure this isn't a waste of your weekend?" I asked Tae as we boarded the train.

"Are you kidding me?" Tae beamed. "I don't know a succubus alive who doesn't like a good shopping excursion."

Tae has an infectious smile. It could be because she exudes confidence and oozes sensual perfection in everything she does. The chick is smoking hot and has a mind that could knock the socks off even the best conversationalists. However, I prefer to believe she makes me smile because she is such a kind and light-hearted person. Even though Tae was shorter than me, she tended to be larger than life. I could scarcely blame other fae for being distracted when she walked down the aisle ahead of me, all curves and shimmery dark skin. Something about succubi made their skin look like it was mixed with a fine glitter that sparkled as they moved. Did I mention she's gorgeous? Next to Tae I feel like a prune left out in the sun too long.

We took our seats, and again I wondered how this ordinary train was going to bring us to the fae realm. Tae grabbed my hand and firmed up her grip "I can't believe this is the first time my girl Lanie travels to the fae realm. I'm so excited for you."

We both squealed. I felt light-headed as if I had just downed a glass of champagne. Soon enough the train announced our departure from the station. I braced myself for something amazing. The train vibrated as the locomotive powered up. Soon the horn was blaring, and we were moving. Willow's Edge slowly rolled by at first, then the train lurched forward at a heady speed.

We left Willow's Edge and entered the countryside. We passed rolling hills, then forests and farmland. It was all quite ordinary. Soon enough, between the vibrations of the locomotive and the unremarkably mundane passing landscape I nodded off. This was just a train ride after all. I don't know what I was expecting to happen, but it wasn't this. Maybe something more like –

"What in the world?!"

I gasped as my stomach lurched like it was flipped inside out. Thick, impenetrable fog blanketed the outside of the train, blotting out my view of the countryside. I wasn't sure how long I'd been asleep. It seemed like only minutes, but my head felt groggy and disoriented.

"Here. Chew on some licorice root," Tae offered. "It'll help."

I greedily shoved a piece in my mouth, eager to fight the sudden nausea. My ears popped. I always relished that feeling, like when you're driving up and down a mountainous area and your ears delightfully pop. I know most people hate it, but I find it refreshing, like nature's way of resetting your eardrums.

The fog outside the window parted in little pockets giving me a tiny glimpse of the landscape. I spit the licorice root onto the window when I swore. Both my hands turned into a pantomime of frightened cat claws, one digging into Tae's thigh, the other my armrest. Through the holes in the fog, I could see the world in miniature detail, the way one would through the clouds on a plane. You might think that an odd analogy. I did too, until I realized with no uncertainty that we were indeed thousands of feet above the ground, barreling through the clouds in a train with no wings. Because trains don't have wings. Because trains should not fly!

Tae giggled and rubbed my forearm. I looked over at her and realized I was still digging my fingernails into her thigh. I let go, fumbling on an apology, but she laughed it off.

"I would have worn a different dress if I knew we were going to engage in a little S&M."

The way she winked at me was so comical, it suddenly took the air out of my fear. I looked around the rest of the train car. All the other passengers were entirely calm, some snoozing, others reading.

"Why is nobody freaking out that we're thousands of feet in the sky?"

I have never enjoyed flying. Any time I've been in a plane was filled with either pretending it was okay or drugging myself to sleep. The slightest turbulence makes me break out in a cold sweat. This was nothing like that. The train cut smoothly through the sky as the world below went by in miniature detail.

Soon, a soft pastel pink bled into the clouds, followed by a pale yellow and then a softer blue. The colors were beautiful, swirling around and making the clouds resemble cotton candy. Suddenly, brilliant bursts of color crackled inside the core of the clouds, like firecrackers with no sound. I watched them with awe as I pulled the licorice root off the window.

"The clouds are so pretty," I said. "Where are those lights coming from? Is someone lighting fireworks in the sky?"

Tae looked quite pleased with herself. "The world really is wonderful, isn't it? The best I have ever heard it explained is that we are entering the fae realms. What you see is the byproduct of us pressing through a sort of membrane that shelters the fae realm from its human counterpart."

I snickered. "Are you saying there's a giant force field around the fae realm?"

"More or less," Tae said in all seriousness.

As ridiculous and sci-fi as it sounded, it made sense. I had once used my magic to create a forcefield of sorts. It was a prismatic bubble that I used to deflect the changeling's killing blow from reaching Sacha. I reasoned this could be similar just on a far larger scale.

"But why doesn't anything like this happen when we enter Willow's Edge?" I frowned.

"You have to remember," Tae said patiently, "Willow's Edge is a province, a place that exists between both realms. By its nature it touches and belongs to both the human and fae realms. The provinces act as a conduit between them. Without the provinces, this trip wouldn't be possible."

That still didn't make sense to me, but I let it go. Soon the clouds cleared and with them the crackling colors. The sun was high, casting brilliant light over the world below. I gasped as a swan as large as an elephant suddenly swooped down from above, opening wide its delicate wings so it drew up level with the train.

"There's a knight riding that swan," I said in disbelief.

Tae peered around me to get a good look. "Oh neat. That's a soldier from the Summer Court."

She waved excitedly at the man who was clad in shiny silver armor, with white wings on his heels and helm. A lance hung from the swan's saddle. It was easily one and half times the length of the gargantuan bird. The soldier waved back at Tae and swooped his swan sideways, falling back toward the rear of our curving train.

"What was that all about?" I asked, unable to maintain what I can only describe as a shit-eating grin. If I had seen anything like that four months before, I would have promptly checked myself into psychiatric care. These days I only wanted to know more about this amazing world I had stepped inside of.

"All four of the great houses own a piece of the bazaar," Tae explained. "The Summer Court owns the rights to sky travel, so they are equally responsible to ensure those skies are safe. There's probably a few more soldiers out there with him, escorting the train since we entered the fae realm."

"Safe?" I glanced back out the window, scanning the horizon. What could be out there that would require a swan knight to keep it at bay? An involuntary shudder danced down my spine.

Tae patted a delicate hand on my lap. "There's nothing to fear. Now look at that. We're almost to the bazaar." She pointed out the window.

The first thing I noticed was we were no longer alone in the sky. There were tracks below us in the open air and another train miles below them, aimed in the opposite direction. Beyond that were a myriad of flying objects. Some were pill-shaped giant zeppelins that cut through the sky. There were giant hot air balloons dotting the area and even a galley fit for a pirate. I had never seen a galley at sea, let alone one flying across the sky. It was breathtaking, with billowing sails that drank the wind and a prow that looked like a wooden mermaid reaching for the sun.

And then I saw it. My first glimpse of the fae realm. Our destination was an enormous floating island.

I could see the port of entry, a harbor of sorts, where we aimed to land. What looked like elaborately constructed ivory scaffolding worked in crisscrossed patterns down the cliffside of the island. The cliffs stretched from the bustling harbor to the horizon beyond as far as my eyes could see, and then staggeringly curved back on itself upward into the air, like the lush green ring of a god. It was an impossible landscape that defied all known laws of physics. I had to stop tracing the horizon upward as I suddenly felt dizzy and insignificant in its wake.

Better to focus on the rapidly approaching harbor. All manner of vehicles came and went as we slid into port. The harbor was the best example of organized chaos I'd ever seen. There were no lights for traffic, nor signs to direct people, and yet everyone seemed to know their place in things. It was like watching an elaborate ballet performed by winged people, giant swans with riders on their backs, trains that moved across the sky as well as land, flying galleys, hot air balloons, zeppelins …

"Come on. We have to get off now." Tae tugged my sleeve.

I realized it wasn't the first time she had said that to me. "Sorry. I was so entranced by everything I guess I zoned out."

She giggled when she saw me blinking back to the present. "Oh Lanie, I'm so happy you brought me with you for your first time at the bazaar," she said with a broad smile.

I was glad too, but I did not want to look like one of those mooncalf tourists who visit New York City for the first time. I gathered my composure and hopped to my feet.

"I'm happy, too. Now, let's go make some money."

Grab your copy of Light's Lost today to continue the story!

Something sinister is happening in Willow's Edge

All Lanie Alacore wants to do is make her new apothecary a success. But she quickly realizes that there's more to protecting the province than mixing a couple tinctures.

Now fae youth have been disappearing all over the province and Lanie finds herself caught up in the mystery. With her claim to her grandmother's wardenship contested, her best friend in a coma, and a werewolf and prince vying for her attention, Lanie sets out to track down a missing teen.

Can she solve the mystery in time or will Lanie become the next victim…